When it Rains

When it Rains

by
Laura Cuthbert

When it Rains
copyright © Laura Cuthbert 2002

Turnstone Press
607–100 Arthur Street
Artspace Building
Winnipeg, MB
R3B 1H3 Canada
www.TurnstonePress.com

Turnstone Press gratefully acknowledges the assistance of the Canada
Council for the Arts, the Manitoba Arts Council and the Government of
Canada through the Book Publishing Industry Development Program
and the Government of Manitoba through the Department of Culture,
Heritage and Tourism, Arts Branch for our publishing activities.

The Canada Council | Le Conseil des Arts
for the Arts | du Canada

Canadä

Cover design: Doowah Design
Interior design: Sharon Caseburg
Printed and bound in Canada by Friesens for Turnstone Press.

National Library of Canada Cataloguing in Publication Data

Cuthbert, Laura, 1966-
 When it rains

 ISBN 0-88801-269-1
 I. Title
PS8555.U8465W43 2002   C813'.6   C2002-910053-4
PR9199.4.C87W43 2002

Special thanks to Jennifer Glossup and Pat Sanders for all that they taught me, and to Todd Besant of Turnstone for patience and perseverance.

This novel would not have been completed without the encouragement and advice I received from those who read earlier versions: Carol, Andrea, Maureen, Jodi, Anne and David. Thanks also to Kurt, who gave me the original idea and weathered many changes.

When it Rains

Chapter
One

THE TRICK IS NOT TO MAKE EYE CONTACT. Don't look, don't flinch, don't let them smell your fear. Just walk down the stairs and out of the SkyTrain station. Control your breathing and don't walk too fast. No big deal, just life in the big city. When I left the station, it took every muscle in my body not to turn around and see if the man with the gap-toothed grin was still leaning against the wall.

He was just a flasher—part of Vancouver life, like losing your umbrella. It was the sort of incident my parents cautioned me about when I left my hometown of Grand Forks, BC. Remembering their warnings and their certainty that I would come running home after my first traffic jam only strengthened my resolve. I may have grown up in the sticks, but some loser showing off his inadequacies wasn't going to throw me. After all, I was a tough woman, a worldly, unshakable reporter. I would turn around and laugh in his face, point mockingly and make jokes about shrinking in the rain. Then I would make a citizen's arrest....

I reeled in my thoughts before they ran away from me. People call me a daydreamer, a worrier. I'm the first to admit that although I work with facts at the *East Vancouver News*, my imagination has free rein over the rest of my life. Faced with a flasher, I had to ignore the disastrous scenarios vying for my attention and concentrate on leaving the SkyTrain station like the rational person I knew I could be.

I was celebrating my poise when I was forced to pause to steady my legs. I stole a quick glance over my shoulder. Convinced the flasher hadn't followed me down Commercial Drive, I continued, hustling past the Italian coffee shops, ducking my head against the sheets of rain, swerving to avoid the shrunken welfare dogs towing their dreadlocked owners. Two men lurched unevenly toward me and I crossed my arms before they could leer at my chest. My favorite panhandler cracked his leathery face into a grin as I passed. My smile was so weak I dropped a toonie into his waiting hat as compensation. He yelled his thanks to my back as I turned onto Second Street.

I vowed never to go shopping after work again. I couldn't help checking my back one more time. The flasher could be following me, brandishing a knife, crazed eyes aglow with uncontrollable rage. I knew he was only a man whose thrills depended on my predictable reaction, but the trees lining Second Street suddenly threatened me. I couldn't wait to get home.

I chose to live near the Drive because it seemed like a real neighborhood, the kind of place where locals still gather in coffee shops or grocery stores to talk about the Canucks. Eavesdropping in the neighborhood has given me loads of really great material for the *News*. With its mishmash of traditional families, punk kids, and wannabe artists, Commercial reminded me of New York City, and one of my favorite fantasies involves me making a living as a promising young writer in New York's East Village. I think my studio apartment, on the top floor of an older house, has the funky but cosmopolitan feeling I associate with the big-city writing life. On summer evenings, I visit the delis, listen to the street bands, nurse iced lattes for hours at a sidewalk table, or drink whiskey on my porch and wave to the evening strollers. Those nights, I feel proudly urban, a million miles from Grand Forks and the shy bookworm I was when I lived there.

That evening in February, I was just glad to be safely in my own place. I kicked off my sopping shoes and collapsed in a sagging chair. When I closed my eyes, the man in the SkyTrain station reappeared. A violent head-shaking got rid of him; in his place stomped my editor, May Lee, waving her finger over my copy and clicking her tongue till my words shriveled up and disappeared. After a week's worth of hard work, May had slammed my needle exchange story hard. What a day. A quick tour down Robson Street in search of black boots that belonged in the style purgatory between teenaged fashion victim and middle-aged matron hadn't helped, either. To top it off, the rain had turned my hair into a frizzy bird's nest. I could see myself in the mirror across from the couch. Thanks to the fear lingering on my face, the paleness of fatigue, and the disaster of my hair, I looked more like a sixteen-year-old who'd just failed a driver's test than a sophisticated city reporter who intimidated editors and frightened politicians. Because of my often-cursed baby face, I always look as if I should be shopping for a prom dress, not pushing for quotes.

A ringing phone cut into my self-flagellation. I picked up the phone and groaned hello. It was my neighbor, Dede. Since she had moved into the suite across from me six months ago, we had discovered we both liked to relax with a drink and some jazz after work. Our early evening meetings had become a ritual, a chance for me to bitch about my workday and Dede to vent about her romantic disasters.

"Can I come over? I'll be right there." She hung up without waiting for a response.

She burst through my door two minutes later, just as I was pouring myself a glass of whiskey.

"I'm feeling down, Cait. I have a serious need to drown my sorrows in whiskey and jazz. Let's babble a bit. I'll tell you about my date last night and you can tell me about your thrilling evening in front of the tube. I tell you, that's what happens when you only date men in this city. You become very familiar with prime-time television." Dede always bugged me about my sexual drought, despite my insistence that I would rather be single by choice, thank you, than struggle through her roster of failed relationships. She insisted that a revolving door of women was the way to go romantically; I insisted I wasn't frigid, I was just waiting for the right man.

"I could use some relaxation, too, you know," I told her. "My day sucked. I wanted to quit my job today."

"Be thankful you have a job, that the powers that be don't object to your hair and your lifestyle." One of Dede's pet peeves was the inability of potential employers to overlook her burgundy buzzcut.

"Well, I object to their lifestyle sometimes, to their whole philosophy of journalism," I said. "I had my needle exchange story ripped apart today—too bleak, too negative, May said. Goddamn, the city has a problem and they want me to flog the paint job on the city hall." I gulped my whiskey and licked my lips as it burned down my chest. "I just want to write something that will make a difference."

"The *News* is a rag, Cait. You need to be freelancing. Face it, you're boring." Dede rambled on, planning my life, but I focused on the whiskey. I knew I was stagnating at a small community paper and had a non-existent social life, but I didn't need an unemployed photographer to remind me. Dede never stopped pointing out that my life was dull, as if I needed the tip.

"Dede, hon, I just want to go to bed," I surprised myself by saying. Most nights, she was my career coach and I was her Dear Abby. We didn't let the fact that she didn't have a job and I didn't have a social life stop us from solving each other's problems.

"Well, chin up, sweetie. Tomorrow you'll knock 'em dead." Dede sprang up and disappeared out the door.

I eyed the leftover whiskey, then poured myself another glass and flicked on the television. The local news depressed me, since the anchor always seemed to be a fellow journalism school graduate making big money in a high-profile job. As usual, the lead story centered on rain, flooding, and wind. Did any Vancouverite talk about anything else? I grabbed the remote, then hesitated. A fresh-faced reporter was standing on the Drive near the SkyTrain station. She stood with her back to the strip of bush and railroad tracks that ran under the Commercial Drive overpass. Locals called it the ravine. I passed it every day, although stories of wild parties and roaming gangs had kept me from venturing down the bushy paths.

"The body was found by two fourteen-year-old boys. Police are not releasing the name of the victim tonight, although they will say it is a fifteen-year-old female. Police spokeswoman Sergeant Sandy Leslie told us the victim was sexually assaulted and died as a result of knife wounds. More information will be released tomorrow." The reporter flashed a toothy smile before the camera cut to the anchor desk.

There had been a murder in the ravine: a sex-slaying blocks from my house. My heart accelerated until it seemed to leap out of my chest. I rose from the couch, secured the deadbolt, and steeled my mind against an invasion of images. Knife wounds. Sexual assault. A body lying beneath a tangle of branches. My imagination moved from the ravine to a deserted road in Grand Forks and I was a frightened fourteen-year-old again.

"He'll always be with me," I whispered to my empty apartment. A squeak on the balcony, a knife on the dinner table, a terrifying newscast, all these could bring him back. Every time a car slowed down beside me or some lout flashed me, he was there. And every time I heard that something awful had happened to a young girl, I wished I could hold her hand, offer comfort, and tell her I understood. I had been there.

I turned off the news. I wanted to pick up the phone and talk to someone about my memories, but I had never told anyone, not my parents, not my friends, not the police. To tell someone, I would have to open the maze of memories always lurking behind my stone face. I would, I imagined, begin with a disclaimer, "I've never told anybody this," as if silence somehow proved my strength of character. A few simple phrases could unlock the gates, but I kept them deep inside. I was tough, after all. I had almost convinced myself. I checked that I had locked the door and went to bed.

Once I was safely between my sheets, I began scolding myself. When I was hired by the *News*, they'd pointed out that most reporters need a car. I'd retorted that what I lacked in transportation, I made up for in ambition. Give me any story, I swore, and I'm there, by bus, cab, or my own blistered feet. I told them my student loan was too big to buy a car, but they didn't take the bait and offer me a raise. I didn't tell them what really kept me on the bus was fear, fear of the constant Vancouver traffic, the cars careening across the narrow bridges, darting between lanes, and flying blithely through red lights. I was afraid to drive, but not afraid to go after any story any way necessary. I was tough, remember? But when a woman was murdered four blocks from my house, what did I do? Retreated to my bed.

Gary, the paper's more senior reporter, would probably end up covering the story anyway, since he seemed to get anything with any grit. Only the day before, I had cursed after May assigned him a prime West End drive-by shooting story. I could hardly go down to the ravine alone in the dark, and there was no guarantee the television crew would still be there. I was doing the right thing, I told myself. After a good night's sleep, I could find out more tomorrow. I pulled the covers tighter and listened to the rain drum on my window until my alarm went off.

Chapter Two

"DON'T CHANGE THE WORLD, CAIT, just give me the story."
May glared across the desk, her small fist wrapped tightly
around my needle exchange story.

"I want ten inches of copy, with facts and quotes, not an
editorial, not a feature, just a solid story," she continued.
"You've taken too much of a stand here, and your emotion
clouds your objectivity."

I lowered my eyes and reached across her desk for my
butchered article.

"I just wanted to create some support. The Women's
Center is running out of money, you know." I grabbed the
papers with more force than I had intended. For a few seconds, we glared across the desk at each other.

"Finish the bike ID assignment, then we'll talk," May
muttered.

Bicycle identification! I kicked the wall beside my cubicle.

We'd covered it before in articles that were essentially feel-good ads for the police, written in response to the publisher's requests for "positive" local news about hard-hitting issues like garden shows and charity drives. Who would read it? Or care? I stared at the floor for a few minutes and took some deep breaths to cool off.

I'd entered journalism school filled with visions of becoming a feminist Bob Woodward, a hard-living woman uncovering sexism and corruption in Vancouver's elite. In my off-hours, the fantasy went, I would write travel pieces based on holidays with a series of attractive and equally successful men, and work on long, *New Yorker*-style articles that would be praised for both their literary merit and their uncompromising politics. Instead, I was rotting in this office, writing fluff pieces for a paper that would end up lining bird cages.

"Cait, can I see you again in my office?" May stuck her head around my partition. "Right now?"

Resisting the urge to stick out my tongue, I followed her high heels into the office. Although May was under five feet tall, when I had to talk to her I always felt like a little kid called to the principal's office.

"I just got a call from the police station. They're holding a press conference at five about that girl they found in the ravine."

"What else did they say?" She has to give this story to me, I thought. I had to know more about the young girl raped and murdered so close to my house. Even if it brought up some unpleasant voices deep inside, I could handle it. Really.

"Fifteen. Young girl, raped, stabbed." She shook her head slightly. "Pretty grim. Some note about babysitting found on her."

Babysitting. My stomach did a balletic flip-flop.

"Pretty heavy stuff for the *News*." It was a dig at our marshmallow editorial policy, but she didn't get it.

"I'd like a story by tomorrow. I know it's not your usual assignment, but Gary is busy with that drive-by shooting. I'm sure you're capable. Just remember to stick to the facts." May returned to some paperwork without saying good-bye.

Back at my desk, I imagined what the anonymous girl had been thinking when she realized what was happening, when she knew a simple babysitting job was turning dangerous, and when she saw the knife and realized she was alone with a psycho. Ten years before, on a Grand Forks road, I had drafted a mental note to my parents that I planned to write in my own blood, blood from the knife pointed resolutely at my chest. I had never thought I'd live through it. My hands began to shake with the memory until a ringing phone brought me back to the newsroom.

"*East Vancouver News*. Cait Whyte here." I tried to sound professional.

"Cait! Steve here. Are you heading to the press conference? Need a ride?"

"Will you be in the car?"

"Cait, you know you want to see me. I'll be in the lot at ten to five."

Steve Wilson and I met in journalism school. I had pegged him as a poser, a not-too-bright kid who hoped to use his degree as a stepping stone to a career as a lawyer or politician. A frat-boy who seemed to strive for a minor in keg parties, he distinguished himself in class with questions that revealed his ignorance of current events—the ultimate social faux pas in journalism school. The fate of the alphabetical class list made us partners for many assignments. During our last semester, I suggested a feature on heroin addiction for our final television class assignment. It seemed like a good idea, but it turned out to be a nightmare. Not surprisingly, few junkies were willing to be interviewed on camera. The night before the assignment was due, Steve brought one of his paler girlfriends to school. With some pilfered syringes and a careful reading of *Trainspotting*, we passed her off as an addict for the assignment. My only dishonest story. That night cemented our friendship, and Steve was the only person I'd kept in touch with from my school days. I had one major reservation, though. Steve had landed the best job of our class as a crime reporter with the *Province*. It was handy knowing someone with a car, however, and we often violated inter-paper rivalry rules by arriving at press conferences together.

He didn't pick me up until five, the same time we were due at the police station.

"We've got lots of time. This car can cruise." He had just bought a new car, thanks to his overly generous salary. "I've got to be at GM Place at six, but I can drop you off near your place if this doesn't ramble on too long."

"I know a busy reporter like you can't afford to dawdle," I teased.

"Jealousy, Whyte, jealousy," he retorted, with perhaps less irony. "If that rag you worked for gave you some real stories, you would be busy, too."

"When was your last real story? Certainly not in journalism school, unless those C papers were just misunderstood."

"I tell you, this jealousy just isn't working for you, Cait." He placed his hand on my thigh. I brushed it off. Condescending bastard, I thought. Why do I hang out with him?

"Get your reporter face on, Whyte," he said as he slipped into a handicapped parking spot, five minutes late but unperturbed. I shook my head and followed him to the cop shop.

Sergeant Sandy Leslie, the communications officer for the Vancouver police, was talking when we entered the room.

"At this point, we haven't established a time of death, although we do know her body had been moved from the site of her murder. She was found on Tuesday and had been reported missing by her brother, Paolo Sabato, on Monday."

Sergeant Leslie picked up a glossy piece of paper from her podium. "This is the picture we'll be releasing to the press. Claudia Sabato, age fifteen, of Burnaby."

I forced myself to look from my notes into her face. A typical school photo: blood-red lips leapt off the page, outshining her full cheeks and downcast eyes. She could have been any of the teenagers I shared the SkyTrain with every morning.

Sergeant Leslie put the photo down and picked up a day book. It was exactly like the notebooks made by a street vendor who sold his wares on a sidewalk near my house. He numbered every book he made with large gold numbers on the front cover. Claudia's was number 193.

"This book is the only thing found on her. The entries are standard for a girl her age—talk about homework, movies, and the like. On the day she went missing, the word 'babysitting' is written across the page. Unfortunately, she didn't give any more information. Her parents didn't allow her to babysit. They thought she was too young. They're extremely upset. I'm sure you can imagine." She sighed as she replaced the book.

I bet she has children of her own, I thought. She hates her job and wishes she could stay home and protect them from what she sees every day.

"Any questions?" Her voice was cool as she scanned the room.

"Was she sexually assaulted?" Steve's voice rose from the chair next to me.

"Yes, she was."

As the questions continued, my stomach began to contract in waves. I put down my notepad and redirected my energy to controlling the spinning room. The institutional smell of the station threatened to overwhelm me, and I blinked at the surprise of tears stinging my eyes. I couldn't shake the image: the young girl in the picture, a knife at her throat. As the knife moved closer to her soft flesh, her face became my own.

I had to escape the shrinking room. As Sergeant Leslie wrapped up, I stumbled out ahead of Steve, gasping for air.

"Don't give you too many tough stories at that rag you work for, do they?" he said on the way home.

"Shut up," was all I could say. I deserved that, I thought. I lost my self-control.

"How are you going to cover Bosnia? You lost it on a Burnaby girl."

"How can you say that?" I exploded. "Of all the god-damned ignorant male things to say. She was someone's daughter, she was … she was.…" The words sputtered to an end as more tears escaped. "It's not funny." I wound down my rant in a weak voice.

"Hey there, Whyte, don't get your panties in an uproar." He punched me lightly on the shoulder.

"Typical tabloid expression. Why don't you lead with it?" I pulled back into our familiar banter until he dropped me off at Commercial and Broadway.

I fumed as I stormed along the Drive toward home. Why had I cried? I never lost my cool. I was tough and worldly, I reminded myself. I worked hard at it. This was my chance to escape my memories, to be objective, to write the best story of my career—as long as I didn't break down. Damn Steve. Why were we still friends? Arrogant and chauvinistic, at his worst moments he was everything I hated about reporting.

I should buy a car, I thought. Nothing fancy, just an old beater, so I won't have to bum rides off Steve or take the SkyTrain. A car would mean strange men couldn't flash me on my way home. If hundreds of teenagers could drive around the city in their parents' cars, surely I could drive. It was time to get over my fear of the road if I was ever going to live up to my fantasy of myself. I pictured myself zooming around town, perhaps in a pickup truck or a sporty convertible. I could take auto-maintenance courses, impress men with my mechanical skills. Maybe a car would provide the kick-start my romantic life needed.

Fueled by the enthusiasm of a new idea, I turned into a newsstand and surveyed the patchwork bulletin board. There was an ad for an '88 Tercel for $1000. Was that a good deal? Before I could decide, a strange noise caused me to look away from the board to the sidewalk outside. The street vendor who sold the notebooks like Claudia's was drumming loudly on a pile of them, his eyes closed and his body swaying. I shuddered and wondered if he remembered selling Claudia Sabato her book. Perhaps the police had talked him already, if they knew where she got the book. She had been here, I realized, right in my neighborhood. We may have passed each other on the Drive, neither knowing that I would one day write about her death. I forced my attention back to the notices in front of me. Other cards offered bikes, another option. I could get in shape, buy some new clothes to accentuate my biker-buff body. A '91 Mazda for $2000. I reached over to tear off a phone number when my eyes froze on a small piece of paper.

"Single parent looking for babysitter. Call Pete at 555-9462."

Her parents didn't know she was babysitting, so it couldn't have been for any of their friends. My mind rewound the press conference. Handmade notebooks exactly like Claudia Sabato's were sold right outside the newsstand. If she'd bought the notebook, odds were she had also stood here, reading this bulletin board. I pulled off the ad and stuffed it into my back pocket, then hustled home.

Chapter
Three

THE BODY OF A FIFTEEN-YEAR-OLD GIRL was discovered in the Commercial Drive ravine on Monday. Police have identified the victim as Claudia Sabato of Burnaby. Sergeant Sandy Leslie of the Vancouver police said Sabato died of knife wounds to the torso area. Leslie also said Sabato had been sexually assaulted.

"At this time, we have no suspects, but we are pursuing several tips," Leslie said Tuesday. A special investigative team has been set up to investigate the death. Anyone witnessing unusual activity near the ravine over the weekend is asked to call the Vancouver police or Crimestoppers.

Sabato was a student at Centennial High in Burnaby. Her parents, Don and Mary Frances Sabato, own the Viva Italiano Deli in New Westminster.

After I arrived home, it only took a few minutes to write a story based on the press conference. I tried not to let my feelings color my story. I didn't need any more flack about being emotional from May or Steve. When I finished, however, something was missing. The article had the essentials: when she died, how she died. But it read like a recitation of facts and contained nothing that wouldn't be on the local TV news. I thought back to the picture I'd seen. Who was Claudia Sabato? The question was such a cliché that I had to smile.

Only an hour earlier, I had lashed out at Steve for treating her like just another dead body. I was just as guilty if I wrote a story that didn't give her a voice and a personality. Maybe it was a weakness in my writing, but I didn't know how to paint a better picture of her life without the sort of unprofessional sentimental descriptions that would annoy May. All I knew was that she probably shopped on the Drive and that she babysat. I had a hunch she had found babysitting jobs from the bulletin board near my house, but I could never prove it. Were those ads screened for nut-cases? Could anybody advertise? Feeling a bit ridiculous, I picked up the pink piece of paper and dialed the number.

"Pete Lloyd," a male voice answered. He had the voice of a smoker. I could hear a child yelling in the background.

"I'm phoning about your ad for a babysitter?" Nervousness put a question into my voice.

"Sure. I'm still looking. Any experience?"

"Yeah." It wasn't really a lie, I told myself. The experience was a long time ago, but I was sure I could handle it.

"When can you sit?" he asked.

"Only at night and on weekends. But any time then."

"Why don't you come over tomorrow? I'm just grocery shopping, but it would let you get to know the kid. Plus, I could relax, instead of chasing the tiny demon through produce." He punctuated his little joke with a nervous laugh.

"What time?"

"About eight. I like to avoid the dinner crowd."

I gave him my name, wrote down the address, and hung up the phone. To steady my quivering hands, I poured an inch of whiskey into a glass, then came down to earth. Babysitting? What was I doing? I didn't need the extra work. When I calmed my imagination down and tried to think rationally, I figured it was pretty unlikely that Pete Lloyd was remotely connected with the Sabato murder. I'd made a rash decision, and no doubt I would regret it when I spent the next evening with a screaming brat. Still, watching Barney videos would beat voluntarily entering the house of a killer.

At least it would be a night out. I could lie and tell Dede I had a date. Which brought up a question. Which did I fear most: coming face to face with a potential murderer, or going out on a date? My dating skills were as archaic as the computer I used at the *News*. My bad luck had started in my last year of high school, when a boy I'd had a crush on for months had surprised me with a kiss. I was so surprised, in fact, that I had just sat there numbly while his waxy lips brushed mine. The next day, he had told the entire school that I was a bad kisser.

Journalism school was probably the high point of my post-high-school social life. I had a few empty one-night stands to prove that I was capable of physical contact with a man, but the encounters only depressed me and confirmed that I was better off sleeping alone. In my final year, I dated another student, Mark Simpson, a goateed, wire-glasses type who was fantastically well read and had the sex appeal of my couch. Our dates consisted of long, literary conversations. He would pore over the books in my apartment, making judgments on my character according to my reading tastes. Sometimes, my books would move him to passion, but more often we would end the evening by watching *Nightline*—*Letterman* was "too facile"—and he would leave. I had been fascinated, then bored, then frustrated. He was in Hong Kong now, hoping "to witness the evolution of a new society," and making tons of money doing it. I liked to imagine him running across my name in the future, after I won a major award, and shaking his head sadly, wondering what had happened to the two of us. She was so talented, he'd say to himself, why had I never listened to her opinion on anything?

Since Mark, I had been on the occasional date: Dee's brother, who arrived drunk and passed out on my couch before seven; an extremely handsome programmer who was moving to Siberia the next day; a friend of Steve's who told me he was actually gay, but hadn't worked up the nerve to tell Steve. No wonder an evening of babysitting actually had me excited. Dede was right: I did need to get out more.

Not that the babysitting date didn't have its own possible thrills. Just imagining introducing myself to Pete Lloyd sent a course of adrenaline through my blood. Even if my rational mind figured he wasn't the killer, there would always be that niggling doubt to add some wild imaginings of terror. Maybe my excitement would spill over to my story, which obviously needed an injection of something.

I picked up the phone book and turned to "Sabato." I knew the names of Claudia's parents, Don and Mary Frances, from the press conference, but I had no intention of phoning them. Even if they answered the phone, I couldn't face bereaved parents. Sure, every day some reporter sticks a mike in an unknown victim's face. It's standard reporter behavior, encouraged at journalism school, applauded in the Press Club, and guaranteed to get air time on network television. But I couldn't do it, at least not now and not with this story. I couldn't help but picture my own parents at the other end of the phone, quietly searching for answers to give a reporter. I scanned the rest of the listings for some other relative to give me an insight into Claudia's short life.

The first number I tried, belonging to an A. Sabato, was picked up by an answering machine. The quavering voice on the machine belonged to an elderly woman, possibly a grandmother. Not my best bet. The next name was Paolo Sabato. I remembered that Paolo was the name of her brother, the one who reported her missing. Figuring he must be the family member taking control of the impossible tasks that surround a young girl's death, I dialed the number. Once again, my call was answered by a recording, this time with a low, faintly accented voice.

"I'm spending this difficult week with my family. If you leave a message, I'll get in touch with you." The phrasing was awkward, but there was a tension in his voice that almost made me think twice about leaving a message.

"My name is Cait Whyte. I'm a reporter for the *East Vancouver News*. I'd like to extend my sympathies to your family. I'm writing a story about your sister and I was wondering if we could talk. I'd like more information about Claudia, information that would make my article be about her life, not just a recitation of facts around her death. I can be reached at the *East Vancouver News*." I gave the number, offered more sympathies, and hung up with relief, glad to have finished my contact with Paolo Sabato's machine. I reread my article. Although there wasn't much I could do until I had more information, just hearing her brother's voice convinced me it was too cold. I imagined her family reading the paper. With a picture of tearful parents in the back of my mind, I picked up a red pencil and added a few words.

When I'd finished, I called Dede. She answered the phone sleepily, Ella Fitzgerald wailing in the background.

"Dee, did I wake you?"

"Just dozing a bit. Do you want to go out later?"

"Probably not." It was almost eleven. "Well, where are you going?"

"Don't know. Just for a beer maybe. I need something to pick me up."

"Hey, can I read you a story?" I was pretty nervous about my revised article, and Dede was a critical audience and born skeptic.

"Of course. I'm kinda sleepy, though, so I may not be totally on my game."

"I'm writing about Claudia Sabato, that girl found in the ravine. Have you heard about her?"

"Yeah. Awful stuff."

I began: "At age fifteen, young Claudia Sabato has become yet another young victim of violence against women. The North Burnaby student's body was found in the Commercial Drive ravine Monday. She had been sexually assaulted, according to Sergeant Sandy Leslie of the Vancouver police, and died of knife wounds to the torso.

"The murder has terrified Commercial area residents, particularly the area's women, who already have had so many frightening reminders of their vulnerability. Leslie said the police do not have any suspects but are pursuing several leads." I took a deep breath.

"Sabato's parents, Don and Mary Frances Sabato, are devastated by the tragic and needless death of their young daughter. If you noticed any unusual activities near the ravine, call Crimestoppers or the Vancouver police and help bring her killer to justice. Vancouver women have put up with enough fear." I paused, slightly out of breath from my rapid recitation.

"Heavy stuff, Cait. Makes me want to run out and bag him myself. Way better than most of the garbage the *News* prints. More feeling, more guts."

"Some would say too emotional, with far too many adjectives," I said. "And expressing an opinion on women's safety is generally considered bad form, believe it or not."

"How can you be too emotional about a murder? Go for it, I say." Dede's voice was becoming more and more animated. "Still interested in that drink? I met a woman who might be able to give you some advice. She's really political. I might go to some meetings with her next week. She's into violence against women. You should talk to her. She's cute, too."

"*Into* violence against women?" I said. "And since when are you 'political'? I thought we agreed that sex and politics shouldn't mix."

"I liked some of what Janet said. And I like her. I was

21

almost thinking it might be time to narrow the field to one woman, if you know what I mean. You in for a drink?"

"I should sleep. I'd love to hear about your thoughts on romance, but it's been a rough day again. Sorry to wimp out on you two nights in a row."

Although she was always frustrated by what she saw as my nun-like existence, Dede liked to go out with me. Thanks to our shared enthusiasm for a few drinks and a good argument, our political, sexual, or esthetic debates had often lasted till the wee hours. In fact, she had converted me to whiskey, nursing me through my first gagging sips by convincing me that it was the perfect tough reporter's drink. Although I occasionally thought longingly of the peach cider I drank in college, I'd come to agree with her, comparing brands with the enthusiastic research skills of an investigative reporter. Sometimes I worried that I drank too much, but rationalized it was part of my rough, urban lifestyle. I wouldn't have any whiskey tonight, though. Claudia Sabato's story had drained my last reserves of energy and I doubted I would be up for Dede's new "political" pal.

Maybe Dede had the right idea, though, I thought as I lay in my bed, listening to the rain. She was grabbing all that life offered her romantically, she once told me. According to her philosophy, the more variety in relationships, the better. She wondered how I could exist without the excitement of a sex life, relying only on a frustrating job for stimulation. Maybe she was right. My life was in a rut. And just when it was becoming obvious that I needed to take more risks, I had the perfect opportunity. The Claudia Sabato story filled me with terror and excitement. It was almost like falling in love: I could take a leap and become more involved in the story, meeting her relatives, trying to find out who she was babysit-ting for, exploring her world, and remembering my own, or I could tell May I would prefer that she assign the story to Gary, after all.

But why, I wondered as I drifted off to forgetfulness, was I so interested in a girl I had never met? For years, I had tried to pretend nothing bad had ever happened to me. I had sealed my memory as effectively as I had frozen my voice. Why now, as I struggled to prove my strength and put away my fear, was I becoming obsessed with a story that brought it all back?

Chapter Four

"CAIT, I WANT YOU TO REWRITE your Claudia Sabato story. It's too emotional, the voice is juvenile, there are too many adjectives, and you're speculating. Facts, remember, at this paper we stick to facts. If you want to make things up, write for Harlequin." May slapped the story on my desk.

"I like the story. I want people to think more about the victim." It was a risky statement, but the rewrite had made me bold.

"Not in our paper. That's not our job. You know that." She paused a second. "The Sabatos are having a press conference at the police station this morning. I think you should go. This might give you the angle you need. I'll give you another day for the follow-up story."

I gave her my best smile. May would never admit that I might be right, but by suggesting I write about Claudia's parents, she was allowing me to flesh out my coverage.

I had a few phone calls to make about the new paint job on the city hall before the press conference. Another earth-shattering story that was no doubt an important step on my road to international acclaim as a ruthless investigator and prose master, I thought with a grimace as I proofed the story.

Finally, I called for a cab downtown. I hadn't talked to Steve since the press conference the day before and I had little desire to initiate a conversation. I was still embarrassed, and I thought he might be uncomfortable. Male friends, in my experience, don't like to see women cry.

The conference was a lot like the previous one, with the same generic-looking police officers facing the same disheveled reporters. Steve entered a few minutes after I did and took the seat beside me.

"Whyte." His greeting was curt. He looked distracted, his myopic eyes darting around the room.

"Steve," I whispered back. "Sorry I yelled yesterday." I always apologized first.

Sergeant Leslie walked in the room and took her place in front of the podium. A tall, blond cop with a huge mustache followed her, accompanied by a middle-aged couple, the woman leaning on his arm for support. The Sabatos. I leaned forward to get a better look. Their eyes were fixed on the floor, as if they couldn't bear to look up into the expectant faces in front of them. The set of Claudia's father's shoulders, solidly squared but carrying the weight of his family, made him look both beaten and determined.

"These are the Sabatos, Don and Mary Frances. They've requested a press conference because they have something to say to the public. They will not be answering questions afterwards." Sergeant Leslie's voice was gentle. Mary Frances stepped to the podium.

"Claudia was a nice girl. She didn't run with gangs, do drugs, or any of that. She had no enemies." She stopped and closed her eyes briefly. Her husband placed a hand on her shoulder.

"No young girl should die the way my daughter did. I don't know who would want to do this to her, but somebody must have. Somebody sick. If you know anything about who killed her, please contact the police. I beg you, call the police."

A battery of flashbulbs went off as Mary Frances brought up a hand to wipe her eyes. She blinked and looked around the room until her eyes found the TV cameras. Would my mother have had the strength to meet the camera squarely like that?

"She was a beautiful girl. Imagine it was your daughter."

She turned into her husband's arms and the blond policeman led them away.

"That will be all." Sergeant Leslie followed them.

"That was short." Steve stood to leave. "I could have got that by phone."

I ignored Steve's pragmatism. I was mercifully dry-eyed but shaken once again. I didn't need to agitate myself any further by examining his lack of compassion.

"I've gotta go, Steve."

"Going out tonight?"

"I don't think so," I said.

"Sitting home and contemplating murder and other cheerful subjects?" If I didn't know better, I would have said there was a faint note of concern in his voice. Was he joining Dee's campaign to get me off my couch and on a date? The Committee to End Cait's Celibacy didn't really need another member.

"Don't worry about me." We opened the door to pelting rain. Instinctively, I took a step back inside to stay dry while I unfolded my umbrella.

"Excuse us," someone said behind me. A hand tapped on my shoulder. "Could we slip past you?" I turned around to face the Sabatos.

"Certainly." But my open umbrella continued to block the door while I searched for words.

"I'm very sorry about your daughter," I murmured. They'd probably heard it hundreds of times already, but I was sure they knew it was heartfelt.

"Thank you. We hope she is happy where she is now," Mr. Sabato said.

"She was a wonderful girl." Mrs. Sabato smiled weakly. "I know she would have made something of herself."

"I'm very sorry." I stepped out of their way and watched them walk to their car together, hands entwined, leaning toward each other for support against the wind and rain. I turned to Steve.

"They seem like nice folks," he said.

"It's so sad." I shook my head and walked away, my open umbrella hanging by my side as the rain quickly drenched my hair and ran in tiny rivers down my face.

Back at home, I made myself my standard can't-think-of-anything-else-but-a-can-of-spaghetti dinner and sat down in front of the television. I was too nervous to eat, so I paced around the living room. Suddenly I was no longer so certain my hunch about Claudia's babysitting was so ridiculous. What if Pete Lloyd was the killer? I wondered briefly how I could call the cops and explain my theory without sounding like one of those weird psychics who always try to get involved in murder investigations. At the very least, I thought, maybe I should tell someone where I was going. Too complicated, I decided. I would have to defend myself if anything happened. But could I? I dug out my Tae Bo tape from the bottom of my closet and spent a few minutes kickboxing. Movement helped release my adrenalin, and if I was forced to take action, at least I would be warmed up, with some punches fresh in my mind.

At a quarter to eight, I boarded the bus to Burnaby. I found the house easily, but I paced in front for a few minutes. If I wrote a story about the house, it would be hard to find an angle: all the blinds were closed, there were no plants, and while the paint wasn't peeling, it wasn't exactly shining, either. The lawn had a few toys scattered about and there was an old blue Toyota in the driveway. I took a deep breath and knocked.

A small, blond girl answered the door. She was wiping chocolate stains from her mouth with one hand and clutching a threadbare blanket with the other.

"Are you Cait?" she asked, pale blue eyes fixed on my face. "Who are you?"

"I'm Ally. Dad!" She turned and ran out of the entrance hall, flashing smooth skin through a large hole in the rear of her flannel pajamas.

"Hey, pumpkin, I'll be right there." The male voice seemed far away.

I let myself into the living room and sat on the only piece of furniture, a corduroy couch. I looked directly at the bookshelf. I had to agree with my ex-boyfriend on one thing: to a reader, books are always the barometer of someone's character. My eyes scanned the titles: *Diet for a New America,* a shelf of cookbooks, some child psychology books. Did a tattered Patricia Cornwell point to an interest in grisly forensic crime novels? A red flag went up in my mind. Perhaps I should have told someone where I was going.

"You must be Cait."

With a start, I turned to the kitchen door and smiled at a unshaven, brown-haired man with a hand on Ally's head. I stood up and moved to shake his hand.

"I'm glad you could make it. I take it you've met the monster." He patted his giggling daughter on the head.

"No problem." I tried to meet his eyes, but they were flicking around the room. His brown eyes, circled with a network of fine lines, looked older than the rest of him. His bangs stood straight up from his forehead. If he'd been in a downtown band, the look would have been trendy; in a Burnaby kitchen, it just looked disheveled. Still, he was attractive in an almost punk rock sort of way. When he turned around, I caught myself looking at his butt and jerked my eyes away. Maybe I did need a man in my life, but a potential killer wasn't exactly what I would ask for in a personal ad.

Even if he was innocent, a single father was only a marginal-ly better match than a killer for a child-fearing woman like myself.

"I'll be back in about an hour," he said, interrupting my thoughts just as I was imagining losing prize-winning stories because Ally had the chicken pox. "Shopping is much more efficient this way. With the little princess here, I could be gone till midnight."

He gave me a quick smile, his eyes flitting somewhere over my left shoulder, then turned and clicked the door behind him. The room was silent until I exhaled loudly.

"Let's watch *The Princess Bride*." Ally broke the silence.

"You start the movie, I have to go to the bathroom."

The bathroom was dirty but bare. I found toilet paper under the sink, soap scum around the taps, but nothing unusual for a busy single-parent family. I opened the door and looked toward the living room. Ally was singing to her-self. I tiptoed out of the bathroom and backed toward a closed door. With one ear on Ally's singing, I inched the door open and slipped inside. Bingo. His room. A double bed, a simple bureau, and some jeans thrown on the floor. There was a small bowl on top of the bureau, but a quick finger sift revealed nothing but change. I walked over to the bed and hunched on my knees, lifting a wad of disheveled covers to reveal what was under the mattress. Dust, a rolled-up sock....

"What are you doing?"

Shit. A tiny voice. How could I explain this so she wouldn't tell her daddy?

"I thought I'd play hide and seek, Ally. But you've already found me. I bet I can find you, too."

An hour later, I had explored every corner of the house in search of my small charge. Pete Lloyd was in dire need of a housekeeper, but unless dust was a weapon I found nothing that would suggest he was capable of murdering his babysitter.

As the hour grew to a close, I realized that he could come home to find me looking behind his couch. I wanted clues to his character, but I didn't want to upset him. And I didn't want him to think I couldn't be trusted. Using child-care strategies I thought I had forgotten, I called Ally into the kitchen for a glass of milk, then lured her to the living room to watch the movie. She had just slipped her tiny body under my arm when I heard heavy footsteps on the stairs. I sat up straight and pulled Ally closer. He could lock the door behind him, take out a knife. . . . Ridiculous, I scolded myself. It was a weird hunch to begin with and there had been nothing to back it up. Surely a man with kind lines around his eyes and a nice rear end wouldn't kill his babysitter. Plus, I reminded myself for what felt like the hundredth time in two days, I was tough, a survivor, and I'd learned the hard way to be always on my guard. I was ready for whatever he had to offer. Wasn't I?

I planned to make a quick exit, just in case.

"Anybody home?" Pete walked in, weighed heavily with groceries. "Holding down the fort, pumpkin?" As he reached down to hug his daughter, he winked at me over her shoulder.

"Was she easy on you, Cait?"

"Huh?" I was busy replaying the wink in my mind.

"How did it go?"

"Great! Ally was great."

"Can I give you a ride home?" he asked.

I froze. For some reason, I hadn't anticipated this question. Was he trying to lure me into the car, so he could drive somewhere quiet and deserted? I had been there before, as my pounding heart and trembling hands could attest. I steeled my mind from slipping back to that spot and tried to focus on what I had learned since then: I was in control of my body, my safety, my life. All I had to do was assert myself.

"No thanks," I squeaked. I took a step toward the door.

"You sure? It's no trouble."

"I've got things to do downtown. But thanks. See you again, Ally."

I was halfway down the block when I realized he hadn't paid me.

Chapter
Five

I SHOULD TALK TO MAY, I THOUGHT. Walk into her office right now and tell her she may be right about the Claudia Sabato story. My article had appeared that morning, edited with May's heavy hand. Reading the revised copy, I wondered if I really had been too emotional. If I couldn't get my feelings in check, I'd be covering city hall paint jobs for the rest of my life.

I pictured myself in twenty years, graying, fat, and bitter, surrounded by young and ambitious reporters.

"*How* long has she worked here?" they would ask each other, vowing they would never end up like me.

Hannah interrupted before I'd added up how much whiskey my older self would have to drink to dull the pain of unrealized dreams.

"Cait, there's a call for you on line two."

I picked up the phone, trying to take my thoughts away from my crumbling ambitions.

"Cait Whyte here."

"Cait Whyte? Is this Cait Whyte?" The voice on the other end was deep and, I guessed, about my age.

"How may I help you?"

"My name is Paolo Sabato. Claudia's brother. I got your message. I just read your article in the *East Vancouver News* and I wanted to thank you for thinking of our family." His voice had a faint lilt and just a hint of the accent that colored his parents' speech.

"Thank you. My sympathy goes out to your family. If there's anything I can do, please let me know."

"Miss Whyte, could we meet for coffee? I'd like to talk to you about my sister."

I decided to overlook the "Miss." He was going through a hard time, after all. And he sounded nice.

"Sure. When's a good time for you?"

"Could we meet today? When do you finish work? I would like to start right away."

"Sure. Meet me at five at Joe's on Robson for coffee. I'll be wearing a red kilt and I'll be right inside the door."

"Thank you once again, Miss Whyte."

After I hung up, I picked up my copy of the article. I was glad the Sabato family had no complaints, but I knew any further involvement with them would annoy May. In her mind, the story was over. Until they caught the killer, we'd given enough space to a murdered teenager. I could have coffee with the bereaved brother, but, for my career's sake, it would have to end there. In my mind, though, it wasn't over. Just hearing Claudia's brother's voice ignited my desire to do more with the story, to unearth my investigative reporting skills. In one sense, I owed it to Claudia. I could prove that I was strong enough, tough enough, mature enough, to help other young girls. And if I uncovered the killer in the course of the story, I wouldn't be a victim any more; I would be a hero. And I would prove to Dede, Steve, and myself that my life wasn't really so dull after all.

I had several calls to make about some sorry excuses for stories, but instead I looked for Derek Malone's number. Derek had just moved from traffic to the homicide squad. Newcomer or not, he was bound to have information not available at the press conference. And Derek was always very willing to talk to me, for reasons that I suspected were less than professional. During my first week with the *News*, I had interviewed him about a Granville Street car accident. That weekend, by chance, I ran into him at a party Dede had dragged me to and we'd spent the evening comparing work stories. A tall man whose boyish face was incongruous with his official uniform, Derek had become my ally in the cop shop. More than once, I had detected a faint reddening around his ears when our conversation turned to the personal. I was sure I didn't even know how to flirt, but I wasn't above being extra-friendly to Derek to get some information. It didn't help that he was pretty cute, in a Dudley Do-Right sort of way. He was almost a fantasy version of the ideal man to bring home to Mom: chivalrous, respectful, and clean-cut. I certainly could feel the pull of those qualities, although five years ago, I probably would have found them dull. Although I generally didn't go for that all-Canadian kind of charm, I was attracted to him. His interest in me always made me feel somehow protected, secure, in ways I would never admit to Dede.

Derek answered his phone on the first ring. His voice was young and rang with enthusiasm. If I hadn't known him, I would have assumed I had the wrong number. He couldn't fake that world-weariness that distinguished so much of the police force, so he still sounded excited just to be answering the phone.

"Are you free for a couple of minutes to talk? It's Cait." Derek was always too polite to tell me he was busy, and I didn't want to interfere with his investigation.

"How are you doing? I read your article this morning. Pretty good stuff. Maybe reading it will inspire someone to come forward."

"Thanks, Derek. I wasn't too happy with the article, so it's nice to hear positive feedback."

"Have you met her brother, Paolo? He called the station yesterday. Seems he's not too happy with our work. He seems to think the word 'babysitting' in her journal should lead us right to the killer. He wonders why we haven't arrested anyone yet. I'm sure he wants the whole city to know how incompetent we are."

"It must be hard on her family."

"Yeah, she sounds like a great kid, too." He sighed.

"Did she suffer?" Where did that question come from? I resolved to keep the conversation more professional. There was a long pause on the other end.

"There's no easy way to be raped and stabbed. I wish I could say she didn't suffer, but…." As his voice trailed away, I could hear the beginnings of the bitterness that seemed to increase with every year a cop spent on the job.

"My buddy Ron is in charge of the case. I'll keep you informed. He was with the family at the press conference." I remembered the tall, blond, mustachioed cop holding Mrs. Sabato's arm as she inched to the podium. I'd heard Derek mention Ron before, a police veteran who seemed to have taken Derek under his wing. Despite the admiration Derek didn't even try to conceal, Ron actually sounded like a bit of an asshole, the kind of cop who didn't think women should be on the force and used words like "member" and "perpetrator" when "cop" and "thief" would do.

"Are they focusing on the babysitting angle?" I knew he couldn't tell me much, but I wanted to know if the previous night's babysitting adventure was the big waste of time I suspected it was.

"I'm not too sure, to be honest. Pretty hard to prove anything without a name. They're interviewing some of her friends."

"Thanks a million, Derek. I'll probably talk to you soon."

"Let's meet for coffee sometime, Cait."

"Anytime." I hung up. Maybe a date with Derek would be just what the Dating Doctor ordered. He was good-looking, earnest, and would probably treat me like gold. But despite the subtle attraction, it was hard to commit to romance. He lacked something, an air of sexuality, of what I liked to call danger. No edge, I decided, using a term that was drilled into my brain during journalism school. My dream lover would be a reporter, hardened, detached, worldly, but literate and secretly sensitive. A cynical attitude, a weathered voice, and serious eyes—these were the features that filled my sexual fantasies and Derek just plain didn't have any of them. But Dede often accused me of searching for faults in prospective suitors in order to avoid having to take action. Was I being too harsh on the man?

Hannah's voice interrupted my pondering once again. It was a good thing she wasn't a mind reader.

"Cait, another call on line two."

I picked it up.

"Great article, Cait. Glad you could pull it off without losing your cool." It was Steve.

"Thanks. Yours was good, too." The *Province* had run Steve's article the previous morning. It was just a simple recitation of facts, but at least he hadn't slipped in any of the offensively sexist remarks he was prone to.

"Do you know if they have any suspects yet?" Steve sometimes forgot we worked for rival papers and couldn't exactly quote each other.

"Why?" I decided to be vague and string him along.

"I'm a little involved myself. Hope they catch the bastard. What do you know?"

"Actually, I don't think they have any leads."

"The perfect crime. But if I was going to kill someone, it would be a runaway, a lonely runaway without any friends or family contacts. At least this little cutie was probably better looking than most runaways, judging by her picture. But who knows what she did in her spare time? Maybe more than band practice, if you know what I mean. A good age, though. I would probably choose a young victim like that."

"She was just a normal teenager." This was just speculation, but I couldn't keep the snap out of my voice. "And you know that a woman's background or history or family should have nothing to do with her personal safety. Nobody deserves this."

"You're pretty obsessed with her, Cait. Relax."

"For God's sake, Steve," I sputtered and hung up the phone. I sat back and tried to breathe deeply.

"Cait, can I see you in my office?"

Damn. It definitely was not a good time for one of May's lectures about adjectives, professionalism, or pleasing the advertisers. I kicked my garbage can and slunk into her office.

"Look alive, Cait," May said without looking up from her terminal. "I've got a story for you. They're adding veggie burgers to the menu at GM Place. Can you go there after work and check it out? It could be an interesting angle— health consciousness of the west coast meets the meat-and-potato hockey fans and all."

"I'm meeting Paolo Sabato right after work. I don't have his number, so I can't cancel." And I wouldn't anyways, I added to myself. Veggie burgers. For God's sake.

"Cait, I thought the Sabato story was over."

"I think there may be another story in it. Seems her brother is unhappy with the police investigation." May always liked a municipal politics angle, although, of course, she would prefer something praising the police.

May pushed herself away from her desk and looked up at me. "Cait, don't get too involved. I've said it before. It's tragic, I know, and frustrating, but it's out of your hands now. And if you think about it, you'll go crazy. Believe me. When I started, I took it all too seriously, too."

"How can you take a fifteen-year-old murder victim *too* seriously?"

"Just be careful. And don't let the brother manipulate you into writing his version of things." I decided that was her way of letting me know I could skip GM Place and meet with Paolo Sabato.

I left work early in order to arrive at Joe's by five. Walking down Robson, I replayed my conversation with May. Did Paolo have a personal agenda in mind? He sounded earnest and upset. It was only natural that he would want to talk to someone. I could help him spread the word about his sister and he could help me with my story, according to the somewhat twisted relationship between crime and the media.

Joe's was packed. I scanned the beaming faces and foaming drinks. Most latte-drinkers were paired off—the old Noah's Ark thing single people like me always noticed. Off in a corner, I spotted a lone espresso drinker, about my age, tall and dark, scanning the room with a puzzled look. I smiled and waved slightly as I approached, but his brows knit together in a bewildered expression. Despite the confusion on his face, I couldn't help but notice a trim haircut and the kind of sideburns that take weeks of careful shaving to perfect.

"Paolo? I'm Cait Whyte." I extended a hand.

He blinked a couple of times as if something confused him, then smiled.

"Paolo Sabato." I felt a pleasant twinge deep in my belly. I have a weakness for good voices and Paolo's had a slightly raspy, honeyed tone.

We shook hands briefly, then he stared at me for an awkward second. He opened his mouth as though he were about to ask me an important question, then paused and continued to stare. My appearance seemed to throw him off, as if he had been expecting someone else. His stare didn't feel rude, perhaps because I was so taken by his eyes, which were a shock of bright blue in his olive-skinned face and framed with fatigue. I smiled again, then looked down at his leather shoes. They were an expensive brand, I noticed, and carefully polished.

"Can I get you something?" He touched my elbow lightly to guide me to my seat.

"An iced latte. It's my favorite drink in the world, even in Vancouver in February."

When he returned, he looked at me again and started talking right away.

"How long have you been at the *News*?" he asked.

"Are you questioning my ability to handle the story?" I answered, smiling so my answer didn't seem harsh. Maybe that's why he looked confused—once again, my youthful appearance was working against me. "I've been there three years."

He shook his head. "No, I'm sure you're more than competent. I was under the impression maybe you had just switched careers, that's all."

I decided to leap right in and impress him with my investigative skills.

"So, I hear you're not too happy with the police investigation," I began.

"I'm not," he said. "I think they're treating her like some punk kid. Like some runaway who deserved what she got."

"Nobody deserved what she got. It shouldn't matter who she was."

"It's my sister, though. A good kid. They're focusing on who she knew on the Drive, thinking she might have got mixed up with a bad scene, run away, joined a gang, or something like that. That sort of thing just wasn't her." He was leaning forward and staring at me as if he was afraid I was about to run away myself. "What about her babysitting? That's more likely. She could be taken advantage of. It happens with babysitters, you know. Her notebook told us she was babysitting. It had to be for someone she didn't know, whom my parents didn't know—some freak luring young girls who want to make a little extra money."

You don't have to describe the scenario to me, I thought, forcing what I hoped was a sympathetic smile.

"That's why I wanted to meet with you today. I have a couple of story ideas to bounce off you. I liked your article.

Maybe you'd be interested in doing some more stories after talking to me."

I'd heard this approach before. Nice to meet you—please write about my great-aunt, my struggle with my neighbor's barking dog, my campaign to lower library fines. Experience had taught me the best strategy was to listen politely, take careful notes, promise to follow up, then forget about it. If anyone phoned back, wondering why they hadn't read about themselves, I blamed my editor. This, though, could be different. Paolo was filled with passion and bitterness and determination that his sister not be forgotten. Was that such a bad thing? Also, I could listen to him talk all night. His voice was exactly the sort that filled my fantasies: deep but soft, faintly accented.

"Maybe an article about babysitting safety." He waited for my reaction. "Remember Clifford Olson? That's how he met some of his victims."

"I've thought about doing an article about the safety of babysitting before." I'd obsessed over it, in fact, but I certainly wasn't going to confess that in Joe's to a handsome, grieving brother. I couldn't deny that I was responding to his intensity, to the way he looked at my eyes when he asked me a question. Already, I was making a mental outline of the proposed article. I was making less noble plans, too, plans that involved red wine and soft music.

"And maybe a profile of my sister. In depth. There's a lot to say. You could write about my family and how we're doing."

An article exposing his own pain was not a typically male request. Although I'd just met him, he struck me as too intense and proud to follow through with it. I wondered if I could hold him to his idea. There was no doubt that he might hold the attention of the *News*'s female readers.

"But the most important angle, I think, is the police incompetence. Why can't they catch my sister's killer? She had a goddamn diary on her. Wouldn't that give them something? They don't even have a suspect yet." He pounded his fist on the table, rattling the foam on my latte.

"I'm sure they're doing their best. I'd need more specific examples of what you feel they've done wrong," I said.

"Why haven't they put up more signs, started a Crimestoppers ad?"

"I'm not defending the police. I'm just trying to consider all angles. I can't do a story with only one side."

"I know." He rested one hand briefly on mine. "You'll have to excuse me. I'm under a lot of stress. My parents are falling apart. Claudia was their baby. I have my own grief, but I also have theirs. It kills me to see my father cry."

He looked so sad for a moment, I wanted to touch his perfectly sculpted cheek. I had to admit, as I faced his sorrow, that I was being less than objective about Paolo Sabato as a source. He was as classically handsome as Pete Lloyd was disheveled, and as smolderingly sexy as Derek was wholesome, but I was starting to realize that I was attracted to all three. Too bad all three were linked to a murder case that kept me up at night.

"Did Claudia hang out on the Drive?" I asked a question to bring myself back to the story. My neighborhood was filled with suburban teenagers experimenting with drugs and the dangers of city life, kids who thought smoking pot in an urban park would make them Jack Kerouac.

"She went for coffee there sometimes, yeah, but with her friends from Burnaby. We don't think she knew anyone on the Drive, and she wasn't a regular at any one coffee shop. She didn't hang out too much. She was a pretty busy kid. Very focused."

He stared directly at me for almost a minute. While I tried not to squirm under the directness of his gaze, I could almost see wheels turning in his head. Perhaps he was remembering his sister as she ran out of his parents' house to take the bus into the city; perhaps he was wondering what he should say next to the stunningly attractive young reporter across from him.

"But enough about me." He interrupted my fantasy just in time. "Do you enjoy reporting?"

"Yes and no. I'd like some harder stories, less local politics, less Go Vancouver stuff, and more investigative journalism on more relevant topics. Maybe that's why I enjoyed writing the article about your sister." Whoops. Had I just implied I was enjoying his misfortune? "I didn't mean. . . ." I struggled to take my words back.

"I know what you mean." He smiled slightly. "I can understand."

Change the subject, my racing brain urged. "What do you do for a living?"

"I do some consulting, help out my parents. I went to theater school." He looked vaguely embarrassed. I wasn't surprised he was interested in acting. He had the looks, I reasoned, and he definitely had the voice.

"Claudia was interested in acting. I tried to encourage her, but my parents. . . ." His voice trailed off as if he was afraid he would say something unpleasant about his parents when they were at their most vulnerable.

"Let's just say we argued about it a lot. Claudia was their favorite. They didn't want her wasting her time acting. She was going to be a doctor, as far as they were concerned. I thought she had some potential as an actor, but my opinion never really counted for much. Too much history. But let's not think about that right now."

With an abrupt about-face, he switched the subject away from his family. The local arts scene was oppressive, he told me, oppressive and filled with pretentious cliques.

"Not that I can't be pretentious," he cautioned. "Ever so pretentious, dahling."

I guffawed, then sat grinning at him. The man at the table next to us shot me a look of contempt. That guy thinks I'm a bimbo, I realized. I abruptly wiped the inane smile off my face. I was in date mode. I was practically hitting on the bereaved brother. Despite my shy and nunnish lifestyle, I was hoping to charm this poor man right back to my apartment when we had finished discussing the death of his sister. Could I sink any lower? Maybe suddenly finding myself attracted to three different men was bringing on the appearance of the regressive flirt gene.

"I should go." I sat up straight and put down my coffee, careful to keep my mouth frozen in a straight, non-flirtatious, line.

"It's been a pleasure, Cait. I appreciate your taking the time to talk with me." He extended his hand toward me and looked directly into my eyes. A voice *and* manners, I noticed. And a way of looking at me as if I were the best reporter in the city.

"I only wish we had met under better circumstances," I said. Christ, I groaned inwardly, what a cliché.

"Can we meet again? To follow up?" he asked.

"I'll see where I go with your ideas." But you can bet I'll give you a call, I added in my own mind.

I'm a fool, I'm a fool, I chided myself on the bus ride home, a fool for throwing myself at poor Paolo. May would have my head if she knew what thoughts were burning inside me. Getting too close to a story, indeed. I'll get close to this source, real close. I closed my eyes for a second, imagining exactly what I had in mind, but I quickly put the brakes on my runaway fantasy and forced my eyes open. My head jerked back in surprise as I re-entered the world of the bus. Directly across from me, two narrow gray eyes were fixed on my face. They belonged to a man about my age, with floppy blond hair and a brown leather jacket with a tear down the sleeve. His face was wooden but I could feel hatred burning through his eyes. I leaned back into my seat, hoping to disappear in the stiff vinyl cushions, and glanced out the window until we came to my stop.

It was a tough walk home. I'm just paranoid, I kept repeating. It's natural to feel vulnerable after meeting a murder victim's brother, especially if you're me and any trivial upset can lead to a litany of imaginary disasters. Still, I couldn't shake his face from my mind.

I arrived home sweaty, agitated, and anxious to invite Dede for whiskey. I could bitch about men, I figured. I was certainly in the mood, even after meeting with a charmer like Paolo. The man on the bus had to be one more example of Vancouver louthood. Like the flasher I had seen in the SkyTrain station, he must get off on making women uncomfortable. But something about him and the way he didn't even blink as he stared made me wonder if his hatred wasn't aimed directly at me, Cait Whyte. I racked my brain, but I couldn't place his face. Someone I had interviewed and somehow misrepresented?

Then it hit me: it was the guy sitting next to me at Joe's, the man who had thrown me the look that seemed to brand me as a scarlet woman. Of all the buses in the city, why did he have to end up on mine? And why did he think he could judge me? I fumed. If he only knew the sorry state of my romantic history, surely he would cut me some slack for a being a little coy in an interview. I decided to phone Dede to vent instead of letting my imagination take over. When I picked up the phone, I noticed the blinking light of my answering machine.

"Hey, Cait, Pete Lloyd here. Wondering if you're free on the weekend for some babysitting. Could you give me a ring?"

I picked up the phone. Could I balance babysitting for Pete and writing stories for Paolo, all on top of my regular job? Fortunately, both men were good-looking. I would find a way.

Chapter
Six

"LIGHTEN UP, BABE!" Dede and I were at the Railway Club and she was in rare form. I was sure she winked at the waitress and drank her whiskey like a thirsty horse only to annoy me.

"I just feel that I'm being held back. There's more to the story, I'm sure, and May and those suits at the *News* won't let me explore it. It's frustrating. I'm tired of being told what to write."

"Patriarchal capitalism for ya." Dede raised her eyebrows. She knew what my response would be.

"Give it up, Dee. That's old news."

"Hey, speaking of patriarchs, how's your friend Steve? Still striving for that job at the *National Enquirer*?"

Dede and Steve had met once during an interminable evening of bickering and thinly veiled personal insults. Ever since, each made a point of using an overly polite voice when asking about the other.

"Steve's fine. He's done some better stories recently. Maybe he's finally learning how to write. He's being a complete ass about the murder story, though."

"Steve? An ass? I can't picture it." She laughed. "Whatever has he done?"

"He jokes about the victim. Not in a funny way, but in, well, a weird way. And he's totally unsympathetic whenever I get upset about it. It's not an easy story to cover, you know. But he makes jokes about it, jokes that transcend the normal Steve jerkiness."

"How could he joke about that? The little prick."

"Who knows what he's thinking? I'm not going to talk to him about it any more."

"You know he likes you." Dede raised her glass in my direction.

"Steve? You're raving!" I shook my head.

"He wants you. Everyone can tell."

I finished the rest of my drink and motioned for another. If Dee was going to be completely ridiculous, I might as well have another whiskey.

"Steve is not interested. We talk about girls all the time. He likes blonds with big boobs. That's his only criteria. I hardly qualify." I pointed to my own chest, which was rising timidly under my black turtleneck, then grabbed my decidedly mouse-brown hair.

"Trust me, Cait, he likes brunettes." Dede winked at the waitress as she set down my whiskey.

"Busy night?" Dede asked her.

The waitress looked around the empty bar and snorted.

"She's charming," Dede deadpanned.

I giggled. The whiskey was working its way down, warming my center and replacing my leg muscles with lead. Glowing heat filled my heart; I looked around the empty bar and sighed with contentment, then reached over and grabbed Dede's hand.

"Let's call a cab. I have a big day tomorrow. I'm babysitting after work."

"Babysitting?" Dede looked as if I'd announced I was planning to bomb BC Place. "Do you need to borrow some money, Cait? Is everything all right? No, I know what's up—your biological clock is kicking in. Really, I'm sure Steve would oblige and save you from borrowing other people's kids."

"I'll explain later." I couldn't explain the reasoning that led me to the Lloyds, not even to myself. "There is a perk to it. I have to admit, the father is kinda cute."

"Did I hear you correctly?" Dede looked around the room dramatically. "Did our Cait Whyte, nun-in-training, actually admit she was attracted to another human being?"

"Shhh…." Even though it was a slow night at the Railway, I didn't want anyone to hear. "Actually, I don't what is happening to the men of Vancouver, but the city's sexual market value is rising." I gave her a quick summary of the interview with Paolo and my potential date with Derek.

"Cait! I'm so impressed." Dede grabbed my hands. "You're entering the real world, at long last. This calls for another round."

An hour later, I was flopped on my bed, trying to control the spinning walls by focusing on the telephone. When it surprised me with what seemed like an unusually loud ring, I was sure it was trying to tell me that my staring was making it uncomfortable.

"Cait? Steve here," the receiver said.

I suppressed a giggle. Steve. Perhaps he wanted to ask me out on a date.

"Cait, you okay? Did I wake you up?"

I tried to collect myself.

"I'm fine. I've just had a few drinks with Dede. What's up?" I glanced at my clock. One o'clock in the morning. Didn't Steve know I had to be at work early? Was this any way to seduce me?

"I thought I'd call you before someone else did. I just got a call from my editor. He said they've just found a body on East Hastings, at the Western Rose Hotel."

I registered this slowly. East Hastings. Skid Row. Heroin overdose? Robbery?

"It's another young girl. They found her in a hotel room. A prostitute. She'd been raped and stabbed, like Claudia Sabato."

With a start, I pulled myself out of my stupor and into the conversation. Steve's voice was warm and calm, without his usual ironic edge. He knows something else, I thought, something he's afraid to tell me.

"Do they think it's the same guy? In that area, it could be anything. Could be a trick gone wrong, an overdose...."

"Well...." Steve was at a loss for words, something I'd never heard before. "The killer pinned something on her body. It links the two victims. Actually, it links you. He ... it was ... he pinned your article about Claudia Sabato to this girl, to her naked body, right through her skin."

"My article?" I was awake now. I clutched the phone like a lifeline. "What the hell?"

"That's the only clue they have. Maybe you should go to the press conference tomorrow. Shall I pick you up?"

"That would be fine ... will be fine. Pick me up. That's just fine." I was repeating myself, but my mind was in a hotel room on East Hastings. My article—not Steve's, not the *Vancouver Sun*'s, not anybody else's—my article was pinned to the body of a dead woman. Somewhere downtown, in a fleabag hotel room, my carefully chosen words had mingled with her blood.

Chapter
Seven

"WE MAY BE DEALING WITH A SERIAL KILLER. Or a copycat crime. Given the appearance of the newspaper article, we can't rule that out." Sergeant Leslie paused and shuffled through a stack of photos.

Why did she have to mention the newspaper article? I scribbled some meaningless words in my notebook so I could avoid making eye contact with anyone. Don't look at me, I willed the other reporters. Beside me, Steve nudged my elbow and winked. I narrowed my eyes and sent a thousand invisible daggers his way.

"How long had Ms Bennett been working as a prostitute?" a radio reporter asked.

"We don't have that information yet. She was known to police, though, and is known to have worked in the sex industry. We can say she appeared in at least one locally made pornographic video."

A murmur rose from the room of normally stone-faced reporters. I scribbled "porn actress?" diagonally across my page, circled it three times, and added a circle of stars around the question mark. Steve put up his hand.

"Have you considered the possibility that her death was being filmed? As a sort of—what do they call it—snuff film?"

I drew an angry face in my margin.

"At this point we haven't ruled anything out," Sergeant Leslie answered Steve.

According to Sergeant Leslie, none of Shelly Bennett's friends had heard from her for a week. That wasn't too unusual, they had told the police. Shelly was a private woman, with few close friends. The word her friends used most often to describe her was "shy." In the mug shot released to the press, her eyes were hidden by her lashes and her mouth was set in a grim line, out of sorts with her garish blue eye shadow and pink lipstick. I wondered what sort of life she'd had, what combination of circumstance and free will led to death in an East Hastings hotel room. Somehow her life, seemingly marked by hardship and solitude, had inter-sected with the privileged and protected life of Claudia Sabato.

"That was a pretty tacky question, Steve. Poor woman," I said as we exited the press conference. I wasn't letting him off the hook.

"I was just pulling for a good quote. Besides, nobody ever thinks porn is made in Vancouver. I thought it could be a dif-ferent angle. The dark side of the city and all that."

"But Steve." I wanted to wring his skinny neck. "Why plant an idea in all those reporters' heads that might not be true?"

"Other reporters won't have the story I'm going to have. I have some sources you would kill for."

I ignored the bait he cast my way.

"You just don't get it, do you?" I asked instead.

"Need a ride, Ms Betty-Do-Good-on-the-News?"

"I think I'll take the bus, Mr. Hard Copy."

"You know I'm joking, Cait." He reached out for my hand.

"Whatever." I wanted to be far away from the police station, from Shelly Bennett, and especially from Steve. "See ya."

I had turned a corner in the hall of the station when I heard Derek's voice behind me.

"Cait! We have to talk."

I turned around. Maybe I was feeling vulnerable, but the blue uniform fairly shouted security to me. Between his uniform and his concerned expression, he was lucky I didn't run into his arms.

"Cait, are you all right?" he asked.

"I'm fine. Should I be worried?"

"Not at all. We do want you to come in to answer some questions, though, to say where you were when she was killed. Nothing serious."

I was shocked.

"You guys don't think I could have anything to do with this?"

"Of course not. We're just trying to rule out absolutely every little angle. Seriously, he's probably using the article to taunt us. He's leaving a message: 'If you'd caught me after the first one, this one never would have happened.' We're trying to figure why he chose your article, instead of one from a more popular…." Derek stopped and looked at his shiny black shoes. "I mean, instead of one from another paper."

"One with more readers," I said. "Let's be honest—the killer was probably one of six people who read my story. That should narrow the investigation."

"Do you still want to meet for coffee?" he asked, just as I was about to turn and leave on the heels of my small joke. "Maybe tomorrow night?"

How often did I have two coffee dates in one week, even if one was with a victim's brother and one was with an investigating officer? Dede was going to be amazed.

"Sure. We can talk some more about my articles, if that's okay with you." I didn't want to offend him. I was sure there was a person under the uniform, somewhere, who had other interests.

I half expected Derek to suggest that law enforcement favorite, Tim Hortons. Instead, he suggested Joe's. He was going to be on Robson anyways, he told me. I was going to get a reputation with Joe's baristas if I wasn't careful.

I returned to reality when I arrived at the office. I kept my eyes lowered, trying to ignore the curious glances from my co-workers. It's just a coincidence, I wanted to yell. Just because all my work and worrying about Claudia ended up pinned to another victim's body doesn't mean I have anything to do with the murder. I couldn't even think about Shelly Bennett without picturing my article pinned to her body. I felt dirty, complicit, somehow responsible for her death.

May decided to write about Shelly Bennett's murder herself. It would be inappropriate, she told me in crisp tones, for my byline to appear. It might look as if the *News* was capitalizing on my tremulous association with the murders. I handed over my notes from the police press conference reluctantly, but I could see her point. And I didn't want to tempt fate. Already, my imagination had considered the possibility that if I wrote another article, it would appear on another body. It could turn into a series of murders with a strange journalistic twist. And I would never sleep peacefully, or write another word, again.

I called Paolo as soon as I got home. To bolster my confident-sounding façade, I repeated Derek's statement that I was not at risk. Just a coincidence, I assured him in what I hoped was a breezy tone.

"I'm sure you're not in danger, Cait," Paolo agreed. His

own voice made me feel as if he was personally guarding my door.

"To be perfectly honest," he continued, "I don't think they're related. I think some creep was playing a sick joke on the police."

"It does seem strange," I agreed. "I mean, your sister and Shelly belonged to different worlds."

"It happened when she was babysitting," he said. "I'm sure of it. I don't know why the police don't get it."

"I thought about what you said," I told him. "In fact, I did check out a possible lead." I hesitated for a split second. Could I tell him about my evening at the Lloyds' without sounding like a wannabe Nancy Drew? Would he laugh? Or would my efforts somehow offend him? I decided to bite the bullet. Leaving out my anxiety, second thoughts, and sweaty palms, I told him how I'd followed up on my hunch about the babysitting ad.

"That's wonderful, Cait," he said when I'd finished, "that you'd do that for my family. I don't know how to thank you. You put yourself at risk and took more initiative than the police will ever take. But you really shouldn't do it again. What if he was the killer? It was very brave of you, but a little stupid, too, don't you think?"

I agreed. I'd gone over my decision to call the Lloyds many times, and I still couldn't believe I followed up on my suspicions. I had paranoid suspicions all the time, but rarely did I do anything but stew in my bed at night.

"I don't think I'll phone any other strange men and volunteer to go over to their house," I told Paolo. "Although I am babysitting for the Lloyds again tomorrow night."

"You're sure he's safe?" Paolo asked. "You should give me his address just in case. And make sure he's aware someone else knows where you are."

"You'll call me if anything strange happens?" he asked after I gave him the address.

"Of course," I said. After I hung up, I sat back in my chair.

He was probably only doing what he wished someone would have done for his sister, but that night, whenever my thoughts crept toward the scene of Shelly Bennett's murder, I remembered he had said that I could call him.

The next night I had more time to think on the bus to Pete Lloyd's. It was a bit of a trek from Commercial, but I needed the time to examine what I was doing. Shelly Bennett's murder had made me question my suspicions about Pete even further. I couldn't explain why I was dismissing my theory, but I was aware that I was definitely entering the realm of the paranoid if I thought he had mutilated a body in order to leave a sick message for the police. I was pretty sure I wasn't going to have to make any frantic calls to Paolo. I couldn't decide if that was a good thing. Maybe some other kind of call would be in order.

I have to put the Pete-Lloyd-as-killer theory to bed, I told myself, but surely there was a story idea somewhere. I could ask him why he trusts me, a virtual stranger, to look after his little girl. Instead of a story that asked "Is babysitting a safe job?" I could do "Are your kids safe with a babysitter?" I liked the first idea better, though. Aside from any personal obsessions, in today's panicky climate, I had read a lot about children's safety. The safety of the sitter was relatively uncharted territory.

I was chewing over a possible focus for an article on the safety of babysitting when the bus neared my stop. I picked my way carefully up the aisle, which was slick with rain and dotted with umbrellas and soggy packages. I was almost at the exit when my feet left the floor. If there's a graceful way to wipe out on a crowded, wet bus when you're wearing a short skirt, I'd like to hear about it. My hands hit the ground first, then my knees.

"Damn," I murmured, then I began to pull myself up. I must have tripped over an umbrella, I told myself. As a born klutz, I know the anatomy of tumbles, and this one had been more of a blockage than a slip. I brushed off my knees, then smiled apologetically at the seats surrounding me. "Sorry." I addressed the bus, feeling the warmth of a serious blush spread across my face. "Long day." An elderly woman smiled, a young mother nodded. Beside them, I could see a blond head buried in a copy of the *East Vancouver News*. The *News* wasn't the sort of paper people usually read on the bus—it was short enough to read before the bus left the stop. I strained to get a look at our dedicated reader, but he raised the paper right in front of his face. The top of his head looked familiar. He reminded me of the man who had stared so intently at me the other day. This man's leather jacket had the same rip, but without a better look, it was impossible to say for sure. He was practically licking the *News*, it was so close to his face, though, so I began to move. Trying to recover some dignity, I exited the bus, knees wet, pride crushed. I watched it inch away from the stop.

Ally was thrilled to see me. She bounced around the living room, powered by ideas for our time together.

"Let's go to the park," she exclaimed, jumping up and down on one leg.

"Maybe," I murmured, feeling a bit overwhelmed.

Her father appeared after a few minutes. "You just let Cait make the decisions, pumpkin. Maybe she's too tired to go to the park."

Ally stopped bouncing and looked up at me. "Can we watch a movie, then?"

"I'll be back in about one hour," her father told me, grabbing his jacket off the back of a chair. He flashed me a big smile. "Be good, you guys."

Alone again with a five-year-old. It had been years since I'd talked to a kid. My career plan didn't allow for one, and I didn't think I'd ever meet someone I wanted to share genes with. My parents swore otherwise and tried to convince me I'd be a caring, loyal parent and they'd be the sort of grandparents kids would beg to visit. I was hoping my brother would provide them with this opportunity. I could picture myself as a cool aunt, joking with his kids as they confided in me things they couldn't tell anyone else. I'd take them on trips, buy them stuff, read their letters to my friends, who would also be childless, of course.

Ally brought me back to reality by tugging on my hand. "What should we do?"

I looked down at her. Her lips were ringed with chocolate milk and there was a long scratch across her left cheek. I guessed her hair hadn't been combed yet.

"Let's go to the park," she said. There was a small park with a few slides and swings around the corner.

"It's not too wet?" In the dark, wet night, the park didn't exactly look like Disneyland to me.

"It stopped raining. I go every night after dinner," she assured me.

I'd be a pushover as a parent. "Sure," I told her. She grinned and rushed to put on her shoes.

I sat and watched on a bench while Ally tore up and down the slides. We were alone, but I never took my eyes off her. How could parents ever relax? Maybe I was feeling morbid, but it seemed kids were in peril the minute you took your eyes off them. I could see myself at the police station, tearfully calling Pete Lloyd to tell him I'd lost his little girl.

After about forty-five minutes, Ally came over and sat down beside me. "Are you having fun?" she asked.

"Yeah, sure." I wanted to wipe some new dirt off her cheeks, but I was afraid to reach over and touch her tiny face.

"Why don't you slide with me? Mommy used to slide with me."

I couldn't give her a good reason for not climbing on the slides, other than a lack of energy and a desire not to look uncool in my short skirt, so I rushed to change the subject.

"Where is your mommy?" I asked, realizing as the words slipped out of my mouth that it was a rude question.

"She's in heaven. She's watching us right now."

She said the words calmly, with a child's simple happiness.

I wondered what images her father had used: perhaps her mother floating around with angel wings, watching her daughter to make sure she behaved. I licked my index finger and wiped a smear of mud from her chin.

"It's dark and your daddy's going to be home soon. Let's go surprise him," I said.

A few minutes later we were enjoying mugs of cold milk in the kitchen. While Ally chatted, I heard the door open. Just be alert, I reminded myself. Don't let him surprise you.

"Anybody home?" His voice was cheerful. I sat up straight, clenching my mug tightly as Pete entered the kitchen.

After giving his daughter a hug, he turned a shy smile to me. His breath smelled faintly of beer. Since he'd also picked up a bag of groceries, I figured he couldn't have had more than one or two drinks in the time he'd been gone.

"Want to hang around for a cup of coffee, Cait? Or a beer?"

"I should be home soon." He's lonely, I realized. The winks, the invitations, they all arose from loneliness. If Ally remembers going to the park with her mother, she must have died recently.

Pete was tossing Ally's hair and gazing down at her, his eyes wrinkled at the corners. "We're glad you were able to come by, aren't we, pumpkin?" But Ally disappeared without replying. Pete shrugged and smiled at me again.

Once again, I declined his offer of a ride home. I wanted to be home quickly so I could sink into my tub and forget about Shelly Bennett's death and Pete's and Ally's loneliness, so I hustled to the bus stop, hoping for a quick connection.

By the time the bus arrived at Commercial, the weather had really deteriorated. I hurried through the rain, wondering where I had left my umbrella. But when I reached Commercial and Fourth, something caught my eye. At least twenty sheets of neon pink paper were stapled to the fence on the corner. The wording was simple; in bold letters, the posters warned, "Urban Women Warriors. It's a war out there. We're recruiting."

Recruiting. I wasn't too sure how to interpret the call to arms. I would have to consult with Dede, who was usually much more informed about neighborhood happenings. There was so much to tell her, I realized. It was really time for a girl-to-girl, wine and chocolate and bad videos sort of evening.

She was clearly on the same page—there was a message from her on my answering machine.

"Hey, Cait, heard about the other body and your article and all and I wanted to see how you're doing. Give me a call when you get in, babe."

Sweet, I thought as I dialed her number. She must know how upsetting the story is to me.

"Dede, it's Cait," I said. "Thanks for your message. Hey, did you see those signs on the fence? What's up? I think they're a new level of stupidity for graffiti in the neighborhood."

"I like them." I could hear the tension in her voice. "I think it's kinda cool. Sorta a reversal on the usual, male military, superhero bullshit."

"But don't you think it sounds exactly like the same bullshit?"

"Cait, we're appropriating their language, okay?"

That was so unlike the Dede I knew, I had to laugh.

"Did you say 'we're'? Since when are you interested in sexual politics? And when did you start using words like 'appropriate'?"

"Mellow out. I've always been interested. You just never asked. Hey, I have a call on my other line."

You have not "always been interested," I thought. I had to find out more about this new "political" woman she was hanging out with. Dede and I had always agreed on sex and politics, despite our different lifestyles. Or so I thought. I felt like a chastised child. While I was regressing, I decided to call my parents.

"Cait, honey, we're so glad to hear from you," my mother greeted me with a torrent of words as soon as I opened my mouth. "We just heard about that girl and your article. We've been so worried. Why don't you come home for the weekend? Relax a little, take care of yourself."

My mother has made worrying into an art. I could tell she was trying to be cheerful, but it was hard to miss the tension in her voice.

"Mom, that article has nothing to do with me. It was just a coincidence."

"Honey, we're worried. Living alone and working with murderers."

"I don't work with murderers, Mom. I work with other reporters. I'm in an office most of the time. Frankly, I'd love to work with murderers. It would be a great story." It was cruel, but I liked to tease her. "Mom, everything that could happen here could also happen in Grand Forks."

"But you're so far away." She sounded so sad, I wanted to hang up and hop on the bus right away. My tiny mother, whose bird-like frame made me feel like an Amazon, worrying and helpless all those miles away.

"Forget about it, Mom. How's Brian?"

For another fifteen minutes, we chatted about my brother Brian, who had just made the big move to Nelson, about my father, who was thinking about retirement, about my old friends, who seemed to still move in the same predictable patterns they'd adopted in high school, about Grand Forks politics, and about the weather. It was like getting a private edition of the *Grand Forks Enquirer.*

"I love you, Mom," I made sure I told her when I hung up. My mother is the only demonstrative member of the family. I know she's starving for signs of affection, but I've inherited my father's reserve.

It was time, I figured, to step out of that reserve for a while. What good was an Oscar-caliber fantasy life if my daily existence was strictly at the level of syndicated sitcoms? Still,

I had to give myself a small trophy for venturing out to the Lloyds', for seizing control of my imagination for once and actually seeing if my wild wanderings could stand up in the real world.

For once in my life, I was going to take control. I was going to help find Claudia's killer: for her, for Paolo, for myself. And possibly, I had to admit, for my career. Forget the BC Newspaper Awards; if I led the police to a serial murderer, I could send my resume to CNN without shame. Everyone could say good-bye to timid Cait and her distaff Walter Mitty world: this time she was going to enter the land of the living. And I knew just what the next step of my investigation would be.

Chapter
Eight

Some hotels will never appear in a guidebook. The Western Rose was one of them. Vancouver scenesters were fond of hanging out in rundown dives when they went bar-hopping, as if their Cosmopolitans were somehow cooler when served by a woman with a lined face and a bad perm. But while it may be hip to drink beside a man with no teeth, it would never be cool to sleep in the same hotel as him. The Western Rose smelled like hangovers, bad breath, and hopelessness. The paint was peeling, and even in the morning light, the lobby was dark, the fading wallpaper and lone light bulb doing little to brighten things up.

I arrived at the hotel about 9 a.m. A police car was parked in front, but I didn't see a cop when I walked up to the front desk. To my surprise, the woman at the desk was young and friendly-looking.

"Help you?" she asked.

"Actually, I'm a reporter for the *East Vancouver News*. We're writing about the woman found here…." I couldn't quite bring myself to say "murdered." And I didn't want to get into too many details with the article, since I wasn't the one actually writing it. I wasn't here on assignment. I had made the trip to East Hastings because I had to see the room where my article was found, attached to a body about which I had to know more.

"What's your name?"

"Cait Whyte," I murmured. If she had any knowledge of the body found upstairs, she would know my name and ask about my article.

"No kidding," she exclaimed instead. "That's the same name as one of our permanent residents. She just moved out."

That wasn't what I expected to hear. "Cait?" I asked. "I spell mine with C." I knew I didn't have the most original name in the world, though I always thought my spelling set mine apart. I wasn't "Kate White," a perfectly nice though common name, I was "Cait Whyte." Sure, I had to spell it out every time someone asked, but it set me apart.

"No, I think hers was the usual way. She was cool. I'll miss her."

I stood motionless in the lobby. Had she just said that someone with almost the same name as mine lived in the hotel where the body was found? Could that have anything to do with the article carrying my byline? It seemed like too much of a coincidence.

"How long ago did she move?" I asked.

"Couple of weeks, I guess." The desk clerk was getting bored with our conversation. "Now we've got cops crawling around this place, talking to everyone. She's lucky. It's pretty creepy, too, all that's going on. But I can't talk about that, you know? The boss said to shut up about everything."

I didn't tell her that she'd already given me a tip so huge I could barely restrain myself from leaping over the desk and forcing more out of her.

"I'd love to meet someone else with my name," I said instead. "Do you know where this Kate lives now?"

"Sorry," she shrugged. "And I couldn't tell you if I did. She's pretty cagey. I do know she has a new job at the Bear Pub in Burnaby. That's why she moved. Finally could afford a place with her own bathroom, if you know what I mean. Once she left the business for good, I guess she wanted to move away from her old friends."

I knew the pub. It was a couple of notches up from East Hastings; Kate must have been excited to leave the Western Rose's neighborhood. I wasn't sure what "the business" was, but if it was based in this hotel, it probably wasn't charitable work.

The clerk turned to answer the phone, and I started for the door. As soon as she bent over the desk to write something down, I ducked up the ramshackle staircase that rose from the lobby.

The halls of the Western Rose weren't a great improvement over the lobby. The wallpaper was the same patchy flocked velvet; the carpet the same pea green shag. Only the smell changed: while the lobby reeked of stale cigarette smoke, in the halls, the odor of burnt dinners took over.

I wasn't sure what I was doing, roaming the halls of a fleabag hotel, as if some clue to my article's appearance would appear around each dark corner. Maybe the victim had dropped a clue in the hall—my business card from an earlier meeting for a story, an article I had written she had liked and clipped. I figured the more of the hotel I was able to explore, the more likely it was that I could find something to link me to the discovery of a body within its musty walls.

When I reached the third floor, I saw the yellow ribbon of the police investigation blocking a door halfway down. Several men in suits were standing outside the door, consulting notebooks. I could talk to them, but I knew from past experience they would only give me the standard "we're doing what we can, go to the press conference" spiel. I decided to climb up to the fourth floor.

I had just rounded the landing when I became aware of steps behind me—fast, heavy steps bearing down quickly. I picked up my pace slightly—only five more stairs, then four, then three. I just reached the frayed carpet of the fourth floor when a hand grabbed the belt loop of my jeans.

I froze, one hand on the banister. It must be the cops, I thought, stopping me from going any further. I didn't really look like a resident, after all.

I turned around, ready to apologize, then jumped back. Staring intently at me, hand gripping my waist, was the man I had seen on the bus after my interview with Paolo. His expression hadn't changed. His eyes made me feel as if I had been caught with my hand in a bank safe, as if I had been doing something illicit, but I didn't think walking through a decrepit hotel was a crime.

"Going somewhere?" he hissed. I stared back, too numb to come up with a good excuse.

"I don't think you live here," he continued. "We've got it covered."

"Are you a cop?" I stammered. "Because I'm Cait Whyte … the author of the article. I was trying to find the crime scene."

"Don't worry, Cait, we'll contact you. Like I said, it's time to leave."

He was still a step beneath me. I shifted slightly, and his hand shot out to the banister to grip my left hand.

"I don't think you're going to find anything here," he continued. "Just turn around and we'll let you go."

I began walking slowly down the stairs. I heard his steps behind me as I descended. When I reached the lobby, I paused and turned around. He kept walking past me, past the desk, then disappeared down a staircase with a "Private Property" sign at the top. Cops must have immunity from such warnings.

I walked out of the hotel into the gray drizzle. The gloomy day actually seemed bright after my time in the Western

Rose. The bus stop was right outside the hotel, thank God. Even on a sunny day, I don't enjoy winding my way down East Hastings, a stretch of urban decay that never fails to make me feel guilty for my relative wealth and security. It has to be the most depressing strip of pawn shops, bars, and hotels in North America.

I was pondering my role in the Vancouver poverty cycle when it hit me. I had seen the man on the stairs on the bus the other day, but what self-respecting cop took the bus? Most of them were as attached to their cars as they were to their right arms. He could have been working undercover, but why had he focused his surveillance on me? As I boarded the bus, I made a note to ask Derek about him.

Back at work, I faced a routine story, one that could hardly compete with the adventure of the morning. How many coffee shops on Commercial offer wheat-free pastries? May had asked. What vegan options were available? May had grabbed Vancouver's interest in healthy eating and wouldn't let it go. The result would be the kind of article I hated: too light for the *Globe and Mail*, too dull for *Cosmo*. Sometimes I wondered if May was testing me.

"Cait, the *Province* is on line two." Hannah interrupted me just before I started my list of health-conscious coffee shop contacts.

I picked up the phone. I knew it was Steve before he barked in my ear.

"Whyte! Meet me at the Press Club after work. We have to talk."

"Why?" I sighed.

"Cait, my girl," he said. "You're the talk of Vancouver media. Are you scared? Have the police talked to you very much? Your story, man, *it's* a story."

"I have something to do," I told him. There was no way I was giving up my after-work mission of finding out more about this Kate at the Bear Pub.

"We need a drink, babe."

"Steve, I'm busy." I didn't have the patience for Steve.

"Have we hit the big time, now? Too newsworthy for old friends?"

"Get over it." I hung up. I really was taking control of things. Two weeks ago, I would have spent more time on an elaborate apology than Steve ever spent on a story. Hanging up was easier, another strategy I was beginning to wish I'd learned years ago.

My muffin story was going nowhere. Not that anyone would ever read it, just some old biddies with nothing to do but sit around and read about gluten allergies. As soon as I established that May was in a meeting with an advertiser, I opened my Internet search engine and considered the best way to approach the quest. Finding anything about a Kate White or Whyte was going to be next to impossible. Shelly might be easier: I knew she had worked in the porn industry, although probably not under her real name. Still, that was about all I had to go on.

I entered "Vancouver" and "porn" and "movie" and sat back. The search engine produced thousands of hits. I wondered how long May's meeting would be, and if the *News* monitored employee Internet use.

Fifteen minutes later, I had learned a lot about Vancouver porn. To my surprise, it was a flourishing local industry, proving that Vancouver was competing with Hollywood in many genres of film production. Different articles argued for the legitimacy of the industry, while others took a more tawdry approach and described the details of the child-porn recruitment that apparently took place right under my nose. Why hadn't the *News* ever written about this? I knew the answer, but there was a wealth of stories to be uncovered in the disrobing of Vancouver's would-be actors.

I opened an archived *Georgia Straight* article. They could usually be counted on for a different approach, something with more edge than the mainstream media like the *News*. The article was called "Can Vancouver's Porn Stars Cross the

Border to Legitimate Acting?" I scrolled through. Apparently, many people in porn felt it was just a stepping stone to a "real" acting career.

"But at least one veteran of the scene has different aspirations," I read. "Kate Whyte has been acting for ten years. Unlike her costars, she isn't interested in leaving the industry to walk the red carpet at the Oscars. Instead, her dreams are filled with book signings and publishing contracts. Whyte dreams of becoming a writer."

I almost fell off my chair. Kate and I had more than our names in common, even if we were taking different routes to winning the Pulitzer. Any doubts I had about making the trip to the Bear Pub were erased: I had to meet this woman who had lived with Shelly Bennett, performed sexual acts for a living, and wanted to write.

I scrolled down further to find a black and white picture. The cutline said, "Kate Whyte: Naked Novelist." Kate Whyte, naked novelist, looked nothing like Cait Whyte, repressed journalist. Soft blond curls tumbled down her shoulders and her lips were full and pouty. She had the thick eyeliner that porn actresses seemed to favor, which made her look both cunning and somehow clueless. She wasn't smiling, but she didn't look unfriendly or bitter, like some of the others profiled in the article. I could barely restrain myself from leaping off my chair and heading to the Bear Pub. Never had writing about whole wheat cinnamon buns been more painful.

At five o'clock I boarded the bus to Burnaby. My mind was racing, turning over possible questions. Did she ever feel she was in danger? Of course, I had developed a mental picture: Cait and Kate, reporter and porn model, comparing lives and trying to determine how the choices each had made had led them into their respective careers. We would recognize similarities in our lives and puzzle over the differences. Of course, we would stay in touch afterwards. I could introduce her to some contacts and pull her out of the swampy mess of the skin trade. The bus arrived just before I won a BC Newspaper Award for the ensuing articles.

Looking around the Bear Pub, I saw one table of bellowing college students and a rogue's gallery of downward-gazing, middle-aged men framed by faded velvet wallpaper. I took a table as far from the college students as possible and looked around the dimly lit room for the waitress. A few minutes later, the bartender, a young East Indian male, came over to my table.

"Can I help you?"

"Double Jamesons, please. You alone today?"

He gestured around the bar. "Not much need for anyone else. I've got it under control. The waitress will start in about half an hour. By then we'll have the beginnings of the after-work crowd. Why do you ask? Are you unhappy with the service?"

"I'm looking for work." I congratulated myself for my quick thinking. "In fact," I continued, "I think we've worked together before. What's your name?"

"Ray. I don't think I recognize you, though. Where have you worked?"

I ignored the question, instead answering the one I'd hoped he would ask.

"My name's Cait Whyte." I extended my hand.

"No way! That's the waitress's name. Couldn't hire you— it would be too confusing." He shook my hand jovially while I gave myself an imaginary high five. Without telling him I was a reporter, I had found out that Kate Whyte did, in fact, work at the Bear Pub.

It turned out Ray had a lot to say about the bartending industry. For about twenty minutes, he supplied me with tips for my imaginary job hunt. Just as he was warning me about sexual harassment in the business, he raised his hand in a wave.

"Kate!" He aimed his greeting over my left shoulder. "There's someone here you should meet. She's looking for a job and has the same name as you."

"Must be a good worker." She had the raspy voice of a long-time smoker and sounded older than I'd expected. I did a double take as she rounded the table. The woman in front of me had the same long blond hair and unseasonable tan as the picture in the *Straight*, but her eyes and mouth were lined with tiny wrinkles, and her cheeks, high and rosy online, were now sunken and pale beneath her orangey tan. She may have had a porn model's body, but it was hard to tell beneath the ratty Cowichan sweater and faded black leggings. Only the white leather fringed boots hinted at flashier possibilities.

While I took all this in, she looked me up and down appraisingly.

"You worked in many bars, sweetie?" The "sweetie" told me she was skeptical that I, in my v-necked sweater and flat shoes, would be able to deal with the Bear's rowdier clientele.

"Not really." I couldn't continue to invent this alternate career. "I just thought I'd ask around. Do you look for a lot of experience?" I knew I sounded lame. I was starting to sense the job application route may not have been the best approach.

"We like at least five years in the industry. So, you're also Kate Whyte? I spell Whyte with a Y."

"So do I, but it's Cait with a C." All these letters were confusing.

"You're not also a reporter, are you?" Her voice was lower, suspicious.

So, she knew.

"Yeah. I work for the *East Vancouver News*, but I was hoping to make some money in the evenings." I couldn't completely back out of my original story without looking like a fool.

"Yeah, yeah." She was uninterested in my quest for a supplemental income. "Are you the same Cait Whyte that wrote that article about that girl in Burnaby? The article they found with Shelly Bennett's body?"

"I wrote that," I said. I waited for her to continue.

"I knew Shelly. It was pretty weird to hear about that article with my name on it. Let me tell you, I had to tell a lot of people I didn't write it. I spell my first name differently, I told them, but they thought I was just being fancy. Some of the losers I hang out didn't even know how I do spell my name. Hell, I couldn't have written something like that, anyways. I write all the time and I want to be a real writer like you, but I'll never get a real job. I seem to be stuck in dumps like this."

"Did it scare you?"

"Scare me? What? Why?"

"The killer might have thought you wrote the article. Maybe he knew you and Shelly. When he saw your name— or almost your name—on the article, he might have thought you wrote it, especially if he knew you liked to write. Maybe he chose that article to pin on her body because of you. Of all the articles written about the murders, why did he pick the *News*? It's definitely not the most widely circulated paper in town. I can't help but think it was because of the name."

I was piecing the various possibilities together as I spoke. I was no longer speaking to Kate, I was trying to put myself inside the killer's mind. I didn't edit my words for her sake or consider that I might be frightening her.

It didn't matter. Kate was hard to scare. She considered my suggestions for a split second, then shrugged.

"Maybe. I'm not afraid, though. I can take care of myself." She looked at me. "Did the cops talk to you?" The hostility in her voice warned me not to align myself with the police.

"Well, I was writing a story about the murder, so I did have some contact with them."

"They're all just pricks, anyways. I'm sure half the East Side knows who killed Shelly, but you can bet the police will never know."

"Do you know?" I tried to keep my voice nonchalant.

"No, but I'd sure like to. I wouldn't tell the police. I'd have the bastard killed. No, wait. I'd do it myself. String him up by the balls. She was a great kid. The cops don't know nothing about her."

"That might be a good story," I said. "We could tell people a little bit about Shelly. Show the human side of a murder victim and a part of Vancouver not many people even know about. A lot of people don't think that sort of thing happens here."

"People don't want to hear about it. Well, some of them want to see a lot of it, if you know what I mean. But most people couldn't care less about a murdered girl if she's found on East Hastings. That other girl, the one from Burnaby, she'll be remembered as some sort of saint, just you watch. But Shelly's just another hooker. She wasn't even a hooker, you know. She wanted to be an actress, like me."

"Did you get many roles?" I knew the answer before I asked.

She gave me a small smile, then looked me in the eye. "Nothing you would have seen, I'm sure." She looked at my empty glass.

"I'll get you another drink. On the house, if you promise you won't ever call Shelly a prostitute in an article. I gotta look out for her, you know."

"Do you want to meet me another time and talk about her?"

"I told you, people don't want to read that stuff. And I don't want to talk about it. If I hear anything, though, I'll let you know. You seem more reliable than those losers at the police station."

"Did you talk to them?" I asked.

"Yeah, but I couldn't answer anything. We were close in lots of ways, but she definitely kept a lot hidden from me. I never met her boyfriend, didn't even know his name. He was bad for her, though. If you ask me, once they find the boyfriend, they've found the killer. Don't expect the cops to find him—she could have been dating the manager of the Canucks for all they'll be able to find out."

It was hard to tell whether she was telling the truth. Perhaps she did know the boyfriend and was giving me a broad hint, or perhaps she was frustrated that she knew so much about her friend but still didn't have the crucial information she wanted.

I finished my second drink in silence, trying to decipher her story while Kate sauntered around, serving customers and leaning on the bar to talk on the phone. She never returned to my table after delivering my drink, although she did smile at me from across the room a couple of times. I turned to wave good-bye as I left, but she didn't see me.

I inhaled the outdoors gratefully when I left. People complain about the Vancouver smog, but on a clear day, it sure beats the inside of a bar. I glanced back, thinking of the woman who shared my name but who seemed so removed from the clean, fresh air, as if she'd decided the stale, smoky bar was where she belonged.

I was meeting Derek downtown in half an hour, so I was glad when the bus appeared immediately. It deposited me on Robson just in time. I entered the coffee shop right behind Derek, although I almost didn't recognize him in his suede jacket and trendy boots.

"Hey, stranger," he said when I caught his eye. "You look flustered."

"Yeah," I agreed. This was going to be tricky. It was hard to think of anything but my meeting with Kate, but I didn't want Derek to know we had met. Until I had gained more of her trust, I wanted to keep their two worlds separate.

Derek, however, had other ideas.

"Cait," he began as soon as we sat down. "I need a promise that this is off the record. You're not a reporter anymore as far as Shelly Bennett's murder is concerned. You're now a part of the investigation."

How could I be a witness when I didn't have a clue what happened? I nodded anyways.

"I think I know why it was your article," Derek continued. "Some of the other guys on the team found out about a friend of Shelly's who shares your name—well, it's practically your name, she just spells it differently. She used to be into the same scene as Shelly, but seems to be turning her life around. We figure he was trying to give a warning to this Kate, let her know that she was next."

Next. I sat up with alarm.

"That's kind of a leap of logic, isn't it? I mean, maybe he just thought my story was the best of the bunch." I gave a weak smile. "Surely, there are more powerful ways to threaten her."

"That's our favorite theory right now. He wants to scare her, probably because she has something that could hurt him. That's why we're sure this Kate knows more than she's telling us. Our guys talked to her for an hour and she was practically a mute. Frustrating as hell."

"Are you watching her?" I asked. What if the police had seen me at the pub? Derek would soon find out I was lying.

"All that will have to be confidential," Derek said. "But let's not just talk about murders and threats. Surely, there's more going on in your life."

Even though half my brain was still in the Bear Pub, the hour passed quickly. Derek was always easy to talk to, and he had a gift for listening.

"So, Cait," he asked as we stared at the foamy remains of our lattes, "what would you be doing if you weren't at the *News*? Doing a column for the *Globe*? Anchoring *The National*? What's your dream job?"

"Maybe writing a book of investigative reporting," I told him. "Although none of those other options would kill me. How about you? If you gave up on crime, what would you do?" I expected him to name another traditionally male occupation, one that let him help the needy and wear a uniform.

"I'd be a painter," he answered.

"No way!" I exclaimed. "I expected you to say you'd want to be a fireman."

If he found my response rude, he didn't show it. Instead, he talked with enthusiasm about his love for painting. It was a side of Derek I hadn't expected. Perhaps I had been guilty of stereotyping the poor guy. He had even sold a few paintings, and they weren't the pictures of animals and small children I might have expected. Instead, his work was mostly abstract, he told me, abstract and experimental technically.

"But I'm boring you, I'm sure." He picked up my mug. "It's nice to talk about something other than bodies with articles pinned on them, though." He stared at me for an awkward second, then the familiar blush crept around his ears. Suddenly, he leaned over and kissed me softly on the cheek, leaving a bit of lingering foam from his latte.

"Remember, Cait, you can always call me if all this freaks you out." He stood up, then extended his hand to help me up. An artist and a gentleman, I thought as I rose to my feet. I could almost get used to this. The kiss had not been unpleasant. Maybe it was the discovery of Derek's artistic side, but it wasn't as businesslike as I would have imagined. Instead, it was soft, promising.

I left Joe's almost as overwhelmed as I had been when I left the Bear Pub. After years of blaming my poor social life on the shortage of interesting men in Vancouver, I was deluged with possibilities.

When I got home, I stated my case clearly.

"Dede, I'm torn between two men." I let the words hang in the air like the smell of the fast-food burger I had grabbed on the way home.

Predictably, Dede did a double take from her position on my couch. She looked away from *Comedy Central*, eyebrows raised. I looked down at her as I paced across the wood floor.

"Two men? Cait, call the *News*. They finally have a story worth writing about."

"I guess I have to be honest with you." I stopped pacing. "Remember the other night when I described those three men? I think I've fallen for each of them." I was thinking of Pete Lloyd and the crooked smile he had when he patted his daughter on her head.

"Call hell and check the temperature. It might be freezing over." Dede popped off the couch and gave me a hug. "Tell me all about them, girlfriend. And don't leave out the parts with the sex."

"No sex." I laughed. "Though one of them screams sex appeal. He's Italian."

"A sexy accent? He's the man."

"I don't know. I'm not so sure. They each have a certain appeal." Trying not to gush, I described Pete's ragged charm and gentle way with his daughter and Derek's hidden depths.

"Cait, if you were a character in a movie, each of those men would represent a certain part of you: the long-buried sexual Cait; the Cait who wants to be taken care of by a protective cop; and the maternal Cait longing to take care of a struggling cutie and his daughter. Which Cait will win out?"

"Not so fast." I laughed and threw a pillow at her. "They're all great guys. You're oversimplifying."

"Am I?" she asked. "What you have to do is call this Paolo. You need to run a quick comparison, side-by-side with the others. It's no fair to go out with Derek without immediately seeing Paolo. Pepsi wouldn't run a taste test without a glass of Coke right there.

"Of course," she added, "I'm pulling for the sexy one. I think it would be good for you. From what I know about your sex life, and, let's face it, I know everything you've done in the last year, you're practically ready to reclaim virgin status."

"Call Paolo?" I considered this. "He's got a lot going on right now. Remember, he may be smoldering hot, but his sister just died."

"It's the perfect time to make your move, honey. Get him while he's needy. Call him up. He may want to talk, anyways."

I sat back on the couch. "I could make a business call to offer my support." I looked at the phone mocking me from across the room. "Perfectly reasonable. I'm supposed to be working on an article that he suggested, anyway." I walked over to the phone and dialed.

"Hello?" The voice on the other end was guarded.

"Paolo? It's Cait Whyte, from the *News*. How are you? I'm not calling too late, am I?"

"Cait." His voice relaxed. "I was thinking about you. Not letting that bastard scare you, I hope?"

"I'm fine." Was that all anyone could say to me? "How's your family?"

"My father, he's still pretty bad. I miss Claudia, too. I'm spending as much time as possible with my family."

"I'm still considering the article you suggested. I was wondering if you wanted to meet and discuss it?" How transparent. From across the room, Dede threw a pillow at me and stuck out her tongue.

"Is tomorrow night okay? I'm just about ready for bed, to tell the truth."

We arranged to meet at a coffee shop in the West End at eight. I hung up with relief and grinned at Dede.

"Mission accomplished."

"Very smooth, Ms Whyte," Dede said with what I was sure was a note of admiration.

"He's a real gentleman. I think they have a strong family. Different from Shelly's, I'll bet." I couldn't shake her life from my mind.

"Do you have any idea how they're connected?" Dede asked.

"I can't think of how their paths would cross. I guess it's up to the police to find out."

That's what I was telling people, at least. I didn't tell Dede that I had my own campaign underway to link the two victims.

"Maybe you need to do more research with her brother," Dede leered.

"Very classy move. 'Want to have dinner with me so we can decide what your sister had in common with a prostitute? And how they both ended up dead?'"

"And what your article has to do with them. Do you think you're at risk?"

"I try not to think about it." I had, in fact, been more vigilant about locking my door. And would I have been as freaked by that cop on the bus if he'd been eyeing me two weeks ago? I couldn't draw the line between paranoia and common sense. More than once I'd called the emergency room when someone I was meeting was late, envisioning a terrible accident. The slightest headache was quickly diagnosed as a brain tumor by my industrious little imagination. A wrong number could lead to a weekend sleeping on Dede's couch, and just about anything, from a crow flying above me to a dirty look from a panhandler, was a portent of bad luck. It would not be a stretch, under the circumstances, for me to panic completely.

"Really, Cait," Dede continued, "I'm sure you'd never be the target of some psycho. You're too together. Who could hurt you?"

I froze and stared at Dede. Indeed, why would someone hurt me? I had asked that question a hundred times in Grand Forks as I retreated deeper and deeper into myself the lonely summer after my rape.

"Maybe someone you dissed in an article," Dede continued. "But not while you're covering the new parking lot at Science World for the *News*. When you're writing for the *Globe and Mail*, exposing corruption at the heart of Ottawa, that's when you'll have to watch your back."

"Not everyone likes me, Dede. I'm not exactly beating off social invitations. My love history isn't too stellar, either." I forced a smile. "As you like to remind me."

"Imagine being me. Contempt from men, confusion from women, relatives embarrassed or ignoring you. It's lonely." Her tone was light, but as she spoke Dede shrunk into my couch. I wanted to throw a blanket over her to keep her warm and protected.

"I'm not being followed by any fan club, either, Dee. I haven't had a date in months, my family is far away in their own little nice country world, and nobody at work likes me because they think I aspire to a better job."

"Cait," Dede's tone was light, but she didn't mince any words, "you didn't spend your formative years in a crisis like I did, wondering if you were going crazy because you couldn't quite seem to conform to the norm, no matter how hard you tried. You didn't wonder if your parents would ever speak to you again if you revealed your true self. You didn't feel like you had a secret that the whole world was about to discover, so they could scorn you and paint the letter L on your forehead."

It was quite an outburst for Dede. When she finished, tears hovered on the tips of her lashes. I wanted to touch her hand, but she had curled up at one edge of the couch.

"I know a bit about secrets, Dee."

She didn't acknowledge me, but continued as if she was talking to herself. "When it came to a point where I had to tell my mother I was gay, I wanted to kill myself. I was convinced she would banish me from the house. If there's anything worse than talking about sex with your mother, it's talking about allegedly deviant sex to your mother. You don't know what it's like to suffer so much when you're so young."

Three years of reporting had only confirmed one of my favorite tenets: that everyone has a secret; that behind every calm smile lies a private source of muffled, gnawing pain. The degree of pain varies, but it's never safe to assume that someone hasn't suffered.

"Don't take that for granted, Dede," was all I could say in response.

"With your perfect parents? With about ten other people in your little postcard town?"

I was silent, remembering the summer I was fourteen. We

lived near a lake that was a popular vacation spot. I had sat on the beach every day, filled with envy for the frolicking families around me. I had imagined their lives were as effortless as their swift strokes through the clear water.

My mother had watched me sit alone all summer, worrying that I was battling adolescent insecurities, that I was unhappy with her, with my family, with Grand Forks, and with myself. She'd tried to set me up with her friends' children or with tourists my own age, but I was sure I had nothing in common with the young faces she hopefully presented to me. They quickly decided I wasn't any fun when I didn't want to talk about their boyfriends, sex, or drinking. I only wanted to sit on the beach, alone.

"I didn't have a great adolescence, either, Dede, if that makes you feel any better." But don't ask me why, I added silently, suddenly uncomfortable about having said that much. Just the hint of that summer was making my hands shaky. I sat on my hands so Dee couldn't see them tremble and tried to control my breathing. Don't say anything else and she won't ask, I told myself.

"I understand." She slapped me on the back. "I'm just jealous because you have a date and I don't. I'm sorry if I'm always pressuring you to get out there and meet men. Sometimes I think I want to live a parallel heterosexual life through you."

"It's an interview, Dee, not a date. He just happens to be cute."

After she left, I poured another glass of whiskey. It was an interview, I reminded myself, above all else. My own social life wasn't nearly as important as seizing the opportunity to help Claudia Sabato. I had to write the story of my life.

Chapter Nine

I DRIFTED TO WORK THE NEXT DAY, aware I would be counting the hours till my meeting with Paolo Sabato. I anticipated a slowing of the clocks, mind-numbing story assignments, and a serious problem staying focused. By eleven o'clock, all my suspicions were confirmed.

I perked up when I came back from an interminable meeting in May's office to find a message on my voice-mail.

"Cait, Paolo here. Call me."

He was equally brusque when I reached him.

"Do you want to meet for a drink instead? At seven? At a bar? I don't feel up to the crowds at the coffee shop." He named a small bar in a downtown basement. The dim lighting and lack of clientele held more potential for romance than a trendy and crowded coffee shop, so I agreed to meet him. Only on the caffeine-powered west coast would I worry more about crowds in a cafe than in a bar. At five o'clock I fled the building.

It had been ages since I'd put a minute of thought toward my appearance. At six o'clock, I was standing in my bedroom, surrounded by piles of clothing. A short skirt, I'd decided, was too obvious. A long floral dress, too demure. After several trips to check myself out in my bathroom mirror, I decided on a black velvet shirt and jeans with a pair of old cowboy boots. I rooted through my bathroom cupboard, certain that a can of mousse was rusting in the back. After a few tentative back-combs, I was out the door, actually pleased with how I looked.

Darkness covered my eyes as I entered the bar. As the room came into focus, I spotted Paolo hunched over a drink. For a moment, I thought he was crying.

"Hey there!" I sat down across from him. When he looked up, I could only pray my cheeks would not turn scarlet when he looked at me.

"I'm afraid I'm not in a very good mood," he began. "I've had a lot on my mind."

"I'm sure you have. How are the police doing?"

"Not so good. It's frustrating. I've told you this all before, though."

"That's my job," I laughed, then stopped abruptly. I didn't want to sound like a bimbo again, especially since Paolo was slumped with despair.

"Claudia always had such a strong sense of justice. She was innocent, but was also just a good person. She always thought the best of everyone, even me."

"Even you? I'm sure she was crazy about you."

"Yeah, the big brother." His lips curled in a faint smile. "She's not getting what she deserves, is she, Cait?"

"As we both said before, no one deserves what happened to her."

"All the fights we had, with each other, with my parents, so much I would take back. . . ." He shook his head slowly. "I'm going to be a new man with my parents. They deserve it, to have a son as wonderful as their daughter. We've fought, a lot. They disapproved of everything I did for a while. Then I figured out a secret—just keep ninety percent of my life a secret from them. Now, I'm going to share with them and try for honesty."

"I'm sure…." I didn't know what to say next. The intimate discussion of his family was making me uncomfortable. I wondered if he was talking to me at all. He was looking right over my shoulder, and his eyes wouldn't meet mine as he talked. This wasn't the suave Paolo I'd been looking forward to, and it certainly wasn't the gentlemanly Derek. I had to stop being so selfish, no matter how long it had been since I'd felt really attracted to a man. He was grieving for his dead sister, not starring on *A Dating Story*.

"You don't want to know any of this," he continued. "There are bad things in any family." He stopped and drained his drink. "And we've had this conversation before. Let's change the topic. How's work?" His voice still had a bitter edge.

"Work's fine. Should I go to the bar?" No one had appeared to take my order and Paolo had just emptied his glass. The long-haired bartender was talking to two men, both leaning across the bar and whispering.

Paolo pushed himself away from the table. "No. I'm feeling claustrophobic. Let's go for a walk."

Thank God, I thought. A few more minutes in the dark and empty basement and I'd feel like a character in some kind of Canadian film noir. The Paolo I had met for coffee seemed to have dimmed with the lighting in the bar. I hoped leaving would have the opposite effect.

Outside, Paolo's shoulders relaxed and the lines at the side of his mouth disappeared. We walked to Robson Street in silence, each of us taking in the gangs of flashy, baggy-sweatsuited boys who seemed to have engineered a coup of downtown Vancouver.

"I feel old." I joked to break the silence.

"*You* feel old. I just turned thirty. I count the hairs on my pillow every morning."

"You're an actor. Be thankful you're not female. Men seem to get more interesting roles as they age." I wanted to encourage him to talk about his acting. I felt like a teenybopper, but I had to admit acting was a sexy profession. And part of me might have wanted to compare his feelings for acting with Derek's passion for painting.

"Any roles would suit me. Actually, I've been looking more at the production end of things. I figure if I haven't made it by now as an actor, I should admit defeat." I started to protest, but he continued. "And that's where the real creative control is, anyways. Directing, producing, maybe writing."

An hour later, we arrived back at the bar. The conversation had evolved from the awkwardly personal to local gossip, as we exchanged stories about celebrities visiting Vancouver. I had just finished telling him about the reporter who stalked the *Dark Angel* set when he leaned over and kissed me. His lips barely scraped my own, but there was no doubt it was a kiss. I felt his breath on my ear.

"You're so young and pretty. And it's nice to talk to someone new. Let's get together again."

Ordinarily, I hate being called young, but if that's what Paolo liked I was willing to put my hair in pigtails.

"Of course." I beamed at him. "I'll call you next week."

"Can I drive you home?"

Once again, I cursed my ability to blush and prayed that it was too dark for him to see my flaming face.

The conversation came to an abrupt halt when we got in his car, and we drove to my place in silence, except for my periodic directions. I froze further when he dropped me off. I might have felt braver if he'd kissed me again, but he just pulled over and reached over to open the door for me. I never could figure out how more savvy women made that leap from car to apartment. Whenever I had had a man in my apartment in college, we were both drunk, the man in question couldn't drive home, and we both passed out. I had no idea what sober, adult women did for seduction, and I could hardly ask Dede and Steve for their advice.

Inside my apartment, I ran over the evening's conversation in my mind. I had no real clues as to how he felt. I was sure, though, that there was a loose connection between us, an ease of conversation that suggested we could talk for a long time under different circumstances. I did want to know more about the troubles such a seemingly well-mannered son had with his family. The bitterness in his voice when he recounted his filial failures was the only genuine dark spot on the evening. And I had to admit I was slightly bothered by his fixation on my youth. If he had just turned thirty, I wasn't that much younger.

I could picture us getting together again. I could go watch him in plays, meet his poor parents. He could stay in my apartment. I saw him walking out of the bathroom in my robe, black hair mussed by my own hands. I would slide my hands under the robe....

The phone cut into my thoughts. The damn thing seemed to be ringing a little too often. With a sigh, I picked it up. There was silence on the other end.

"Hello? Hello?" I spoke into the receiver. Shallow breaths told me someone was on the other end, someone listening to my increasingly frantic voice. I hung up. I knew how to deal with crank calls—every paranoid female in the city knew the drill. Picking up the phone again, I dialed *69. I would get the number, call the creep back, and give him a piece of my mind. Or at least I could assure myself it was a wrong number.

A computerized voice told me the number was not accessible. I couldn't get the name, or even the number, of the person who had sat breathing on the other end while I panicked. I put down the phone and poured another inch of whiskey.

I was just about to take a break for coffee the next day when Steve called.

"Hey, Cait. Have time for me today?" He sounded excited about something. "You're not going to believe what I found out."

"Try me." If I could find three interesting men in this city, anything was possible.

"I found out about a woman with your name. Well, same name, but she spells hers with a K. But the cool part is—get this—she's a porn star. Not a very successful one, but a lot of men have seen her naked, if you know what I mean."

"Oh yeah—Kate." I was going to have fun with this. "Actually, I think she's left the porn business."

"You know about her?" I could almost taste the disappointment in his voice.

"Know about her? I had a drink with her yesterday." I was not above embroidering the truth to have fun with Steve.

"How did you find her?" It was killing him, I could tell.

"My secret. How did you?"

"I told you, or at least I've been trying to when you're not too busy, that I've got sources you would kill for. What angle are you going for in the story? Local girl breaks free? A reporter's alter-ego struggles to go legit?"

"Grow up. We're just friends." If there was one thing I had learned from Kate, it was that she did not want to be the focus of a story.

"Is she cute?"

"Steve, I think you can forget about any romantic interest in your centerfold. She's a bit of a hard-ass now. She'd chew you up and spit you out in no time."

Steve was unfazed. "What does she look like? I saw a picture in the *Georgia Straight* from about two years ago."

"Maybe it was airbrushed. Or maybe it's been a tough two years. Trust me, she's not your type."

"Did you give her my name? Do you think she'd talk to me? Is she single?"

"Grow up, Steve." I couldn't see whatever goofy charm Steve possessed going very far with Kate.

"You know you love me, Cait."

I hung up. There was too much on my mind already without having to envision Steve making a fool of himself to Kate.

By the time I got home, I was exhausted. The minute I entered my apartment, I collapsed on my couch and looked around my empty room. The last few days had worn down even my normally inexhaustible imagination. The cop on the bus and in the hotel, Kate Whyte and Steve's creepy interest in her, the doubt and fear and memories lurking at the back of my mind since the whole Claudia Sabato story began, all these were taking a toll. Even the surprise appearance of romantic possibilities on more than one front wasn't enough to overshadow the sordid thread running through my days. What I needed was a long bath. Or perhaps a strong, hot shower would scourge me of the filth that seemed to have settled on my life.

I decided positive male contact would help. And I didn't know a more positive male than Derek. I picked up the phone and dialed his number. He answered right away. I could hear jazz music playing in the background, which surprised me. I'd always pictured Derek as more a Hootie and the Blowfish kinda guy.

"Derek, it's Cait."

"Cait! I was just thinking of you. Holding up okay? You're not worried about things, are you? If we thought you were in danger, we would let you know."

"I'm fine. How's the case?" I would never confess to being scared.

"Frustrating. Nobody will admit to knowing anything about Shelly. Other hookers usually look out for each other, but she seems to have kept to herself."

I was silent on the other end, wondering if I should break down and tell him about my meeting with Kate. I didn't have anything to share, really. She had talked to the cops already and it sounded like she'd given all the information she had— or at least, all the information she was willing to give. Talking about our meeting to Derek would feel like breaking her tentative trust.

"Was Shelly new in town?" I asked instead.

"Nope, just a loner, I guess. Hey, has Paolo Sabato ever called you?"

"I've talked to him. Why?"

"No real reason. We've heard quite a bit from him. Seems he's bent on taking his version of our investigation, including what he sees as massive incompetence, to the media. He really has it in for me, in particular. I wish we were making more progress, too, but he just doesn't see me as an ally in the search at all, just a bumbling fool."

"Don't be silly," I murmured. I could understand that Paolo's intensity could be at odds with Derek's more congenial approach.

"I had a good time last night," he continued, embarrassment creeping into his voice. "We'll have to do it again."

"Yeah." It was time for me to get the bus to go to the Lloyds', but I didn't know how to make a smooth exit. My tentative re-entrance into the dating world was highlighting my lack of social skills.

"Hey," I began. "I have to be somewhere. Can I call you back another day?"

"Sure." He sounded disappointed. I wished I could tell him I wasn't doing anything exciting, just babysitting, but it would be impossible to explain that obligation to him.

"I'll call you when I'm free," I said instead.

Chapter
Ten

ALMOST LOOKING FORWARD TO AN EVENING with Ally, I changed into some jeans, then grabbed a bus. Pete answered their door alone. As I walked in, he placed a finger on his lips and pointed down the hall.

"She's asleep. Just went down. We went to Stanley Park today and it plumb wore her out. I shouldn't be too long. Make yourself at home." He gestured around the toy-studded living room, then waved as he walked out the door.

I sank into the balding sofa and surveyed the chipped coffee table. A Tom Clancy book was sprawled beside a Robert Munsch paperback. Beside the books, a copy of the *East Vancouver News* was spread open. I picked it up. Whoever had read it last left it open to my bicycle identification story. I wondered if he knew I was the Cait Whyte who wrote it. Of course, for all he knew, my name was "Kate Whyte," since he had never seen it written down, but why else would he have a copy of the *News*? Did he wonder why I had to moonlight as a babysitter? Did he follow my stories, now that I worked for him? Maybe leave them in hotel rooms? I looked around the room in a panic, but, as before, there was nothing to suggest anything other than a cute single father struggling to maintain a sense of order in his life. I could feel myself teeter at the edge of panic. What was that word Dede's therapist had taught her? Catastrophizing. I was creating a catastrophe in my own mind. One newspaper was setting off alarm bells and leading me to question my decision that Pete Lloyd was innocent. Next, I would be barricading the door and arming myself with a steak knife.

I scanned the room again until my eyes found a phone. Picking it up, I dialed Dede's number, my heart warming when I heard her familiar voice.

"Dede? It's Cait. How are you?"

"I'm great, Cait. Ya know, that's a rhyme. I'm going out in a minute. Want to join me?"

This was going to be hard to explain. "I'm babysitting again. It's a long story. But I just wanted to give you the address. I got a bit creeped out and it occurred to me nobody knew where I was."

"Cait." Dede's voice rang with alarm. "I'll come and sit with you if you're nervous. Where are you? And I know you said the dad was cute and all, but wouldn't it be easier to just ask him out on a date instead of babysitting?" She spat out the last word with distaste.

"I'm fine on my own, Dee. I'll just give you the address and phone number. Call my house in two hours. If I'm not home, call here. I feel silly doing this. They're nice people. Don't worry. In fact, forget I called." I had definitely overreacted by calling her.

"Are you sure, Cait? I can come over."

"I just panicked for a second." I gave her the Lloyds' address and phone number. "Promise me you won't worry."

"Cait, there's something you're not telling me. I know you too well. What's up?"

"Go! I'm a big girl. You know I can look after myself."

"Take care."

"We'll talk soon." I hung up slowly, then sat and looked around me. Nothing had changed since the last time I sat for the Lloyds, but I noticed the holes in the couch and the chipped paint on Ally's wooden toys. Was it the disarray of a struggling family, or was it a deeper disorder, a disregard for convention or a desire to flaunt all societal laws? I had always had contempt for my mother's insistence on rigorous house-keeping, but maybe she'd had a deeper impact than I'd thought. I was on the verge of equating squalor with murder.

My imagination was off and running again. I grabbed the remote and turned on the TV. A stroke of luck—a prime-time soap, thinly disguised as a social issues drama. I used to watch this one with a group of friends in journalism school. It was a tightly observed ritual: mock the melodrama, the trite dialogue, the cartoonish plastic surgery, but never talk too loudly during an important scene. Just the sort of mind-less nostalgia I needed.

The action was building to the usual unresolved climax when Pete Lloyd appeared in the door. He smiled when he saw the TV.

"What's happening this week in the world of sin and sex? I haven't watched this in a while."

"The usual—lust, angst, crimes against fashion," I said. "How was your night?"

"I was shopping again. It's much easier without the mon-ster." He sat down and pulled a beer out of a brown paper bag. "Want a beer?"

"Sure." I thought it might help me relax. As he handed me the beer, I resolved to remain rational. We were just two adults having a drink in a messy living room, checking out a particularly lame TV show. I glanced toward the screen, just as a shirt was being unbuttoned in a moment of scripted passion to reveal a scrap of lace barely containing a pair of breast implants stuck on a bony chest like two grapefruits.

"Go, girl," Pete laughed. "She's pretty cute. Normally I don't go for blonds. 'Cept Ally's mother, of course. But that's kinda scared me off for life."

I pretended to be engrossed in the show.

"Ever been married, Cait?"

I sat up and looked over. "No." It was all I could manage.

"None of my business, I guess. Sorry. I'd advise against it, though. It's easy to get carried away when you're in love, but the next thing you know, you're throwing dishes at each other and having some sort of sick contest to see who can hurt the other one the most. Nope. Don't recommend it."

Somehow he must have snuck in a few beers while he was out.

"How long were you married?" I asked, trying to make conversation.

"Let's just say that the last six months seemed like six years. You know how it goes. Or maybe you don't. Seeing anyone right now?"

"Just broke up." The lie came easily. "Another reporter."

"Reporter?" He sounded genuinely surprised. "You're a reporter? Where?"

"*East Vancouver News*. I thought you knew." I gestured to the paper strewn on the table.

"I never read that rag. It was in the mailbox yesterday for some reason." He gave me a sheepish look. For a second, he looked like a little boy who had been caught looking at a skin magazine. "But I'm sure it's well worth reading if you write for it. Have I saved myself from putting my foot in my mouth?"

"I've heard worse about the *News*." I laughed. "It's strange that you got one. We never deliver out here."

"You're not sitting for me because you're writing a story?" he asked. "You're not researching single fathers or some such crap like that?"

"Of course not. I would have told you if I was. I just

wanted to supplement my income. My hours were cut back. I thought babysitting would be good because I might be able to write while the kids sleep." I seemed to be doing a lot of lying on my feet recently.

"A reporter." He shook his head. "Never was that great at English myself. Can't write very well. I'm a musician. That's the language I understand."

I had seen a guitar in his bedroom, but hadn't given it too much thought. Now, the absurdity struck me: I was sweet on an actor, a painter, and a musician. I was a walking cliché of female arts lust.

"Don't follow the news much, either," Pete continued. "Too depressing. Do you have to write about grisly stuff? Murders, accidents, that sort of thing?"

"Sometimes. I've been writing about those two young women who were murdered recently." I waited for his reaction. He had used the word "murder" first, leaving the door wide open for me.

"Dad?" We both turned around. Ally stood behind us, clutching a teddy bear with one hand.

"Sweet pea, what's the matter? Are you having a bad dream?"

Ally nodded, her lower slip sticking out and her eyes half shut.

"Come here." In one swift motion, he picked her up. Ally was a pretty big kid—I was impressed.

"Shall we dance, pumpkin pie?" He twirled her around once. "Do you want to show Cait how we dance to sleep?"

Ally nodded sleepily and rested her head against his chest. Pete walked over to the stereo, and put a vinyl album on the turntable. "I'm still an old-fashioned vinyl man," he said over his shoulder.

Frank Sinatra sang out smoothly from under the needle as Pete and Ally waltzed around the living room. It was almost too sweet to watch, the way she nestled up to him and the look in his eyes when he looked down at her. I felt silly standing there, watching them, like a teenager without a date at the prom, conscious that I was intruding on what was obviously a private father-daughter ritual.

"Join us, Cait?" Pete whispered.

I wasn't sure what to do. It really wasn't that different from the dances I had attended in high school: my feet felt nailed to the ground. Suddenly, Pete glided over and put one arm around my shoulder to guide me in their dance. The three of us swayed across the living room, slightly out of step and out of balance, with one of us drifting back to dreamland.

Under any other circumstances, being touched by a man I had suspected of murder would have caused my whole body to rebel, but with Ally slumbering between us and Sinatra singing behind us, it felt natural, right. I could have almost fallen asleep myself, our little circle felt so cozy. When the song ended, Pete tilted his head to kiss Ally on the top of her head. Then turned to kiss me softly on the cheek.

"Sorry," he drew back before I could decide how I felt. "That was totally out of order. I was just feeling comfortable, and, well, you know…."

"That's okay," I answered. I wasn't sure if it was or not, yet, but he looked so ashamed that I couldn't imagine doing something like slapping him. So much for babysitter self-defense.

"I should let you go," he continued. "Don't let an old man like me keep you from your more exciting life. And I've got to put the munchkin to bed before my arms fall off. Hey, I think I still owe you from the first time. Let me put her down, and I'll be right back."

As soon as Pete returned, he reached into his back pocket and pulled out some crinkly bills.

"Don't worry about that." I raised a hand. "It was the special introductory offer."

"You sure?" he asked. "I appreciate that." I followed him to the door.

"Cait. . . ." He raised his hand slightly, then lowered it.

"Well, I'll give you a call again, if you don't mind. Good babysitters are hard to find and you're a great one. I promise I won't do anything inappropriate next time. Honest. I don't have to tell you we're having a hard time here by ourselves. Ally's mother left us a couple of months ago. She just left a note saying she'd met someone else. We haven't heard from her since. I don't even know where she is. I couldn't tell Ally her mother just left, so I told her she died. I didn't want to tell her that her mother left her without a forwarding address. Stupid, eh?"

I smiled back at him, my heart melting. He looked so tragic standing there with a handful of wrinkled money. I walked down the steps with a smile.

The truth was, I had enjoyed the kiss, I had enjoyed the dance, and I even enjoyed the talk afterwards. Pete wasn't as smooth as Paolo or Derek, but his relationship with his daughter was attractive in a way I probably would have found horribly boring a few years ago. Plus, he was a musician. I could imagine the songs he would play: probably rough on the edges but poetic, sweet. Maybe I could go to his concerts, he could write songs about me....

I stopped myself before I imagined him making eye contact with me from the stage. For heaven's sake, Cait, I chastised myself, you've had similar thoughts about two other men. You've been kissed by two other men. Worse, you've enjoyed being kissed by those two other men, and wanted more.

Chapter Eleven

"Cait, a woman from the Bear Pub called. She wants to meet you at WaaZuBee's at six."

Hannah had left the message on my desk while I was at lunch. Since then, I hated my job even more than usual. All my stories—local home renovations, police reports, gardening tips—just stood in the way of my finding out why Kate wanted to see me. My mind was working overtime, but I tried not to fixate on the possibilities: Kate killed Shelly and would confess it to me! Kate wanted me to help her straighten out! Kate had proof the mayor was one of Shelly's favorite clients! There was no way I could concentrate on work with so many possibilities for fantasy.

When I entered WaaZuBee's five hours later, I spotted Kate immediately. Her hair was tied back in a ragged ponytail and she was wearing a shapeless purple sweatsuit with a yellow paint stain on the chest. At her table, a half-empty bottle of red wine glistened ruby crystals in the setting sun. With one hand on the bottle and tears running down her face, she looked like a character in Tom Waits's saddest song.

"What's up?" I tried to look friendly. I didn't know what to say about her obvious pain.

She wiped the tears from her splotchy face. "Sorry. I'm having a bad day. I'll feel better after I talk to you."

"What's on your mind?" Whatever she said, I was certain this was going to be a career-making story.

"I didn't tell you something the other day," she said. "Something you should know. I don't know what it means, but maybe you will."

"I can try." I tried to keep my tone gentle, although half of me wanted to grab her and shake whatever she knew right out of her mouth.

"I just went through Shelly's things again. I have a bag that used to be hers. She left it at my new apartment the week before she died." She poured herself more wine.

"There was something weird in there." She reached into her fake leather purse and pulled out a small, crumpled picture, then placed it on the table gingerly, as if it would shatter on impact.

I leaned forward to get a better look. The naked torso of a young girl filled most of the frame. The girl's face was turned slightly away from the camera, but tears shone on her exposed cheek. Despite the shield of dark hair she was trying to hide behind, I knew her immediately. It was Claudia Sabato.

"Did they know each other? Who took this picture?" I asked impatiently. Kate shook her head silently. Either she didn't know, or she wasn't willing to tell me.

"Why haven't you shown this to the police? They're looking for a link between Shelly and Claudia, you know. This is exactly what they're looking for." I wanted to grab her hunched shoulders and force her to meet my eyes.

"I didn't want anyone to know what Shelly was up to. She has to be remembered as a good person. Otherwise, no one will care what happened to her. The police will give up if they don't feel she's worth their time. Then he'll kill again."

"*Who* will kill again?" I was trying very hard not to yell at her.

"It must be someone in the business."

"The pornography business?"

"Yeah. Someone had sucked Shelly into it. That's gotta be why she died."

"Because she acted in movies?"

"She'd just started making movies, too. Nothing too weird, not snuff films or anything like that, just, you know, movies. Well, she got more involved, not just acting, but making them. It totally wasn't like her. I tried to find out who she was working for, but she just gave vague answers."

"How involved was she?" I knew absolutely nothing about the production of pornographic movies, but I did know when someone was withholding information. Kate wouldn't meet my eyes; clearly, something was on her mind, troubling her, that she was on the brink of blurting out.

"I ran into her once, at the bus station. Shelly was talking to this kid, a girl who'd just got off the bus. All ratty-looking— probably a runaway. Shelly was buying her a coffee and some fries. I couldn't figure out why she was bothering with the kid, but I forced it out of her. We were good friends, after all. She said she was recruiting girls for movies. Sick, eh? She wouldn't say any more, wouldn't give names or tell me what was going on. She was a good person underneath it all." Kate touched Claudia Sabato's picture lightly with the tip of her finger. "I'm sure she wouldn't be involved in any of this," she whispered.

"Who got her involved, then? If it was out of character, who gave her those ideas?"

Kate was silent.

"Did Shelly ever tell you who was directing her to recruit these girls?"

She shook her head and looked at the floor. Clearly, unless my reporting instincts were taking a vacation at a really bad time, she had at least a suspicion.

"Claudia didn't need money," I said to break the expectant silence. "I don't know much about her, but I don't think she would be involved in that stuff." I picked up the picture and turned it over. There were no identifying marks on the back.

"I think we should take this to the police." I tried to make my voice firm. "You won't have to say too much about Shelly. This is too important to keep to yourself. It might help them find the killer."

"I've been having dreams about her. About Shelly." Kate looked away. "I've had bad dates myself, you know. That could have been me, or any one of my friends. I've done some stuff I'm not too proud of." A sob broke free from her shaking voice. "I should just burn this picture."

I wondered how I could comfort this woman whose trembling form held more sorrow than any body should contain. Tentatively, I touched her hands.

"You'll be fine," I began. "There are groups. . . ."

"I'm beyond help." She pushed her chair away and stood up. "I can look after myself." Glaring defiantly at me, she grabbed the picture from my hands and stuck it back in her purse. I watched her ponytail bounce vigorously as she left the restaurant.

Back home, I started to fry some onions for spaghetti sauce. I hadn't even ordered a drink at WaaZuBee's, never mind dinner, and my stomach had started to digest itself. The onions made my eyes water, but I didn't bother to wipe the tears away.

Jesus Christ, I whispered to myself. And I think I have problems. I just don't see how she can do it. I feel as if I carry a big secret, but what if I knew the sort of secrets Kate was keeping? I'd always complained that my life was dull, but surely Kate would prefer my routine to what she faced. The sick thing was, half of me was jealous. If Kate ever did manage to pursue her writing goals, she would produce work with ten times the gumption of anything I could write. I was starting to work out the logistics of a collaboration between her knowledge of life and my knowledge of grammar when I heard a loud knock on my door.

"Who is it?" I yelled, pressing my ear against the chipped wood. A month ago, I would have opened the door without asking.

"Me! Who else?" Dede's voice answered. I opened the door.

"Dede! What have you done to yourself?" Like about ninety percent of young Commercial residents, she had a silver ring looped through her nose. The newly pierced flesh looked angry and red. I touched my own nose protectively.

"I went with Janet yesterday. She was getting her nipple done."

I moved my hand a bit lower.

"Dede! I thought we agreed piercing had passed the point of shock value. Remember, when we talked about stuff from the underground being co-opted by the mainstream, that whole argument. Next, you'll be going for dreads." We both thought dreadlocks were the most ridiculous fashion statement a young would-be rebel could make.

"I think I look kinda cool." Dede's lips curled into a pout.

"Was this Janet's idea?" I hadn't met Janet, Dede's "political" friend, but I was liking her less and less.

"Well, she made the appointment, but I've wanted to get this done for a long time."

News to me. I shook my head and returned to my onions.

"Want to stay for dinner? I'm just having spaghetti, but I think it will be a good sauce." The Italian delis that dotted the Drive had the supplies to raise pasta above the mush I ate when I was feeling really lazy or poor. There was sauce from a can on stale noodles, a meal with the nutritional value of ketchup on white bread, then there was sauce with firm Roma tomatoes, leafy fresh basil, newly grated Parmesan, and handmade noodles in funky shapes. The food was a definite advantage of life on Commercial.

"I could eat." Dede flopped on my couch. "What's new? We haven't talked in a while. You need to fill me in on this babysitting weirdness."

"It was an impulse. Claudia may have been killed while babysitting. I saw an ad she must have seen. I thought I'd see what happened."

"Holy shit, Cait! When did you become Nancy Drew? I can't believe you actually did that."

"Well, it was a bit of a long shot, anyway. I think my hunch is probably wrong. And, to tell the truth, I wouldn't know what to do if I was right." She'd hit a bit of a nerve with the Nancy Drew comparison.

"What is he like, this potentially lethal client and potential love interest?" she asked.

"He's going through a rough time, but I can't see him as a killer, especially after what I found out last time I was there. I think it has to be someone with pretty seedy connections." I gave her a quick summary of my meeting with Kate Whyte.

"This is all too strange, girl." Dede looked troubled. "I'll ask Janet what she knows about porn production in Vancouver."

"Janet?" That name again. "What would she know?"

"She's very involved in violence against women." Dede sounded defensive. "But Cait, I think you should find out more about Claudia. Maybe she wasn't the saint everyone seems to think she was."

"I'd hate to think that," I said. I considered Claudia an ally, a friend. We would understand each other, I had told myself many times over the last few days. I didn't want to know anything bad about a fifteen-year-old victim, one who had found herself in the same unimaginable position I was in all those years ago.

"Don't let your feelings cloud your story, Cait. You know

it looks bad for your girl Claudia. How else could Shelly have ended up with that picture? Claudia had to have taken her clothes off. In front of Shelly, or someone she worked with."

"She didn't look too happy about it," I said. "There were tears on her face."

"Let me find out more about the porn industry from Janet." Dede was all business, apparently unmoved by the thought of Claudia Sabato's tears.

"Steve found out about Kate Whyte as well," I said. "It's strange."

"Leave that creep out of it," Dede warned. "He'd get far too much enjoyment out of the whole thing."

"You're awfully hard on Steve, Dee. He can be an okay guy."

"Yeah, that's what they said about all serial killers. I'd watch your back around him. Hey, have you resolved the love triangle yet? Or is it a love square? A love rectangle? Love trapezoid?"

"Don't be daft. There is no love in any shape or form. They're just three cute guys." Dede was making me defensive.

"You need to explore every angle, Cait. Get into all the nooks and crannies of whatever shape you think it is. Combine a little biology with geometry, if you know what I mean. Speaking of watching yourself, Janet and I are going to an Urban Women Warriors meeting tomorrow. Care to join us?"

"Excuse me? Urban Women Warriors?" Dede and I were definitely growing apart. "I thought you weren't into that sort of thing," I said.

"Janet," Dede began.

"Of course, the wise and all-knowing Janet," I interrupted-ed, realizing as I spoke that I sounded jealous.

"She's been around a lot, Cait. She's political, but I'm not so sure that's a bad thing any more. Besides, she's cute."

"Well, whatever." I waved my hand dismissively. "I think I'll pass on the meeting. I think I'll visit Claudia's school tomorrow. Ask around. Find out if she was the model child her brother seems to think she was." I moved the spaghetti off the stove and tilted it into the colander. Steam poured up into my face.

"I don't know," I said through the mist, "I just have a feeling there's something I don't know about Claudia Sabato."

Chapter Twelve

I WOULDN'T HAVE LASTED A MINUTE at Burnaby North. The stream of babbling students filing past me all seemed about ten years older than I was and the fashion war had definitely heated up. Cliques, I decided, were more pronounced than when I was young. It was easy to divide the students: the trendies were the ones in flared pants, quilted satin jackets, and retro-bouffant hair; the stoners had stringy hair and black T-shirts; the overachievers wore khakis and carried cell phones; the rapper kids also carried phones, hidden somewhere in their oversized clothes. Where would I have fit in? My high school uniform was a bulky wool sweater and loose-fitting cords. Nothing flashy, nothing revealing—that was the style code that governed my adolescence. In comparison, my current wardrobe of short pleated skirts, chunky shoes, and second-hand blazers was downright brazen.

I'd announced I was coming down with a stomach virus

and left work at noon. I arrived at the school as lunch hour drew to a close. Although time was running out, I couldn't bring myself to rise off the bus-stop bench I was sitting on and cross the street to the school grounds. Security was tight in an urban high school, and an unexplained visitor would attract attention. I didn't dare use my press pass since I had left work. The last thing I needed was a suspicious principal calling May to confirm my ID.

A tall girl sat beside me and started rooting through her shiny vinyl purse. After a couple of seconds, she threw it beside her in frustration.

"Can I bum a smoke?" she asked me, her voice pitched to a whining level.

"Sorry. I don't smoke."

"Damn." She leaned back and set her lips into a pout. "I really need a smoke. My day sucks so far."

"What's wrong?" I asked.

"Rotherham. You know what he's like. Won't accept any damn excuses. I was sick yesterday and he doesn't believe me. Don't you just wish he'd be fired?"

I nodded.

"That's happened to me," I said in what I hoped was a sympathetic tone. I was constructing a new, more daring, plan. Obviously, Miss Congeniality beside me thought I was a student and in a large school, no one would notice a new face. After years of complaining about not being taken seriously, I was finally happy to look like a teenager. Perhaps I could go undercover for a week and write about high school from the inside. It was a story with award-winning potential, I decided, before I returned to the task at hand.

"I've got to go." I stood up and crossed the street to the school grounds.

If I'd been halfway cool in high school, I might have known how to approach any of the groups milling around me. Instead, I felt myself regressing rapidly to my teenaged self. I didn't want to talk to these kids as a reporter, only as another kid. The problem was, when I was their age, I never would have had the courage to talk to anyone as stylish and together-looking as most of the students I saw around me. And what exactly did I plan to say? 'Hi, I'm just another student worried about passing French, but have you heard that Claudia Sabato was involved in the porn business?'

Hang it all, I decided. I'd have to tell them I was a reporter. I walked up to two relatively unthreatening girls with cord shirts and bobbed hair.

"Excuse me," I asked, "could I ask you a couple of questions?"

They looked at me warily until I introduced myself.

"Cool," said the shorter one. "Will you take our pictures?" Her hand flew up to her bangs.

"No. I just wanted to ask if you knew Claudia Sabato. Her body was found last week."

"Oh, her." She looked mildly disappointed. "No. Didn't know her. Bummer though."

"It makes me feel nervous walking alone at night," her friend chimed in.

I nodded. "Who did know her? I was hoping to ask some questions about what she was like."

"She hung out with the Italians. They're usually on the front steps." She made a vague pointing gesture with her Diet Coke. "They're real upset. They're pretty tight."

I thanked them and moved on to the front steps. Four girls in fresh pastel outfits and platform shoes were perched on the steps. All four were leaning over one magazine. I approached them tentatively.

"Hello. I was wondering if I could talk to you girls for a minute."

"Why?" the closest one asked, looking at me suspiciously from under a cloud of blond ringlets.

"Did you know Claudia Sabato?" I decided to come right to the point.

"Who are you?" The challenge in her voice told me she would be a tough interview.

I introduced myself and gave her my card. "I wanted to write a more rounded article on Claudia. I want people to know more about her life than her death."

"Yeah? For that paper? Never heard of it."

"It's distributed in East Van, where Claudia's body was found." Maybe if I didn't mince words about her death, they would be moved to talk to me.

"Great part of town." She snorted.

"Did Claudia visit there a lot?"

"We like to hang out at the coffee shops on Commercial." All eyes were fixed on me, but only the blond girl answered my questions.

"I guess the police have talked to you."

"Yeah. We told them we didn't know anything about any babysitting or boyfriends or nothing. She didn't say anything to us about any of that. Stupid, eh? Maybe if she had, they'd catch who did it. We thought we knew her pretty well."

"Did anyone ever approach Claudia about acting or modeling?"

"Claudia?" She laughed. "She was five feet tall. Why would anyone want her to model?"

"Claudia was pretty, Gaby." A small girl with a neat black pixie cut spoke for the first time. "But it wouldn't have been for her. She thought models were stupid. She was kinda feminist. She wanted to be an actress—a serious actress, not someone that used their looks as a substitute for talent."

"Her brother's an actor." Gaby giggled and nudged the girl next to her. "He's a babe. I always hoped he'd show up when she had a sleepover."

"It's not funny any more, Gaby," the small girl said with consternation. She turned to me. "Claudia watched his rehearsals sometimes. She wanted to be an actress, but she was shy."

"What else did she like to do?" I asked.

"Wrote some poetry. She read a lot, but only female authors. She liked hanging out with us. Going to parties. Girl stuff."

"We did go down to the ravine sometimes," Gaby said. "Don't laugh, but we read poetry."

"The ravine where she was found?" I asked.

"Yeah. We used to build fires and talk, read aloud, stuff like that."

"I always thought that ravine was a bit creepy," I told her. "I would have thought kids only went down there to drink or have sex."

"It's not so bad, once you get away from the overpass," Gaby said. "It feels like a bit of a getaway, like a park or something."

"You must all be upset by her death," I said.

"No kidding." Gaby's tone was grim. "I miss her. And it freaks me. I've had a lot of really bad dreams since she died. You just can't think about stuff like that, ya know. You never think it will happen to anyone you know."

A piercing bell broke the silence that followed. The girls jumped up to attention.

"Will you call me if you think of anything else?" I directed the question to Gaby.

"Yeah, whatever." She turned and disappeared into the school. I backed away from the door to avoid the flood of nylon track suits and dyed hair heading my way. I could never go back to high school. I abandoned my high school story idea. There was no way in hell I would go undercover.

On the bus back to my place, I pondered the rest of the day. I could, I figured, return to work and claim a miracle recovery. Or I could go home and brood over this new information. A feminist Claudia just didn't fit with my latest theory—that she had somehow been lured into Vancouver's porn scene. I was certain the kind of girl who would hang out with the stylish, self-possessed "Italian" girls of the front steps, reading poetry, would have resisted whatever tawdry allure pornography held. She didn't need the money, either. Her parents' deli was successful and if they were as dutiful as they certainly seemed to be, they would have supported their teenaged daughter financially. With such a spotless life, Claudia certainly fit the profile of the victim of a random killing. At least, she would have if her picture hadn't been in Shelly Bennett's bag. If she was interested in "serious" acting like her friends said, would she have been naïve enough to believe that pornography could be a stepping stone to a legitimate career? It was hard to imagine, and I would have thought Paolo, with his experience in the acting world, would have warned her away from believing any sleazy promises of success.

I rested my head on the seat in front of me. Trying to fit Claudia's two worlds together was starting to hurt my brain. What I needed, I decided, was a vacation. A real one, not just a day spent in bed after lying to May about my health. I decided that a night at home didn't have to be a grim recitation of murder and broken lives while I ate cheap food. I was going to take a break from my life.

I made myself a huge curry for dinner and settled down with Portuguese wine and some international magazines I'd picked up at the newsstand around the corner. Compared to people in Grand Forks, I decided, I had a very cosmopolitan life. And one day I would have a career they all would envy. I could imagine our class reunion. Rumors about my career would ripple around the room. People who wouldn't talk to me in high school would hover nearby, unsure of how to approach me. I would rise above my desire for revenge and be gracious and generous to all.

Even with a good fantasy to fill my mind, I couldn't fully relax, though. I was scheduled to meet the police the next day and still hadn't decided what to tell them. After Kate showed me the picture of Claudia, I knew something the police didn't. But Kate didn't want me to tell them. What were my obligations? All the debates I'd sat through in journalism school suddenly seemed abstract and removed from the real world of reporting. Surely there was a middle ground somewhere, a solution that would preserve my word to Kate but satisfy my conscience when I talked to the police.

The only solution, I decided, was to persuade Kate that

sharing the photo with the police was the best course of action. If she really wanted to find Shelly's killer and protect other young women from the same fate, she would come with me the following morning, prepared to make a full disclosure. No matter how resolute her silence had been, I would have to convince her.

First, we had to meet. I picked up the phone and dialed the Bear Pub. I knew servers didn't appreciate personal calls, but I wanted to arrange to meet her at the end of her shift.

"Bear Pub." The nasal female voice at the other end was muffled by the bar noise, but definitely not Kate's.

"Is Kate Whyte there?" I asked. "It's an emergency."

"Kate?" the other voice asked. "She didn't bother to show up today, so I have to cover for her. Not like I don't have better things to do, you know?"

"She didn't come in?" I hadn't counted on this. "Did she call you? Is she sick?"

"She didn't even call. I guess her majesty has better things to do. Not really like her though. Not like the girl we had before her—she was always slacking off. Kate's never even had a sick day before. We tried to reach her—my kid has soccer practice and I didn't want to come in—but we couldn't find her. Left about ten messages, but no answer."

"Do you have her home number?" My desire to reach Kate was growing with every word.

"Honey, you gotta know I can't give that to you. Especially Kate's. She's pretty private. Two guys were in looking for her on her day off and she totally freaked out when I told her. And you should have seen her after the police were in."

"Who was looking for her? Did they look suspicious?" I asked.

"Not really," she answered. "One had a pretty nasty expression, as if his face had frozen that way. But we get worse in here."

"I'm a friend. Can you tell me where she lives? Give me a hint?"

"Yeah, if you were a good friend, you'd know, eh? Look, I have to go. We can't sit around and chat. I have drinks to serve."

I hung up with a stomach full of knots. Kate was missing. The police thought she was next on the killer's list and she was missing. She seemed like such a survivor that it was hard to imagine her as the victim of any sort of crime, but the fact that she hadn't even phoned the pub raised the hair on the back of my neck. I knew it was too early to call the police and report her missing, but the news that she hadn't shown up for work and that someone else had been asking about her confirmed one thing: tomorrow I would have to come clean with Derek about everything she had told me. If she really was in trouble, her secrets would have to come out. I may have the knowledge that could help her, wherever she was.

After a predictably restless night of sleep, I got up at the crack of dawn and went down to the station. My nerves were on edge as I rehearsed what I had to say and consoled myself that I really was doing the right thing. I wanted the police to take Kate's absence seriously, to find her as soon as possible, and they would need all the help they could get.

There are a million stories in here, I thought as I took a seat in the station's lobby and looked around. Beside me, a young girl shook and sobbed while her boyfriend tried to comfort her. A wrinkled man slept on a chair, raising his head every few minutes and crying, "Mama." I wondered if he was homeless and had come into the station not to file a complaint, but to dry off.

"Cait!"

I jerked up. Derek towered above me. He looked different; less boyish, perhaps, than the last time I'd seen him. He led me down a maze of hallways into a small office.

"What's up? How's the writing?"

"Actually, I'm here because I have some information on the Sabato and Bennett murders." I winced slightly as I spoke. "It's about Kate Whyte. She didn't show up for work yesterday and she didn't phone. And the woman I talked to said two men had been looking for her—not the police."

"I wouldn't panic yet, Cait." Derek sat down beside me. "She's probably feeling sad about her friend and decided to lay low for a while. But we can look into it."

I took a deep breath. "There's more, though, stuff that makes me think she knows something dangerous. I promised her I wouldn't tell you, but...."

"Cait, if she really is in danger, everything you can tell us will help. You may have the clue that points us to her and helps us get to the bottom of what she knows."

I prayed quickly that I was doing the right thing. "Kate found a picture of Claudia Sabato in Shelly Bennett's things."

"Her things? In what? How did we miss it?"

"A bag Shelly had left at her place before she went missing. It was a bad picture ... not very, well, nice. She didn't have a shirt on."

Derek's eyebrows shot up about six inches.

"Cait, that's pretty interesting information. I can tell you, a lot of people are going to be very interested in what you have to say. I'm going to have to get another officer. Sit tight for a moment."

I looked around the office after he left. Two paintings hung directly over my head. They were watercolors of what seemed to be the ocean, although from certain angles subtle shapes moved beneath the blue waves. When I shifted in my chair to get a better look, I noticed a signature: D. Malone. So these were Derek's. I had raised a finger to trace the watery swirls when he entered, followed by the blond officer who had stood with the Sabatos during their press conference.

"Cait, this is Ron, another officer on the case. He's been working a lot with the parents."

I remembered his arm supporting Mrs. Sabato as she faced the press.

"That must be a hard job at a time like this. They seemed so devastated."

Ron shrugged. "Normal grieving parents."

His wording was not lost on me. Compared to Derek, he seemed jaded. He even looked hardened, with his mustache hiding his mouth and tinted glasses shielding his eyes.

"Ms Whyte," he began.

"Cait," I corrected him.

"Ms Whyte," he continued, "we have talked to this alter ego of yours. She wasn't helpful. Obviously, we have to find her to talk to her again. How did you get acquainted with her?"

"I went to the Bear Pub," I whispered.

"The Bear Pub, eh?" He made a note. "You just ran into her and got talking and she decided to give this to you?"

"I, um, found her at the Bear Pub. Then she called me to arrange to meet to show me the picture. Maybe something I'd said had bothered her, who knows? But she definitely didn't seem to know as much as I expected. Unless she's lying."

"Did she seem upset?"

"Very. I honestly think she was trying to help when she showed me the picture."

"What made you want to talk to her? Was it for a story?"

"Don't you think it's a coincidence that the killer chose an article written by someone with practically the same name? I wanted to find out more. I mean, to tell the truth, I was a bit scared. I thought she might have some answers."

"You'd be a great cop, Cait, if you ever get tired of reporting," Derek interjected.

Ron shot him a look that sealed his lips. "Ms Whyte, you'll have to leave us your number. You've given us a new angle on the Sabato murder and I think this Kate will open up more once we tell her what we know. After we've tracked her down, we may have to ask you a few more questions."

"I've got her number. Thanks for coming in, Cait," Derek added.

"Ms Whyte, anything else to say? Or anything related to the investigations you'd like to ask us? Any other secret information you're harboring? You realize any further inquiries of your own could compromise both your own safety and our investigation. If I hear more about your activities, the first thing I'll do is call your boss. Understand?"

Do you have to be so officious? I wanted to ask Ron. Instead I smiled and stood up.

"Always a pleasure, Derek. And if you get tired of working down here, I think those paintings have real potential." I didn't think I should give any hint that we ever exchanged a word outside of work. Ron didn't seem to be the sort to approve of cops dating reporters.

I returned to my own job filled with doubt. I had betrayed someone I thought I could help, but I still held a thread of hope that I'd done the right thing. I had committed the ultimate reporting breach of trust, but I had to believe what I had done would protect Kate. Maybe I was just rationalizing by over-inflating the significance of what I'd told the police, but I couldn't help but feel I may have made the difference between life and death. Assuming she was still alive.

I could have pondered this possibility all night, examining the various "what ifs" and "what would happens." Fortunately, Dede appeared at my door five minutes after I got home from work. She was holding a bottle of whiskey. By the way she threw her head back when she laughed, I guessed she'd already had a few shots.

"Maybe you're interested in sharing this," she said as she rummaged through my cupboard for a glass without waiting for a reply. "I've got to update you on my life. You think the soaps are full of intrigue?"

"How's Janet?" I tried to keep the sneer out of my voice.

"She's cool. You want to come out with us later? Of course you do."

"I've had another bad day. I may just hang low and brood." I outlined my moral dilemma to her.

"She could even be the killer, Cait. Have you thought of that? That's why she's disappeared, before they get too close.

You did the right thing, giving her name to the police. Or she could be a ruthless criminal bitch, so mad at being double-crossed by you that she'll become a killer." Dede punched me on the shoulder.

"Nice try, Dee. She could also be a perfectly nice woman who thought she could trust me and will never confide in a reporter again."

"I think that she's a woman who needs help from the police. Or a woman who will give the police the exact missing piece of the puzzle they need to find the killer once they find her. Don't sell yourself short, Cait. You know you did the right thing. Now stop worrying and go get changed so we can paint this town red."

Half an hour later, I was fastened into the passenger seat of Dede's Volvo, at the corner of Smythe and Howe, trying to tune out the monologue Janet was intent on performing in the back seat. Her parents, she insisted on telling us, favored her brother because his firm commitment to heterosexuality had led to grandchildren, as if, Janet scoffed, that was any sort of accomplishment for a man.

"All he had to do was have sex with a fertile women, and now, wait until my folks' will comes out. I bet his kids get it all, just to congratulate them for having been born and proving that my brother has slept with the *opposite* sex like a good boy. Vile offspring. I can't stand them, and I'm expected to be nice when they visit."

I tried to sneak a wink at Dede. We've always claimed contempt for this sort of conspiracy theory. She was staring out the window at a young girl in zebra tights and pink stilettos.

"How old do you think she is?" Dede addressed the question to no one in particular. "Doesn't she look about twelve?"

"Men like them like that." Janet settled back in the seat with the satisfaction of one whose pet theory has just been confirmed. "Better watch it, Cait. You'll be too old soon."

"Cait does okay for herself. She's got three men on the go." Dede grinned at me.

"Three men?" Janet grunted. "From what my straight friends tell me, there aren't three single men in Vancouver. How did you meet them?"

I wasn't about to tell Janet that one was a cop, one was a story source, and one was a babysitting client. Instead, I tried a more acceptable summary. "One's an actor, one's a painter, and one's a musician."

"Art slut!" Dede exclaimed.

Janet laughed. "Cait, have you ever considered that you're attracted to these artistic men because your own artistic ambitions haven't been fulfilled? What you want from those men, you can get from yourself."

"I don't think she can get everything from herself. Especially not what she wants from that Paolo Sabato," Dede winked at me. "He's hot, Cait says, and I think he's got the hots for her. You know me, I vote for the hottie. Forget the others."

"Is he related to that girl who was killed?" Janet asked.

"Her brother."

"That's kinda sick, isn't it, Cait?" she asked. "That he's thinking about sex right after his sister is killed?"

"I didn't say he was thinking of sex. Maybe in Cait's dreams, hey, Cait?" Dede said.

I grimaced slightly. "Do you know him, Janet? He's in the film industry." According to Dede, Janet was a set designer and knew practically every aspiring thespian in the city.

"Only from the news about his sister. I don't think I've run into him. What has he done?"

"I don't know," I admitted.

"You should phone him, stupid," Dede went on. "That's your assignment for tomorrow, sweetie. Find out more about his acting career and report back."

I sat back as Dede wove through the nighttime traffic. If she insisted, who was I to deny her?

Chapter Thirteen

THE NEXT MORNING, I WOKE WITH A CAT in my mouth and a jackhammer in my head. Only five pints of draft beer and I was reduced to a pathetic shell of a human being. No wonder I usually stuck to whiskey. I stretched out in bed and reviewed the evening. It hadn't been so bad, after all. Janet was much more bearable after the conversation switched from sexual politics to film production and gossip about actors. She even gave me some story ideas that didn't involve the Urban Women Warriors. I also had to admit that Dede seemed to enjoy her company and she was quite attractive. With a painful shake of my head, I staggered out of bed to make some coffee. For me, a cup of coffee was the best hangover cure. I had settled down with the Saturday *Sun* when the phone rang.

"Cait, Paolo here. I didn't wake you up, did I?"

"No, I was just reading the paper. I was going to call you today." I figured I might as well just come out and say it.

"How do you feel about sushi for lunch?" he asked. "I've got a craving."

To me, every bite of sushi tastes like the entire Pacific Ocean condensed into a bite-sized circle. I'd sooner eat all the kelp washed up in English Bay. In fact, given my hung-over condition, I would rather have crawled under my bed and licked the dust off the floor.

"I'd love to," I told him.

At one o'clock, I was heading down Davie in a short flow-ered skirt, big sweater, and clunky boots. I caught a glimpse of myself in the Royal Bank window and smiled at my reflec-tion. Usually, I turn away before I start to think I look fat or notice my tights have a run, but thanks to my impending date, my confidence level was flying. Lust was a hangover cure worth patenting.

Paolo was waiting at the restaurant door in a burgundy wool blazer. His hair was slightly damp and tousled, as if he had just gotten out of bed.

"You look lovely. So fresh and pretty," he told me in the voice I recognized from my fantasies. He took my elbow and guided me through the restaurant. Suddenly, sushi was my favorite dish.

The queasy feeling returned to my stomach when the sushi arrived. Slime, salt, seaweed. I lifted a tentative chopstick and tried to change the subject.

"We might have a mutual acquaintance," I began. "Do you know Janet Cook? She claims to know every actor in town."

Paolo shook his head. "I don't know too many people in the scene, to tell the truth. Do you like Italian food better than Japanese?"

"Can you tell?" I dropped my chopsticks, glad to end the food charade. "I thought I'd give it another try. Seems silly to live on the west coast and not like sushi. I'll admit I'm much more interested in Italian food."

The bait was neon orange with sparklers, but he bit.

"I'll make you dinner, then. How about next week?"

"Love to. Just don't include any seaweed."

The conversation switched to Italian food, to prosciutto and provolone and the wisdom of drinking white wine with seafood lasagna. Maybe it was the disappointment of the sushi, but before long my mouth was watering at his descriptions of the Sabato family's meals.

"My mother's starting to resume her normal life," he told me. "But none of us will be normal again. It's like walking around with an arm missing, when a family member dies."

"You seem very close," I told him. I still wanted to know more about their relationship.

He shrugged in response, his eyes focused about four feet over my head. "Family is the key to Italians." He raised his glass in a toast. "Hey," he continued. "Did you read the *Sun* this morning?"

"Just skimmed it," I confessed, not wanting to go into too much detail about my fuzzy-headed morning. Truth be told, I'd never got beyond the front page after his call.

"The police said they've got a lot of tips from the public. Do you know about any of them? They haven't shared too much with us. Not as much as we feel we deserve."

"I'm just as baffled as the rest of you." That was certainly true. "Maybe they don't want you to get your hopes up. I think the police get a lot of tips from weirdos who are just trying to get in the spotlight." Technically, I hadn't actually lied to him.

"So, tell me more about your acting career," I said. I was curious. After talking to Janet, I felt a bit silly that I hadn't found out more. I could imagine myself in a theater audience on opening night, front row and center, while Paolo bowed and winked at me, but I couldn't take the scene any further without more info.

"Tell me about you instead," he answered. "What kind of meals did you eat in Grand Forks? What do you cook now? Anyone making you meals on a regular basis?"

"Contrary to what you've witnessed today, I'm not a picky

eater. I don't eat big meals too often, though. I'm too busy and it seems so pointless when you live alone."

"Have you always lived alone?" It was a direct question. I felt myself flush.

"I've never lived with anyone. I'm not exactly what you'd call lucky in love."

"I'm sorry to hear that." He seemed to be searching for words. "Do you ever talk to the police? I'm still pissed at them. I don't want to put you on the spot or anything." He was smiling, but I noticed with regret the light flirtiness had left his voice.

"Not often."

"You'd tell me if they told you anything, wouldn't you? Things they won't tell us, even though we're family. I'm still stunned they haven't caught anyone yet. They just radiate incompetence whenever I'm at the station. This one guy, Malone, he doesn't look old enough to order a drink legally. And he's supposed to avenge my family? What do you think about the investigation?"

"They wouldn't tell a reporter anything that wasn't going to be public knowledge. I'm the enemy, remember. They'd tell you before they told me."

"It's all too frustrating." Paolo motioned for the bill. "I've got to go. I'm meeting my parents."

I worked to catch up to him as we left our table. He stopped at the restaurant door, then leaned over and pecked me lightly on the cheek. For a split second afterwards, he looked directly at me with his blue eyes.

"Thanks for a lovely lunch. Let's keep in touch." His voice. I struggled to find my legs so I could walk away with some dignity. He touched my hair lightly. "I like that you're so sweet," he murmured.

Many questions ran through my brain that night: who did I have a crush on? Paolo was intense and moody. He clearly had issues about his family, he was less than forthcoming about his career, and seemed overly into my so-called innocence. Derek, on the other hand, was open and friendly whenever we talked, but he definitely lacked Paolo's mystique, and his fresh-faced earnestness could get boring. And then there was Pete. He was friendly without the puppy-dog quality that I sometimes felt in Derek. But, if I had met him without his daughter, would I still find him attractive? I barely knew the man, after all. I had originally gone to his house suspecting he was a killer.

The possibility of multiple romances lit a fire under my imagination. I tried to stop my thoughts before I got ahead of myself, but I was already entertaining fantasies of family dinners, traditional Italian weddings, converting to Catholicism, beaming with pride at local plays as Paolo crossed the stage. Or police socials, mingling while Derek's colleagues eyed me warily, unsure of how friendly they could be to a reporter, then going home afterwards and laughing at Ron's pompous speech. Or stepping into the role of the good stepmother, helping Ally and Pete get their lives back together, Pete's adoration only increasing as I became closer to his daughter while he wrote worshipful songs about me.

The next day, Hannah stuck her head in my cubicle first thing in the morning.

"I've got to tell you something. May will freak. I shouldn't tell you...."

Hannah is the worst gossip in the office. She often overestimates my relationship with May, assuming we discuss every office transaction.

"Hannah, I'm kinda busy." It was true. I was busy thinking about my future.

"Cait, you should know this. It involves your friend Steve."

"What about Steve?" I tried to put on an impatient expression.

"Steve the reporter? You're going to be so disgusted." Hannah giggled.

"Give me the dirt, Hannah." I'd had enough teasing.

"He's under review. The *Province* might fire him."

"Steve? Vancouver's answer to Bob Woodward?"

"Apparently, he's been working on an article about prostitution. A sort of undercover thing. But he researched it a little too thoroughly, if you know what I mean. Sounds like he slept with his main source."

"*Steve?*"

"Some hooker called the *Province* to give the dirt on exactly what sort of research old Steve was doing. He says he was researching for a story, and they just fell in love. You know what they say—there's a sucker born every minute. Pretty amazing. May will love this." Hannah always considered it a coup to be the first with hot gossip.

Steve with a prostitute? I'd always considered him morally suspect, but I'd assumed he was just a shy geeky guy at heart, the sort of guy who would never step too far outside the bounds of convention. It was true that he had surprised me with his interest in that world. He had mentioned several times that he had great sources, and he'd wanted to talk more. I had assumed he wanted to brag about an interview with an undercover agent or something routine like that. His eagerness to talk made more sense now. Dede will flip when she hears this, I thought. She'd always hated Steve, even joked about him killing Shelly. I shuddered. Could I ever really know another person? Annoyingly ambitious Steve was willing to risk his reporting future to have sex with a prostitute.

"Cait? Can I see you in my office?" A razor sliced through May's voice. The hair on the back of my neck rose. Not now, I moaned as I slumped into her office.

"Cait, have you heard about your friend Steve? He might be suspended."

"Hannah just told me. I'm very surprised. Steve's a bit of a creep, sure, but I never thought he'd do anything that would hurt his career."

"I know you two are friends. But you don't discuss your stories together, do you? Not in detail? Not confidential stuff?"

"We usually know what each other's working on, yeah. But I don't totally trust him, so I don't give him many details. I didn't know anything about this prostitution story." Although I probably should have figured it out after all the hints he's given me, I added silently.

"Good." May got up and shut the door. "Cait, the police just called. The *Province* asked them to look into the situation, and they found out that the woman Steve was with was also questioned extensively about the Sabato and Bennett murders."

I jumped slightly. "Was she a suspect?"

"I'm not sure. But they thought Steve might be crossing the line, going into police territory. Now, you were pretty involved in those stories. The police officer I talked to somehow knows you two are friends. He's concerned that you and Steve were poking around like amateur detectives. You wouldn't do that, would you?"

That would depend where you draw the line between objective reporting and amateur detecting, I thought.

"Of course not, May," I said. "I'm as confused as you are. I'm not about to run around with prostitutes and potential murderers. You should know that much about me. I'm a wimp, remember? I had trouble covering an anti-logging rally undercover."

"Just be careful, Cait." May looked back at the pile of papers on her desk. Our little meeting was over, but I was still full of questions. Maybe I was in over my head. In every mystery novel I had read, the amateur detective always ended up face to face with danger. I was determined to overcome my past by taking action on this story, proving I wasn't a cowardly victim any longer, but maybe I had crossed a line when I phoned Pete Lloyd about babysitting. Or perhaps I went too far when I went down to the Western Rose Hotel. And in light of what happened to Steve, seeking out Kate Whyte definitely went outside the lines of common sense. I constantly wondered, though, where she was, if the police had made any progress finding her, and if I had done the right thing. More than anything, I wanted to track her down myself, but I had no idea how to start. And it seemed as if every time I turned around, there was a warning to stay away from Shelly Bennett's world.

"No way!" Dede hooted with laughter. "No bloody way! That's too funny."

"Dede," I said, "I knew you'd react this way. I know it proves everything you've suspected about Steve's wicked male ways. But don't you think it's a bit weird?"

"I'm sorry, but you have to admit it's hysterical. That self-righteous little prick! Wait till I see him again." She slapped her hand on the table, almost upsetting my glass of wine. We were having salad and a glass of wine at WaaZuBee's while I filled her in.

"Dee, he's suffering enough. Everyone knows what happened. He's going to have to go before a review board. He could be suspended."

"That'll teach him which organ to think with."

"Well, he might drop by here later," I said. "He left a message on my machine. Don't be too harsh on him if he does."

"You spoke too soon. Don't look now, but Vancouver's answer to Hugh Grant has arrived."

Ignoring her advice, I whipped around to face Steve. With his neon patterned tie and gelled hair, he looked almost the same as the last time I saw him. Only the shadow around his jaw suggested he'd spent less than his usual amount of time grooming himself.

"Dede, Cait," he nodded. In one fluid motion, he pulled up a chair and took a chug of wine right from our bottle.

"Steve. . . ." I didn't know how to begin. "Why don't you get a glass?"

"I'm fine, thanks." He snorted as he spoke. A trail of wine dribbled in a crimson stream down his chin. He didn't bother to wipe it off. "I couldn't be better."

"Steve, what were you thinking?" I had to speak before Dede bore into him.

"Lay off, Whyte. You don't know the whole story." He turned his head around to scan the room. If I knew Steve, he was convinced the whole bar was staring at him in his infamy.

"Steve, do you want to talk?" I tried the confidante approach to get him to relax and open up.

"I don't normally sleep with hookers. You know that, don't you, Cait?"

"I was surprised."

"I wasn't," Dede piped up.

I pursed my lips in her direction.

"I was writing a story. I was totally psyched about it. I knew it could be big, the best of my career. It all started when this woman contacted me. She said she liked my work and that she knew who killed those girls. I couldn't tell you that, Cait. You're so into that story, it's almost weird. I even told her that she should really be talking to you, the obsessive reporter. Sorry." He touched my hand lightly.

"So I met her, Angie, her name is—at least that's what she told me. She's real pretty and friendly. Doesn't seem like a hooker at all. Gorgeous long red hair. At first she seemed reluctant to tell me what she knew. Then she told me about some guy Claudia had babysat for. She swore that he did it. Said she had an eyewitness who was afraid to come forward because they didn't want to get too close to the police."

"You're kidding. I would have killed for a tip like that."

"I contacted this guy, Ed Nelson. I interviewed him briefly, before he got suspicious and told me to bugger off.

He does use a babysitter every Tuesday, though, and he's a bit of a creep. But there was no way it was him. She'd failed to complete her research. Turns out he was picked up on a DUI charge that night and spent the night in jail, and his mother was looking after the kid. I checked it all out. Angie had also told the police, though she failed to mention that bit of information to me. It didn't take them too long to uncover his DUI."

Steve sighed and leaned back in his chair. "When I told her I didn't believe the story, she told me she didn't think I could handle the information she had, that she'd find a better reporter."

"When did she become more than just a source? I mean, is it true what they're saying?" I had to ask a direct question.

"We did sleep together, but we had become friends. I didn't pay her or anything. It wasn't like she made it sound afterwards. I started to feel totally taken advantage of after she dropped me. Used, you know? I phoned her up and told her so, yesterday. I told her I was going to go public about that guy she was trying to set up for the murders. That wouldn't make her look too good. So then she goes to my editor, that bitch, and rats on me. Makes me look like some kind of pervert." He shook his head, as if the reality of what had happened hadn't quite registered yet.

"Why did you sleep with her?" I wanted to give him a chance to clear his name.

Dede looked at me and rolled her eyes. "Cait, remember, he's a man."

Steve closed his eyes for a fraction of a second. "She told me she wasn't a hooker. I thought she liked me. She was giving me story tips. We even kissed. They don't kiss johns, do they?"

"Steve!" I couldn't keep the frustration out of my voice. "And you accuse me of being naive?"

"She saw you coming a mile away, Steve." Dede said. If I didn't know Dede better, I could have sworn there was a touch of sympathy in her voice.

"She was cool. Smart. I believed her. I think she knows some pretty hard-core people."

"Why do you say that?" I asked.

"Cait, I'm not a source, and I don't have to tell you everything, do I? I will tell you this chick had been around."

"Wow." I motioned for another bottle of wine. We were going to need it.

"So, you think she was using you to set up this other guy, Ed Nelson, the one you interviewed? Why wasn't it enough to go to the police?"

"She said they were getting too many anonymous tips. She wanted this one to be investigated right away, so it had to be in the paper, then the police would have to act on her tip." He scratched his forehead. "It made sense at the time," he said. "I want to ask her more questions. Why did she do this to me? She ruined my career."

I reached over and touched his hand. I wanted, at that moment, to do anything I could to help him. I had never seen a man so miserable.

"I'll help you find her. Once you find her, maybe she can help clear your name."

"Thanks," he murmured, filling his glass with the new wine. "You're a pal, Cait."

I have to admit, though, my motives were less than altruistic. I wanted to hear more of this story. I had to meet this woman who claimed to know so much.

Chapter
Fourteen

I WAS SURE MY DREAMS WOULD BE FILLED with conniving prostitutes and murderous men. Instead, as I lay in the netherworld between sleep and consciousness, I acquired the power to fire May. As the new editor, I had changed the direction of the *News*. I was just starting to enjoy my new power when an echoing buzz cut into my head. The phone. Again. I rolled over and lifted it off my night table.

"Cait? Did I wake you?" It was my mother. I groaned inwardly. After the sleazy story I'd heard last night, I didn't have the heart for my mother's concern.

"Hi, Mom." I tried to sound perky.

"Are you okay? We're worried about you."

"I'm fine, Mom. No more articles have appeared on any dead bodies."

"Cait, when you have kids, you won't joke about things like that."

"I'll add that to my list of things to remember when I'm a parent."

"Well, just be careful, sweetie," she said. There was an edge to her voice I had come to know well. She had Something To Say. I had to answer a couple of superficial questions, then she would come to The Point of the call, just as I was starting to let my guard down. Sure enough, she relayed some news about the weather and my brother's new girlfriend, then there was a pause on the other end.

"I had the best news, honey. I thought it might cheer you up."

"What, Mom?" I was prepared for both the trivial—the snow was melting!—or dramatic—my brother was getting married, my father invented a new logging machine that would make millions!

"Do you remember Melissa Jones? That girl who had that terrible thing happen to her when you were in high school?"

Did I remember the terrible thing that happened to Melissa Jones? Only every day. And I not only remembered it, I had terrible thoughts, thoughts filled with so much blame and shame and guilt I couldn't even think them to myself without an inch of whiskey. My mother had no idea what the name Melissa Jones did to me: there was no way she could. She didn't know about my own rape, never mind that "the terrible thing" that had happened to Melissa was my fault.

"Yeah," I said to my mother, "I remember."

"Terrible thing," she repeated. "I couldn't believe something like that could happen in Grand Forks. I hope he's still in jail. Imagine." For a split second, the phone lines were silent.

"But she's done something wonderful, hon. Just goes to show you how anyone can make the best of what they have. She just got hired with the RCMP as a victim's advocate. Won't she be good with other young girls somebody hurts? I just felt so proud of her when I heard that."

"That's great," I said. "Mom, I don't feel too hot. Can I call you back later tonight?" The conversation was on extremely dangerous ground. "Thanks for calling. Take care, and don't worry about me."

"Come visit soon," she said, then hung up.

I sat for a few minutes, staring at the wall. Melissa Jones is braver than me, I whispered to my pillow. I'm a coward. I'm such a coward that it's my fault she suffered in the first place. I never asked my mother if she had any news about Melissa. I couldn't handle the guilt if the answer left no doubt of the pain my cowardice had brought into her life. Unable to remain in my room alone, I threw on a T-shirt and jeans and left the house.

I was on a mission to buy groceries. I avoided making eye contact as I sped along the Drive. Everyone I passed, from the aggressively pierced to the lovingly wrinkled, they all were braver than I was. Stepping around the crowds, I imagined what would have happened if I'd gone to the police, as Melissa did, all those years ago. If I had gone to the police, he would have been in jail. If he was in jail, he wouldn't have raped Melissa.

I crossed the lights at First Avenue. A crowd of bongo players had gathered at the corner, and I had to step around them carefully. As their audience milled on the sidewalk, bodies closed in on me, stealing my air. Too many sweaty people; I couldn't breathe. My legs felt for solid ground as the sidewalk tilted underneath me. I tried to focus on a telephone pole a few feet ahead, but oxygen was disappearing with every gulping breath I took. What if I died in a crowd of neo-hippies? I almost smiled at the thought. I staggered into the first coffee shop I passed.

"I'm not feeling very well. Could I sit down?" I could hear myself spitting my words out, but they felt disconnected from my body, as if they had a life of their own.

The man behind the counter looked up from the latte machine.

"Have a seat. Want a glass of water?"

I nodded.

"I'll bring it out to you. Want me to call anyone? You don't look so hot."

I shook my head, found a chair, and let my legs give out from underneath me.

Dede had had a few panic attacks a couple of months before. I had tried my best to be sympathetic, but I had a few unspoken thoughts involving words like "neurotic" and "hypochondria." Sitting at my table in a clammy sweat, I regretted my hard-assed attitude. My suffering was probably some sort of retribution for my lack of sympathy toward her. For what felt like twenty years on the sidewalks of the Drive, I had been convinced I would die. While I thought about what had happened, my heart slowed and the rest of the room came into focus. More than anything, I wanted to leave the scrutiny of the coffee shop, but I was afraid to go back outside. What if it happened again?

I pushed myself off the chair, then waved a thank you to the guy at the counter.

Groceries could wait, I decided. I needed to cocoon myself.

To my relief, there was a message from Derek on my machine when I returned. He was just the person I wanted to talk to, a solid, reassuring police officer who would look out for me.

"Hey, Derek." I tried not to sound too freaked out when he answered.

"I just wanted to see how you are doing," he answered. "I know you and Steve are friends and you've had some strange things happen to you recently."

"Yeah," I agreed. "Derek, Steve mentioned you'd gotten a tip about a single father that Claudia babysat for. Is that true?"

"It's not a story any more, I'm afraid, Cait, so you can turn off your recorder. We did look at the guy. Our source said he was the one Claudia was babysitting for so we were interested, as you can imagine. But it turned out the guy was in jail that night on a DUI."

"But why would someone try to accuse him?"

"Couldn't tell you. We've talked to the source—she's the same woman Steve was working with. She swears she knows someone who witnessed the murder, someone with too many shady connections themselves to come forward. We figured we'd get the name of this alleged witness out of her, but first we checked into this guy's background. Didn't take us too long to find out that he'd had a few pints too many that night and ended up in jail."

"But why set him up like that?"

"We're looking into every angle, Cait. All sorts of fruit loops come forward at times like these. We've had a couple of other people call in, claiming to have killed her. Frankly, this guy has a bit of a shady history, so anything is possible."

"Is he still being held?" I wanted to know all I could about this man—his story was too close to my initial suspicions about Pete Lloyd.

"We can't hold him just because some pretty unreliable woman claims he did it. The sad thing is, after we heard about that picture you saw, we wanted to ask him some more questions. He used to work in the local porn industry, so we thought he might be able to help us out a little. Also, he denied any prior knowledge of Claudia Sabato and at the time it made sense. Now that we've seen the picture, however, it doesn't seem like such a leap that he may have had some sort of connection. But we had him, and we let him go. Now that we want him back for a few questions, he's disappeared off the face of the earth."

"Like Kate," I murmured. "Have you found her yet? Or any clues as to her whereabouts?

Derek laughed. "Cait, you're a reporter. As much as I'd like to phone you personally with every development, if we get anything big, you'll have to attend the press conference like everyone else."

So much for my delusions of preferential treatment.

There was a pause on the other end. "Let's have coffee

again," Derek continued. "You sound like you need a break."

"Yeah." The morning was starting to overwhelm me. "I do need a break."

"Take care." Derek sounded worried, but I hung up without saying any more.

Curled up in my bed, I relived the morning. How had my thoughts gotten so carried away while I walked down my favorite street? I had to relax more and spend less time obsessing about work. I staggered to the bathroom to pee. I tried not to look at myself in the mirror, but when I washed my hands I couldn't help but sneak a peek. Hideous. I shuddered. My pale skin was appropriate, I figured, to a woman who had just looked death in the eye. But my hair. There was no excuse for the knotted growth above the pallor of my face.

I threw down my brush and stomped to the phone. I knew I was just trying to get my mind away from the morbid and catastrophic, but I had to call in reinforcements. I felt lousy, so I was going to get a haircut.

"Hair's strange, when you think about it," I explained to Dede ten minutes later in her apartment. "It's just dead matter on your head, but you can shape and cultivate it to express some part of yourself. It's dead, after all, but shave it off and you're a skinhead, with suspect political views and an assumed attitude. Or say a guy goes a few months without cutting it. Suddenly, you can't introduce him to your mother."

"Just ask for a trim. You're thinking too much." Dede patted her burgundy buzzcut smugly. "No offense, but your hair doesn't say too much."

"Just because my maintaining my look isn't a full-time job doesn't mean my hair is silent. It says that I haven't read any fashion magazines recently, that I don't watch *Friends*, and that I just don't care enough to bother."

Dede scoffed and handed me the phone. "Just make the appointment."

"But I don't know where to go," I protested.

"Some reporter you are. What about your investigative skills?" She tossed me the substantial *Vancouver Yellow Pages*.

An hour later, I faced three bleached blonds dressed in black. Six eyes were fixed on me with a combination of forced civility and skepticism. I flipped back my own windswept hair and gave them my best smile.

"I guess I need a haircut." I tried not to sound sheepish.

In what seemed like milliseconds, I was trapped in a chair by hairclips, scissors, and a suffocating apron while a nasal voice recited the options available for my hair.

"I'd love to see your bangs in a rich chestnut color." The hairdresser, who'd identified herself as Trixie, ran her pointed blue nails through my hair as if she was inspecting flour for worms.

"Brown?" I asked. "But my hair *is* brown."

"I could make it richer, less mousy. . . ." She stopped and turned around as the wind slammed the door shut. I looked past my shoulder in the mirror. A man with a receding chin and a faded jean jacket was standing in the door. He looked straight at my chair. I turned around to face him and my head snapped back slightly as my eyes met his. He was staring directly at me. Without taking his eyes off me, he seated himself in a purple leather chair.

"Can I help you?" Trixie asked. He shook his head silently. Trixie shrugged and picked up her scissors.

"Something asymmetrical would work on you. You could use those curls."

I shook my head, sending a fine spray of water onto Trixie's leather dress.

"How about just a trim?" I asked.

"A couple of inches all round?" she said, disappointment muting her voice.

As dishwater brown curls fell around me, I felt more and more uncomfortable. The man in the purple chair hadn't moved or broken his stare. I had a sense he would not budge until he talked to me. Trixie continued to describe trends in haircuts but I noticed she was sneaking nervous glances his way. When she picked up her blow dryer, I knew I had to start planning my exit.

"Trixie," I whispered before she turned on the machine, "that man is making me nervous."

Plucked brows crinkling, she looked over to the chair. "Him? Harmless, I'm sure." Trixie took out a tube of gel and looked towards him. Her casual words didn't fool me. "I'll just fluff things up a bit here," she said, squeezing a gooey gob into her palm.

"Please don't." I shook my newly styled head. "I never use gunk like that." I rose from my chair and walked resolutely to the till. While I paid, I noticed the man on the chair get up and leave the shop. I could see him through the window, leaning against a lamppost and lighting a cigarette.

Be strong, I told myself. Just push open the door. It's a busy street. Nothing will happen.

"Cait Whyte?" His voice was low as I walked past. "I was hoping we could talk."

The sidewalk was full of people going about their business. People who would, I had to trust, act as a deterrent to any foul play he had in mind.

"I'm walking this way." I pointed vaguely towards Commercial.

"I'm worried about your friend Steve."

"Steve?" I stopped walking. "How do you know he's my friend?"

"I know. He told me. Your friend doesn't know when to keep his mouth shut."

"You know Steve?" I asked. My reporting buddy, I was starting to realize, had been less than forthcoming with me.

"We've talked. We both know Angie. She tried to use him to set me up for a murder."

I raised my eyebrows. If this was Ed Nelson, the man Angie tried to get Steve to uncover as the killer, I had a lot of questions to ask him.

"You're Ed?" I asked. He just kept walking.

"Why did she go to Steve?" I asked him. "Trust me, he doesn't have much power with the police. Does she really think a newspaper can try to convict a murderer?"

"I guess she went to the police, too. I've never been so thankful for a DUI arrest in my life. But Angie was convinced it was me. Except she didn't know I would be busted on the wrong night."

"Why would Angie want to frame you?" I asked.

"I don't know. I don't know what goes on in that chick's brain. We worked together on some movies—not the sort of thing you see at the Cineplex, if you know what I mean. After that, we started dating. She thought I spent too much time with my daughter. My own daughter—can you imagine the depths of jealousy? Her own daughter is headed for a lifetime of counseling. She claimed she knew that I killed her, that somebody else had witnessed it—someone we used to work with. Maybe this so-called witness killed her and was trying to create a screen, or maybe Angie just wanted to get me in trouble because she's a sick woman. I'll never know, and I'm leaving town before I can find out. All I know is she tried to get your loser friend to write an article about me doing something I didn't do. She used him. Me, too."

I stopped walking and turned to face Ed. His mouth was set in an angry line, but in his eyes I was sure I could see fear. After all, a coward like me knew enough about being afraid to recognize it in others. He wouldn't meet my eyes and his shoulders were set as if he was afraid someone was going to ambush him from behind at any minute.

"What if framing you was a way to protect the real killer?" His musings had created a whole scenario that was beginning to unfold in my brain and was almost too horrible to consider.

"Nope. She's a sick woman, but she'd never hurt anyone. She's gotten herself mixed up with some of the less savory characters in the business. That kind of thing is one reason I'm leaving the industry."

"Could they have killed Claudia?" I asked, more to myself.

"If they had, you can bet they filmed it. But I don't think so. I don't think that's their scene, but frankly, I don't want to get close enough to find out. They're connected enough to do some damage."

"Why are you talking to me, anyway?" I asked him. "What do you care about me? Or Steve?"

"I think Angie's going to try to use you next. She's going to try to use you to set someone else up."

"But I'm not like Steve. I won't sleep with her, for one thing. Why did she sleep with him and then tell everyone?"

"I tell you, stay away from her, or someone will make sure you do," he said, eyes darting behind me, searching for eavesdroppers.

He was nervous, but I was the one being threatened. We'd covered threats in journalism school. We had been taught to stand up for our beliefs and the dignity of our profession in the face of corruption and pressure. We hadn't really learned about standing on a street corner with a small-time crook.

"What if I wrote about these threats?" It seemed like the right response.

"Trust me, you won't." His voice was low. "You won't talk to her and you won't write about anything she says."

"Why are you telling me all this? Why not Steve?"

"Between you and me, he's not the sharpest pencil. I don't trust him, anyways. You tell him to stay away from Angie and you do the same. You tell anyone except Steve and you'll never write another story in Vancouver. Stay away from Angie and stay away from East Hastings. I'm leaving this town, and, trust me, you have plenty of reason to leave, too. In the meantime, I'd recommend you stay away from anyone to do with this story."

He dropped my arm and stepped in front of me, then turned and walked away. I charted the course of his denim jacket until it became indistinguishable from the dozens of others bobbing down Robson Street. He didn't look like someone who had worked in the pornography industry. Despite his efforts to be menacing, there was something about him that reminded me of a nervous rabbit being eyed by a predator. I made a note to do more research on the Vancouver porn scene.

Alone on the sidewalk, I realized my legs were trembling underneath me. I glanced down at the undulating sidewalk, then grabbed a nearby mailbox to steady myself. I forced a few deep, even breaths. I'm fine, I told myself with each exhale. I'm a survivor, after all.

My jelly legs began to move, one step at a time. I had to get to a phone and call Steve.

There was a pay phone at the end of the block. Miraculously, it was in working condition. The instant I heard Steve on the other end of the line, I exploded.

"Steve! We have to talk. Now."

"Whyte! I can meet you at lunch."

"Meet me Joe's at eleven. You've really screwed up. I have a lot of questions to ask you." I hung up before he could respond.

Joe's again. I was scooping foam off the top of my latte with my finger when Steve arrived.

"This better be good, Whyte."

"Steve, we have to talk. What have you been doing?" Words tumbled out of my mouth: bribery, police, threats.

"Who was that creep?" I demanded. "Why does he know so much more than I do?"

"Ed's a rough guy. He's got a record, obviously, but not just for DUIs, and he's worked in porn for years. Not really an outstanding citizen. A good choice to frame, I guess. And Angie's his ex-girlfriend. Who knows what sick stuff happened between them? I guess she saw an opportunity to get revenge for their breakup or something like that."

"Or she's trying to create a diversion from the real killer."

"I think she's just got a beef against her ex," Steve argued. "I've had the urge to frame some of mine, too. Maybe not like this, but we all have exes we'd like to see in jail for life."

"I think there's more to it. And Ed knew my name, stuff about me," I added.

"Goddamn." He looked at his feet, then reached for my hand. "I'm sorry, Cait."

"How did you let yourself get so involved?"

"I liked Angie. I was just messing around, looking for another angle, when we first met. But she was smart, different, savvy. She was pretty sure the police were on the wrong trail with Shelly and Claudia. One night she came on to me. Honestly. I'm not using that same male bullshit line. She was all over me. She seemed sincere. Hell of an actress if she wasn't."

"She's a hooker, Steve. She feigns interest in men for a living." I didn't see the point in mincing words. Things had gone too far for politeness.

"The sex was good." He smiled weakly.

I shuddered a bit. "You are such a pig. And that swineyness has got you in trouble, and maybe put me in danger. Grab some ethics."

Steve jerked back as if I'd slapped him. For a split second, I wanted to forgive him, to praise his investigative skills and tell him he could have any woman he wanted, me being a noted exception.

"Remember journalism school?" I asked in a more neutral voice. "The early morning classes and late night production sessions? Sitting around debating ethics as if we seriously expected to have some once we started working?"

"I hated school," Steve said. "It was so competitive. I never knew if anyone liked me, or if they thought I was a good writer or a total hack. Everyone was always trying to outdo each other for marks. It was harder than real reporting, if you ask me. The whole time, I obsessed about finding a job after graduation. I was convinced the other students would scoop me."

"I still worry about being scooped." I looked at him significantly to let him know I hadn't forgotten his past sins.

"Here we are, talking to prostitutes about murder. Our teachers would be psyched. At least it's real journalism instead of some of that pap you write for the *News*."

"So Angie thought you should focus on the babysitting angle." I brought us back to the task at hand. "I've had other people tell me the babysitting angle is underplayed." I was thinking of Paolo.

"But why bribe me?" Steve asked. "Why not the cops?"

"I think we need to find this Angie woman. Ed told me to stay away from East Hastings. She wouldn't live there, would she?"

"I don't know where she lives, but we met at a bar there once. The Wallowing Whale."

I knew the Wallowing Whale. It was right beside the Western Rose Hotel.

"Well," I put down my latte with force, "get ready to wallow."

When I got home, I had a big decision to make. Ed Nelson had threatened me. A good reporter would ignore the threats and get to the bottom of the story. But a good citizen would report the threats and leave it in the hands of the police. Did I want to go after what could be the story of my life, or did I want to go to the cops?

I had wanted to report my rape. I had walked home that night alone, stars mocking me in the sky. Everything looked the same: the dark mirror of the lake, the gently bending trees. It was the same road I'd walked on almost every day of my childhood, but everything had changed. I stopped for a couple of minutes and sat on a small, pebbly beach, skipping rocks across the water. Sitting there alone, I was convinced the lake was bottomless. If I dove in for a midnight swim, I would be swallowed in its depths. I didn't swim for a couple of weeks after. Instead, I showered several times a day, until my mother complained about me wasting hot water.

But back then, walking along the empty road, I planned to wake my parents when I got home. I had the night planned. They would take me to the police station. Everyone would hug me, comfort me, and the next day he would be arrested and punished. He wouldn't be able to follow through with his threats of revenge if I opened my mouth, so I would be spared the promised torture, repeated rape, and certain death that still reverberated around my head. My parents would make everything okay, and I would return to my normal life.

But when I entered the house to the faint cinnamon of the day's baking, then opened my parents' bedroom door and heard their snorting snores, I knew I wouldn't be able to tell them. Telling would expose the sanctuary they'd created as a sham. Their feelings about me would change. I wouldn't be the same.

At that age, I couldn't even form the word "rape" in my own thoughts. How could I repeat it again and again to my family, to the police? For ten minutes, I stood in the door to my parents' room, listening to their rhythmic exhaling. Then I went into the bathroom and showered, scrubbed hard until my skin was raw and my hands were tingling. Stepping out of the shower, I turned around in front of the mirror, inspecting my lobster-red body. It looked the same—faintly curved hips, flat stomach, small, round breasts. I put one hand on my left breast and squished it against my rib cage. It didn't disappear. Looking down at my hand, I imagined a knife slicing smoothly at the point where breast met bony chest, like cutting the eye off a potato. I put my largest sweatshirt on, then went outside. Sitting on our porch dripping wet, I listened to the sounds of the country for almost two hours. At three in the morning, the noise of the front door opening shocked me out of my empty state.

"Honey, what on earth are you doing?" It was my mother, sleepy-eyed in her flannel nightgown. "You're going to catch a cold. Come inside, silly."

Blinking, I followed her into the house. I didn't dream at all that night. The next morning, I got up and had breakfast with her and went back out into the world.

"What's wrong?" more than one person asked me. "You seem quiet" or "You look tired."

I had said nothing. Now was my chance to speak out, on my own.

Chapter Fifteen

THE FIRST THING I'M GOING TO DO is wash my hands, I resolved. Something about spending time on East Hastings made me want to immerse myself in soapy water. There were trendy restaurants and shops only a few blocks away, but somehow the germs felt different. It may not be a very PC view of skid row hygiene, but I felt dirty.

Steve and I were scouring the few blocks surrounding the Western Rose Hotel. We had two missions: to find Angie and to find someone who might know where Kate Whyte was. Steve said Angie spent a lot of time in a four-block stretch downtown and sometimes drank at the Wallowing Whale, and Kate had lived in the Western Rose. It wasn't a lot to go on, but it was the best we could do.

Beside me, Steve lit a cigarette with affected casualness. We had both dressed for the part: jeans, old leather jackets, big boots. Although he didn't normally smoke, Steve thought cigarettes would give another touch of realism, along with the shots of whiskey he insisted we down before leaving my apartment.

I wiped my hands on my jeans. "We're meeting only drunks here, Steve," I whispered.

He scowled in my direction, then scanned the block stretching out ahead of us.

"I know what I'm doing," he muttered unconvincingly. He stopped walking and turned to face a thin man leaning against a mailbox. The man was surveying the street scene as if he were about to paint a landscape painting, his pockmarked face serious, eyes narrowed, hands stuffed into the pockets of his acid-wash jeans. Steve glanced at me, then approached him slowly.

"Hey, I'm looking for some action." He was trying to sound like a gangsta, but I couldn't help smiling.

"I ain't got nothing." The man's face remained a blank canvas.

"I'm not looking for drugs. A date. I want a, you know, woman. Know anyone?"

"I might." His gaze returned to the street scene.

"I heard about one in this area. Red hair, kinda skinny."

"Christ, man, I ain't a pimp." His scarred face twisted with distaste and he opened the mailbox and dropped a handful of letters into the box. "Get the hell outta here."

We watched him disappear down the block, black boots clicking against the concrete.

"Oops." I grinned at Steve. "Excuse me if I'm wrong. I'm not too versed in street culture, being from Grand Forks and all, but is every rough-looking guy downtown a pimp?"

Steve shook his head. "Hey, man, I thought he was. I had a feeling."

"This is starting to feel like the old needle in a haystack." What I really wanted to do, I almost confessed, was go home and have a bath.

"I expect clichés from a *News* reporter. But I've got a better idea." With a few long strides, Steve disappeared behind the fake-oak-paneled door of the Wallowing Whale. With a deep breath and an attitude check, I followed him.

It took me a few seconds to adjust my eyes to the dark. It was a pretty recognizable genre of bar. The pool table was scuffed and oddly tilted, the tables were sticky with beer and scarred by cigarette burns. I could feel all eyes in the room focus on me as I followed Steve to an empty table. The jeans I had modeled laughingly for Steve an hour earlier suddenly seemed truly painted on. Don't show your fear, I reminded myself. With what I hoped was worldly composure, I plunked my tightly sheathed butt into a chair.

"Damn." Steve looked uncomfortable. "I should have thought ahead."

"Huh?"

"Well, no offense, but how am I going to ask for a prostitute when you're with me? I'll look like a total creep."

"No problem. You're used to it. But I'll take care of your little problem." I signaled to the waitress. "Double Jamesons, please. And one for my friend."

When the waitress reappeared, whiskey in hand, I tapped her lightly on the hand.

"I've got to ask you a question," I began, "but it's a bit personal."

The waitress looked down at me, waxy orange lips pursed with impatience. "You're not my type, honey. That's ten bucks for the drinks."

I put a twenty on the tray and held up my hand before she gave me any change.

"Ditto sweetheart." Was it really me talking? I felt as though I was auditioning for a school play. "I need some information about the neighborhood."

"Well, I don't have all day." She waved a bird-like arm around the bar.

"I'm looking for my cousin. She's a runaway and she's been spotted near here. My aunt's afraid she's hooking. We're trying to find her, but nobody seems to have seen her. Funny thing is, I'm pretty sure we saw her the other day, getting into a car. We lost her, but she must be down here somewhere. We want to bring her home." Whew. I wanted to give myself a round of applause. Steve was staring at me as if I'd offered to buy the whole bar a drink.

"Good luck." The waitress's lips curved slightly in what could almost be called a smile. "What does she look like?"

"It's hard to tell we're related." I might as well acknowledge that. "She's got long red hair, pretty skinny."

"Bright eyes," Steve piped up, with just a little too much lust in his voice. "Her hair's a bit curly. No freckles."

"'Bout six feet tall?"

"Yeah." Steve sat up straight. "When she wears heels, she's even taller."

The waitress tilted her head to one side, nodding slowly. "Angie? That her name? They don't always use their real names."

"Angie. That's her. My cousin Angela. And she had a friend, a blond woman called Kate."

"Honey, I can't get involved in your family problems. I'm just trying to earn a living here." She spotted a raised hand across the room. "Gotta go."

"Wait." Steve stood up. "Where is she?"

"I'm only a waitress, honey." She bustled off, leaving Steve slouched over the table.

"She was helpful," I said, shifting my rear end around to get comfortable. No wonder I usually wore skirts.

"We're so close." Steve shook his head. "We're just circling around her. Maybe another couple of contacts will bring us to her."

"What contacts? I'm not talking to anyone else in this bar." Trying not to attract attention, I waved my hand to encompass the rest of the room. Beside us, a gray-haired man sat with his face planted on the Formica table; at the pool table, a woman in a too-small tube top bent over to make a shot as half the patrons howled their support.

"We'll just finish our drinks. Then I may have other ideas."

"As long as I don't have to use the bathroom." I picked up my drink, then froze. A man in a ripped leather jacket was sitting in the opposite corner. It was dark in the Wallowing Whale and the smoke made it hazy, but I knew his face.

I nudged Steve's booted foot with my own.

"Don't stare," I cautioned. "Don't make a fuss, but look over your shoulder to the left, beside the jukebox. Be slow, very slow."

Steve turned, stared, then pivoted back to me with the speed of a Tae Bo instructor.

"That's the man that I think is following me," I mouthed. It was definitely him, the man who had stared at me with hatred on the bus and grabbed me in the Western Rose. While Steve and I stared at each other, wondering what to do next, he began moving towards us. In a split second, our guest whipped a nearby chair to our table, tossed a leg over it, and straddled the chair, leaning forward.

"I hear you're looking for Angie."

I had to lean forward to hear him. Our noses almost met in the center of the table.

"We're looking for her, that's all." Steve's voice was an octave higher than usual.

"What do you want with her?" the man answered.

"I'm just a concerned friend."

I was watching their interaction with interest. One thing was certain: if this man was a cop, I was Christiane Amanpour.

"You're not a cop, are you?" I tried a direct approach.

He winked at Steve. "Can't put anything past her, can you?"

"You said you were a cop at the hotel the other day." I knew I sounded whiny.

"I didn't say I was a cop, princess. I told you to go home; you assumed the rest."

I tried to remember more of our conversation. He had certainly commanded me with the authority of an investigating officer, but I didn't remember him actually identifying himself. I'd learned in journalism school always to ask for identification to prove a source's credentials. Steve was right: real life was different from school.

"How do you know Angie?" Steve was stuck on one subject.

"Look, buddy, she's finished with you. Her little imagination hasn't concocted any more story ideas. Got it?" Our table guest stood up. "You'll have to find someone else to obsess on, boy. Believe it or not, I doubt she'll miss you. And you," he turned and pointed to me, "you'll have to stick to the stories you're assigned. I don't think your little paper will be running any stories about the Wallowing Whale or the Western Rose. Go back to city hall." With a smirk, he untangled himself and returned to his table.

"Let's go!" I grabbed my purse, stood up, and was out the door with amazing speed, considering the tightness of my jeans.

Out in the sunlight, I could see that Steve's face was white. "Who was that guy?" he asked. "What was he doing?"

"I'm not sure." As I struggled for words, I realized Steve wasn't listening.

"There she is," he shouted, pointing over my shoulder. As I turned, I caught a glimpse of a tall, red-haired woman opening the door to the Western Rose next door. Her hair lit up the gray sidewalk, but judging from the flash of profile I was able to see, her nose was hooked at an odd angle, as if she was smelling something foul.

"That's Angie," Steve said. He grabbed my hand and began to run toward her.

"Stop!" A loud voice rang out behind us. We both froze, looking back and forth between the closing hotel door and the man from the bar bearing down on us. As he advanced, I saw a slash of silver in his hand. He had a knife. I was hypnotized. He was coming closer.

"Don't even think about it," he hissed. Steve looked at the hotel again and, still holding my hand, took a step towards it. As my arm stretched with Steve's movement, I kept staring at the knife.

"Steve, he has a knife." I tugged my arm back. Steve stopped. He saw the knife, then caught my eye. Without saying a word, still clutching hands, we broke out into a run, past the hotel, past the street people, across a sidewalk on a yellow light.

We couldn't keep up the fast pace for long, though. It wasn't so much the tight jeans as the fact that neither of us had exercised in years. I could hear Steve gasping beside me, but couldn't suggest we slow down until I knew we were safe. After a block, we turned around. The man in the ripped jacket was nowhere to be seen. We dropped our hands and stared at each other, dumbstruck.

"I don't get it," Steve began. "I just want to talk to Angie, ask if she can clear my name. I don't know what difference that makes to him. What's the deal? Who does he think he is?"

"He was just trying to scare you, Steve. It's probably a property thing. He's either her boyfriend or her pimp, and he probably doesn't like other men coming near her without an invitation. You should be proud of yourself. You're not a real reporter until someone has threatened you." I was trying to lighten the mood, although my own thoughts were darkening quickly. Fortunately, Steve bought my reasoning.

"You're right, Whyte. Maybe he's even jealous. Bet he thought he could scare me! Ha! I tell you, this whole story is getting more interesting every hour. Too bad you can't work on it. Too bad it's too heavy for you."

I could overlook the false bravado, but not the dig at my reporting.

"I'm interested in this, Steve. I'm involved in the whole story. And I'd like to help you. I need to find out more about that guy in there."

"How do you know him?" Steve asked.

"He keeps turning up: I saw him on the bus downtown, I thought I saw him going out to Burnaby of all places, and I bumped into him—literally—in the Western Rose. I was sure he was a cop, but now he's just giving me the creeps. Maybe he is Angie's boyfriend, maybe he's her pimp. But I've never even met her—what would he want with me?"

"Wow," Steve shook his head. "Sometimes I wish I was a food columnist instead of a reporter. If you ever see that jerk again, I want you to call me right away. Call me, then call the cops. That guy means business."

"Are you still going to try to see Angie?" I asked.

"Looks like I'll have to use my charm to keep my job. It's not worth risking my life for. I tell you, I didn't know men were so possessive about the women who work for them. Maybe that's a story."

"Well," I smiled, "don't forget—you owe me."

"I won't forget," Steve said, with what passed for sincerity. "But if you don't mind, I'd like to be alone for a little while."

"What about Kate?" I asked, more to myself than Steve. "It's driving me crazy, not even knowing how to start finding her. Though if she's really made a break from this world, I don't see her returning to this area."

I said good-bye to Steve with some relief. Four blocks later, I had left the sad sidewalks and entered the land of retail shops and tourists. I could even smile to myself. Our trip had been terrifying, but at least I wasn't alone in facing the dark depths of the murders any more. Despite his cyberporn jokes, the leers, the shaky ethics, I was wondering if I'd underestimated Steve. He did always have a joke to lighten any situation, even if it was usually in bad taste. But maybe he was just fooling me. I'd listened to Dede's theories about Steve too many times not to realize that he was also weird, sexually confused, and incapable of intimacy.

Chapter
Sixteen

"DEDE, I'VE HAD ANOTHER OVERLY adventurous day. Wanna share pizza and compare notes?" I'd shown up at her door, unable to contain the story of my day. I felt as if Steve and I had been working as detectives, probing the dark heart of the city with stealth and subterfuge. We'd even been threatened by a man who must have been a pimp. With a few discreet embellishments, I could entertain Dede all night with my portrait of the young reporter as super sleuth.

"Love to talk." Dede retreated into her apartment. "I'll bring wine. Meet you in two minutes."

I could sense her own excitement the minute she walked through the door. With bright eyes, she paced across my living room, words flying out like staccato notes.

"I went to another Urban Women Warriors meeting today with Janet. Pretty radical, some of it. Cait, I hate to say this, but it's all off the record, isn't it? I mean, you won't go investigating the group for a story or anything?"

"Dede! How could you even ask?" I glared at her from across my raised glass. Privately, though, I had to admit it would be a good story and she could be a good source. I tried to check my reporter's curiosity before I asked more questions, but since I was so charged up myself, it was inevitable that I would fail.

"Seriously, though, Dede, I could check up on the group if you wanted. Find out if they're clean, that sort of thing."

"They're *clean*, Cait. They're opposed to crime, remember. Christ, having a few opinions that go against the patriarchy hasn't become illegal, has it?"

"I'm just looking out for you." I had to let it drop, even the word "patriarchy."

Breathlessly, Dede told me about chants, slogans, and exercises she'd learned at the meetings she'd attended. Pretty predictable, I thought, especially for anyone with even an elementary knowledge of women's studies. Buzzwords were scattered through the group's credo like salt on pretzels. Apparently, Dede discovered, there was a bit of a division in the group over the use of violent resistance. While some members advocated a sort of New Age pacifism, others claimed the time for action had arrived. I was afraid to ask Dede where she stood, so I changed the subject.

"I had a pretty radical day, too. Soon, you'll see me with my own crime show." Using every dramatic skill I'd learned as a writer, I described my trip downtown.

"I never thought I'd see you and Steve trying to crack crime together," Dede laughed. "Bernstein and Woodward, move over. But didn't you find it hard to work with Steve?"

"Actually," I couldn't control the smile dancing on my lips, "I thought it was kind of fun."

"Cait, don't fall for him. I warned you. Don't you have enough men in your life already? Do you think now you've got to have the actor, the artist, the musician, and the moron?"

"Steve is not in the running, Dede. Actually, I was thinking it might be time to call one of them. The only one I haven't seen alone is Pete. I'm trying to figure out how to corner him without his daughter." I faked a leer in her direction.

"Forget Pete," Dede said. "You need to stay away from men with children. I tell you, the one to go for is the sexy one: the tall, dark, and handsome Paolo. Although, do you think he's too close to that Italian, Catholic, patriarchal structure of relationships? I was thinking about this at the meeting...."

"Quit the damn group!" I was only half joking when I threw a pillow in her direction. "They must be punished for dealing in stereotypes."

I arrived at work early the next day and settled into my desk determined to find out more about Angie and make a start tracking down Kate. I had just entered the word "porn" when I heard the distinct click of May's heels. Those clicks usually telegraphed the immediate arrival of an angry boss, so I exited quickly and sat back to accept my fate. Sure enough, in scant seconds she was at the entrance to my cubicle, hands on her hips, scowl on her face.

"Cait, we need to talk. Come into my office."

Whenever I follow an enraged May, I feel large, oafish, and incompetent beside the tiny powerhouse of frustration that is my editor. When I walked into her office, I looked down at my feet. They're only size seven, though they looked like boats in my chunky shoes. May's feet were in resolutely spiked pumps, perhaps a size five. Her heels could do damage in a matter of seconds. My shoes were scuffed and faded. There, I realized, was the difference between us.

"Cait, close the door." May sat down behind her desk. "I had an interesting phone call from the police just now. Some guy named Ron called. He seemed to think your work on the Sabato story had crossed the line from reporter to detective and that you had put your own safety in jeopardy."

"I just wanted to get a different angle on the story." I could hear the weak defensiveness in my voice.

"Cait, is there something you're not telling me?"

Prostitution. Kate Whyte. Angie. Movies. Could I tell May all this?

"Nothing. I haven't worked on that story in ages." Technically this wasn't really a lie. I hadn't written a word about the murders in days.

"Have you talked to the family recently?"

"Just the brother. He's concerned about the quality of the police investigation. I think there might be a good story in there."

"This Ron said you'd been talking to some suspicious characters, people who couldn't have been necessary for any story we would print in this paper."

Because we only go with the police's side of the story, I wanted to add. Because there hasn't been a "suspicious character" or anyone outside the middle class in the *News* since the first issue.

"If you find out anything, I want you to tell me right away. I'll pass it along to another reporter. I have a bad feeling about you with this story. You won't be working on any crime stories for a while. Besides, you've got a ton of other stuff on your plate."

"But, May," I began.

"The police are not the only factor influencing my decision, Cait." May's voice dropped to a near whisper. "You know you're too involved." Before I could object, she picked up the phone and used a pointy fingertip to begin dialing.

Goddamn. Back at my desk, I fought angry tears. The nerve of that woman. In my mind, commitment to a story was a *good* thing, not something to fear. Just because May hadn't felt any passion for twenty years, I wasn't going to let her interfere with my contact with the police. I picked up the phone. I wasn't just May's lackey. I could phone whoever I wanted. Whatever happened to freedom of the press?

"Derek? Cait here," I said the minute he picked up the phone. "I wanted to see if you have any new leads on the Sabato murder."

"Ron and I are heading to Granville Island at lunch. Join us? We can catch up then."

"I'd love to." I smiled as I hung up, surprised at how much I was looking forward to lunch with two policemen, even if one had just complained to my boss.

On a sunny day, Granville Island looks like a child's drawing, with bright, primary colors, bold designs, mountains rising from the water in straight, clean lines. The market gleamed with fresh produce in crisp Crayola tones and everyone seemed to have a smile for me. I forgot about my troubles at work, flashed my own biggest smile, and approached a picnic table a few feet from the ocean, where Derek and Ron waited with fish and chips.

Ron was the only person in a two-mile radius without a smile to share. I extended my hand towards him, trying to overlook his overt copness. Although he was dressed in civilian clothes, he could have had "Vancouver Police Force" tattooed on his substantial bicep.

"Good to see you again," I lied. Beside us, a baby girl began squealing with pleasure as her mother spooned frozen yogurt in her eager mouth.

"Damn kids." Ron looked around. "I told you we should have gone to the Keg." He scowled at Derek, who grinned at me in turn.

"This is my favorite place in the city," Derek said.

"It's filled with yuppie scum," Ron objected. "And there's too much frigging healthy food. Everything I hate about this damn city in one spot." He turned his attention to me.

"I talked to your boss this morning. Hope I didn't get you in trouble."

How very kind of you to be concerned, I thought. It was hard enough to sit beside the man whose words had probably doomed me to a lifetime of covering civic politics and lifestyle trends without discussing it with him.

"She's pretty mellow," I lied. I couldn't give Ron the satisfaction of describing May's reaction.

"Ron's right, Cait," Derek said. "You don't want to get too involved. I know you're serious about the story, but your safety comes first. We will have to stop you from doing any more stories if need be."

Traitor. I lowered Derek several rungs in my romantic rankings.

"Seriously," Ron continued. "Don't go poking around Shelly Bennett's world. We're starting to guess she was involved in some stuff you wouldn't want to get too close to. She didn't exactly run with the Girl Guides, if you know what I mean. Pretty hard-core stuff."

"How hard core? What else do you know?" I sat up, ready to ask as many questions as they were willing to answer. Not surprisingly, it turned out they weren't willing to answer many.

"You know we can't say too much, especially to a reporter."

I wondered how much our research had overlapped.

"Did Kate mention Shelly's boyfriend?" Derek asked. "Several people have mentioned that she seemed to have hooked up with the wrong guy, but none of them had met him. They didn't even know his name."

"She didn't know, either," I told them. "She could have been lying, of course."

"That's what she told us." Derek sighed and looked out over the water. "Unfortunately, Shelly didn't leave a lot of clues about her love life. We can't even look at phone records, since her hotel room didn't have a phone. Somebody must have known her better, known what she was up to."

"Did you find her parents?" I asked.

"Nice folks," Derek said. "From Alberta. Law-abiding sorts. Said Shelly had never given them a moment's trouble until she ran away."

"They *said* that. Probably selective memory in action. No kid just wakes up and decides to become a hooker in the big smoke. There's usually a reason they make that decision. Poor morals, poor parenting." Ron nodded at his own wisdom.

"Not many people decide to become hookers," I said. If what Kate had told me about her was true, someone had to defend Shelly. "And it has nothing to do with morals. Sometimes they don't have any choice. Maybe she wanted a real job here, but couldn't find anything else. Maybe by then she was too far in debt. Maybe she had a history of abuse...."

"What do you know about it?" I couldn't miss the hostility in Ron's voice. "You ever walked the street?"

"She's written about prostitution." Derek said quickly. "She's interviewed some prostitutes, right, Cait?"

"I don't really know too much, though." I had to backtrack before I got in over my head with Ron.

"You from Vancouver?" Ron asked.

"I grew up in a small town in the interior. Grand Forks."

"There you go." Ron looked pleased with himself. "Ain't no crime in Grand Forks."

"We had our fair share—kids with nothing to do, tourists gone bad." Nothing riled me more than people touting the alleged safety of Grand Forks, and not just because of my own experience with crime. Growing up, I'd been exposed to plenty of so-called "big city" incidents—arson, accidental shootings, and lots of driving under the influence as kids cruised through mountain roads powered by a lethal cocktail of stolen beer, boredom, and hormones. A classmate's father had disappeared; although he was officially presumed drowned, rumors of foul play persisted. A girl two grades behind me had been drowned by a tourist. He claimed she'd grabbed his crotch and he'd drowned her in self-defence. A student had pulled a knife on a teacher when I was in junior high. I defied any Vancouver woman my age to top my experience with crime. But I could tell Ron's mind was made up.

"I'd transfer there in a minute," he joked to Derek. "Make sure people pick up after their dogs and other strenuous tasks involving dangerous and dastardly deeds."

Ever the gentleman, Derek tried to change the subject.

"Do you still talk with the Sabato brother? Is he still complaining about our investigation? He knows a lot about police procedure, but he strikes me as a bit naive or something. And I sense there's some bad blood between him and his parents—not sure what, though."

"He's bitter," I admitted. "But he's been through a lot."

"I've taken some of his suggestions to the head of the investigation," Derek said. "They seem like nice folks. Rich as stink, but real folks."

"Rich?" I asked. "I thought they ran a deli." I didn't think there could be too much money in salami.

"Trust me, they're loaded," Ron answered. "I think they work just because they're on a mission to provide the city with good Italian cold cuts. They're hard workers, too. But I have to agree with Derek about Paolo. He wouldn't survive a minute on the force."

"I'm not sure he'd want to," I replied.

"It's a complicated situation. You'd better watch your step," Ron said. He didn't elaborate. Instead, he crossed his arms and scowled at the shimmery waves lapping up on a nearby shore. He looked as though he wanted to arrest them for disturbing his peace. I wasn't about to ask him for more information.

"So." Ron spoke again. "I guess your editor isn't giving you any more crime stories for a while. And I assume you've taken me seriously here. I'm not joking—you'll get in trouble if you decide to take the law into your own hands."

I pursed my lips and counted to ten. Don't answer, I repeated to myself. Don't participate in the conversation. I rose silently, nodded at Derek and turned towards work. Walking away in the sunshine, I felt faintly uneasy. I'm usually comfortable around the police. They can be allies of the press, after all, a source of information no reporter can afford to lose. As a law-abiding, generally paranoid citizen, I figured their job was to protect me, and that they would do it well whenever asked. Now I was definitely at odds with at least one officer.

I've always wondered how I would feel if I'd reported my rape. I'd heard terrible stories about women being greeted by disbelief, or having their backgrounds used against them. Most of the male cops I talked to at work were pleasant enough, if occasionally gruff, macho, or unresponsive. Derek was an obvious exception. Ron, on the other hand, just reinforced the stereotypes espoused by Dede.

When I returned to work, I decided to phone the Bear Pub. Surely, I figured, they must have some idea how I could contact Kate.

"Bear Pub," Ray answered the phone to the sound of clinking glasses.

"This is Kate's sister," I started. "I'm trying to track her down. I have a family emergency."

"Get in line." Ray laughed. "We're all looking for her. People have been in looking for her. She's not around. Trust me, if I know Kate you won't find her unless she wants to be found."

"You don't have any emergency contacts?" I asked, heart sinking.

"Look, why don't you leave a message with me and when she comes back, I'll pass it along. She'll return. I know she's not the type to blow us off."

"You don't have any ideas about where she might be?" I persisted.

"Hey, the police are looking, too. If they can't do it, I can't. I have a business to run. Just leave a message…."

I hung up. The day was becoming an exercise in

roadblocks and frustration. I had some time saved up from interminable city council meetings, so I decided to go home.

"Hey, beautiful." Dede was sitting on the front steps, holding her guitar when I returned from work. "Join me in a song?"

"Like I can sing," I smiled. "Another grim day at the grindstone press. What's up with you? Why so musical?"

"I'm thinking of playing at the Flying Goat coffee house tonight. It's an open stage and I feel like making some noise. Wanna come along?"

"I just might join you. When are you going? I have some things to do."

"Work related?"

"Don't laugh, but I'm thinking of going down to the ravine." I waited for her reaction.

"Feeling adventurous? Or going over the edge? That could be dangerous, stupid."

"I talked to some of Claudia Sabato's friends the other day. They said they used to hang out down there. I was thinking of looking around. Maybe I'll get a better sense of what could have happened to Claudia. Maybe I'll see something the police missed."

"Is this your Nancy Drew complex surfacing again?" Dede put down her guitar.

"I'll admit I'm not feeling great about the police work. And maybe my lust for Paolo has brought me over to his point of view."

"I have a great idea," Dede interrupted my reverie. "The perfect date for the dysfunctional couple that you two are. Call Paolo up and ask him to cruise through the ravine with you. It's perfect. You know I'm on Paolo's side in the battle for Cait's heart."

I shuddered. "Don't you think that's just a tiny bit morbid,

Dee? Exploring the filthy pit where his sister was found? What if he sees something disturbing?"

"Face it, you're not going to find anything. No matter what you think about their investigation, the police have gone over that area with a fine-tooth comb. It'll just be an excuse to poke around the bushes together. Maybe roll around in the dirt a little."

"You're seriously disturbed," I told her. "I don't know. Seems pretty weird. But...." I hesitated. Truth be told, I was a tad nervous about going into the ravine alone. Going with a handsome man might ease my mind. I returned to my apartment and dialed his number.

"Paolo," I began. "It's Cait. I'm thinking of going down to the ravine to see what I can stir up. I thought a visit down there might add some realism to my story. If it's not too painful for you, and if you feel up to it, I was wondering if you're interested in joining me."

"Story?" he asked. "Have you started something new?"

"I'm trying to get Claudia's point of view by imagining how she felt." I told him what her friends had said about the ravine being a gathering place. I neglected to mention that I couldn't actually write about anything I saw, since May had put me back on the civic politics beat.

"I'd love to come with you. But will that be an ethical problem from a reporter's point of view, to have a member of the victim's family with you? I'm not exactly an unbiased source."

"As long as you don't bully me about what I see. Why don't you meet me at WaaZuBee's in half an hour?"

I checked my closet for something casual but flattering, something versatile that would be appropriate for mucking around in the ravine to solve a murder, but not out of place if we went to a pub afterward. I spent the first fifteen minutes cursing my hips, my impractical clothing purchases, and my minimal fashion budget. Then I found a pair of overalls and a tight yellow shirt. Not fully convinced this was the right outfit for an intrepid but lustful reporter, I returned to the front porch. Dede was strumming her guitar, eyes closed, when I sat down.

"Not now, I'm writing a song," she hummed melodically.

"Dee, he is coming with me. It was a great idea."

She opened her eyes. "You look adorable. Reporter turned farmer turned cover girl. But you're missing braids. I'd add some pigtails. Anything else in your game plan?"

"I'll just get a feel for the place. I'm not sure why I'm doing this. I've been banned from writing about this story, but I have to know more. I just want some kind of sense of, you know, what happened."

"Have you ever thought of writing a freelance piece? Or maybe that sort of fiction/reporting stuff? What do they call that? Creative nonfiction? Your ideas seem well beyond the scope of the dear old *East Vancouver News*. And, no offense, but you seem to be treating it a lot more seriously than just a story."

"I'm not sure what I'll do." There was a reason, I knew, behind my interest, but no matter how often I turned my heart inside out and tossed and turned late at night and mulled over my own dark memories, I couldn't even tell my best friend.

Chapter Seventeen

THE PATH WAS STEEP AND I WAS GLAD I'd decided on sneakers, even if they made my feet look big. When we reached the bottom, I stopped to survey the land. We weren't too far from the bustle and attitude of Commercial, but already I felt like an explorer. I could hear the roar of rush-hour traffic on the overpass, but the bushy hills around me were silent. In some places, the bush was too dense for easy walking. Throughout, spaces had been cleared, often around the charcoal remains of a fire. Empty bottles were everywhere and I could see an abandoned mattress in the distance.

"Do you know where she. . . ." I couldn't finish the sentence.

"This way. The police showed me."

I followed Paolo's long legs through blackberry bushes until we came to a small clearing littered with the remains of the police investigation: a broken pencil, an empty cigarette package, and some ragged, yellow "do not cross" tape. The grass had been trampled flat. I stood in silence. Claudia had been brought here. If I was quiet enough, could I feel her presence? Or was I getting carried away? I didn't normally use words like "presence," but it was impossible not to think of her spirit—another word I avoided—hovering through the ravine.

I lowered my eyes to avoid Paolo's gaze. I wanted to imagine I was alone. A condom, glistening with recent use, languished just beside me.

"Look." I pointed down at the limp latex.

"Bastards," Paolo muttered. He had turned around so he was at a ninety-degree angle to me, his strong nose silhouetted in profile against the gravel slope. I was about to turn back to my own thoughts when I noticed something odd.

Paolo was staring at me intently. I was a little out of practice, but if my memory served me, the expression written clearly across his face was one of lust. Lust or adoration. Suddenly embarrassed, I turned so my back was to him and pretended to survey the site some more. Purple wildflowers had caught my eye when I felt an arm slip around my waist and pull me close. When his hipbones pressed hard against my backside, I stepped forward. A stubbled chin scraped my neck.

"Cait," he murmured. "Cait, how can I thank you?"

I'd heard that voice a dozen times in my fantasies, but the circumstances were definitely wrong. Poor soul. I knew people had odd reactions to stress. Was ardor Paolo's way of dealing with loss?

"Paolo, I think we should go." While I'm still able to justify my crush on you, I added to myself.

"Cait, you're so young and innocent." He turned my shoulders around so I was facing him, drew me closer, then extended a finger to my chin, lifting it slightly. His lips touched mine for a brief second, then I felt the beginning of an erection against my hip through my overalls. Without thinking I stepped back quickly and stared at him in shock. Behind us, I could hear some kids screaming drunkenly.

"Sorry," he murmured. "I guess this isn't the best place."

"Let's leave," I said, turning quickly. I walked rapidly up the path, my breath short and shallow, my steps in time to the words I was repeating to myself: creepy, creepy, creepy. Just make it to the street, I told myself, then once we were back in civilization we could talk. What just happened might have seemed bizarre and creepy in the ravine but it could be heavenly in my apartment. Maybe I just imagined the erection. Surely, it had been my imagination conjuring up an earlier fantasy at an inappropriate time, although I could still feel the imprint burned against my flesh. Behind me I could hear Paolo laboring to keep my pace. When we reached the sidewalk, he grabbed my hand.

"Sorry about that," he said. "I guess I wasn't as ready to go down there as I thought. Pretty mortifying. I haven't been myself recently." His cheeks were flushed, either from exertion or embarrassment.

"You had kind of a strange way of dealing with it, don't you think?" I looked at him with a question in my face, but he just stared back, face blank.

"Not that I didn't enjoy it." I smiled. Perhaps a joke would break the strange feeling hanging between us like a plastic shower curtain. "Maybe another time we could continue where we left off. Somewhere else, of course."

He didn't seem to hear me, just looked over my shoulder.

"I'm going to the Flying Goat tonight with a friend. Wanna join us?" I didn't know what else to say, so I filled the silence with an invitation.

"I'll call you, Cait. And I'm sorry. I don't know what happened down there." Then he was gone, legs scissoring rapidly as he disappeared. I stared after him, wondering what else I could have said, then returned home. Dede was still on the porch, strumming her guitar and humming.

"Dede, I just had the weirdest experience." With my reporter's voice, I repeated the events of the last half hour. This time, I didn't even need to call on my imagination for embellishment to astonish Dede. For once, reality defeated my imagination. I had to tell someone. Then I had to have a shower.

"Too weird," Dede agreed. "Maybe he was nervous and that made him horny for you. But, imagine, putting the moves on you in his sister's grave. I mean, I joked about it, but it seems sort of gross now that it's happened. I never expected him to strike in the ravine. I've been forced to revise my opinion of old Paolo. Go for Derek instead. The worst thing a police officer would do is flirt in his car or do something unauthorized with his handcuffs."

"He was embarrassed," I reminded her. "He took off quickly. He's normally very composed."

"Sex and death, Cait. You should know they're related. It's weird, but I guess it could be explained under the circumstances: sister's death, cute reporter, lots of emotions stirred up. It's almost understandable, I guess."

"To a shrink, maybe." I was only half joking.

"Come to the coffee house with me and Janet. I'm in good voice tonight. And you shouldn't sit around and get weirded out. The coffee house is exactly what you need."

Ten minutes after I sat down in the patchouli-ridden room, I wondered if the coffee house was more like the opposite of what I needed. The room was filled with cotton-clad students, each clutching an instrument or a sheaf of poems. How many of them, I wondered, had had the sort of day I did? They were all so anxious to change the world, but how much of it did they see in the movement from coffee house to vegetarian restaurant to school? I felt as I had in high school: detached and conscious that I was carrying a secret no one else knew—that the world wasn't safe.

Dede's set was brilliant. She'd written two new songs for the occasion, both wry accounts of love gone wrong. At least she had a sense of humor, I whispered to her when she returned to her seat, not like the other earnest whale-savers baring their psyches as if the whole world wanted to know about their predictable convictions.

"Cait!" Dede admonished me. "You've become so cynical."

I just smiled. Janet looked at me with barely disguised distaste.

"Do you play any instruments, Cait?" The challenge in her voice told me I shouldn't knock it if I couldn't do it.

"I'm a writer," I said. I wasn't a poet, like the rest of the room, but she didn't have to know that.

"Planning to read something you wrote?"

I was about to answer her when I froze. A tall redhead had just walked in the room. Surrounded by the dreadlocks and earth tones of the coffee-house clientele, her fake leopard-skin coat and knee-high purple boots stuck out like a steak on the coffee-house menu. Although I had just caught a glimpse when she went in to the Western Rose, I knew her immediately. It was Angie, Steve's nemesis and unrequited love. Surely she didn't sing, as well. I couldn't take my eyes off her. She moved through the room as if she knew that every-one was watching her, but her own eyes were scanning the room. When she took out a pack of cigarettes, two bespecta-cled men jumped up to warn her against lighting up, block-ing my view.

"Cait," Dede nudged me, oblivious, "Janet wants you to read some of your stuff. You could start with your last piece, 'School Board Elections Marred by Poor Turnout.'" She was ribbing me, but I ignored her. Instead, I watched Angie cross the room and sit down. I should call Steve, I thought. He'd be here before I hung up the phone. Or maybe I should avoid any potential Steve screw-ups by talking to her myself.

"Earth to Cait!" Dede leaned across the table, waving a teapot wildly in front of my face. "Are you in there?"

I stuck my foot out until it made sharp contact with her shin.

"Angie!" I mouthed, trying to jerk my head subtly toward the red-haired woman. Dede's own head whipped around as she stared, wide-mouthed, at her.

"Be discreet," I hissed. I have to call Steve, I thought, then remembered he'd told me he was "on assignment" for the next couple of nights, trying to win over his boss with a good story before his suspension hearing. I opened my bag and fished out my address book, certain I'd copied his pager number down. But it was too late. Angie had leaned across her table and was looking right at me. Her eyebrows were raised as if she knew me and was waiting for me to say something.

"It's too late," I told Dede, stuffing my address book back in my purse. "She's seen us staring at her." I stood up slowly.

Janet looked even more puzzled than usual. "You're performing, Cait? Seriously?" she asked.

I ignored her and walked across the room as quickly as possible, feeling as if I was, in fact, on stage. Angie's eyes followed my maneuvers around the tightly packed tables. I could be a match for her, I told myself. I could cause trouble. I was up for the task. Sure, she was gorgeous, worldly, and no doubt gutsier than I'd ever be. I could also be strong, confident, ballsy. Before my brain could argue this resolution, I pulled up a chair at her table and sat down.

"Are you Angie?" I began.

"Why?" Her eyes had narrowed and her chin was set at an angle that made her look like an angry gargoyle. Her nose really did have a mean hook to it. I made a mental note to ask Steve why he found her so attractive.

"I think you know my friend Steve." I moved my shaking hands under the table.

"That little geek?" She wrinkled her nose and giggled.

"Did you know Steve is probably going to lose his job because of you?"

"Well, it takes two, honey. Steve wasn't exactly putting up a fight, if you know what I mean."

"What *do* you mean?" I asked. But I knew Steve well enough to guess.

"He thought he was using me for a story. Guess I showed him who was using who." She giggled again. "I've been asked enough questions already. Stupid cops. Stupider reporters. My daughter is smarter than he is and she's only five. You can tell Steve to stop looking for me. I'm going away. He'd better leave me alone, or I'll be there to disgrace him wherever he goes."

"You've been talking to the cops?" Ed had mentioned that Angie had a daughter, but I had blocked out my mental picture of Angie towing around a tot in a matching animal-print coat.

"Yeah. You know cops. They think I know something. Well, I may know a lot, but I ain't telling them."

"Do you come here often?" I asked. It was too much of a coincidence that she had turned up.

"I know you think you're a writer, a female Bukowski. I knew where to find you. I think it's hilarious," she continued. "All these people think they're so radical. As if any of this is real art, or has anything to do with real life." She sneered as she reached for her coat.

"Living on the edge in Kitsilano," I agreed. She had a good point about the coffee-house crowd.

"I came here to invite you to a party." She stopped putting on her coat while she waited for an answer. I knew I should say no. Ron and Ed had both warned me, after all. This was probably exactly the sort of situation they had in mind when they told me not to get involved. But who were they to tell me what to do? If I played it safe the rest of my life, I would never have the answers I was looking for, and I would never write a good story. With my heart in my throat, I smiled at Angie and nodded.

"Sure, I'll go. Can I bring my friends?" I gestured to Dede and Janet, who were both watching me intently.

"Lesbian folksingers?" Angie's nose wrinkled again. "Why

not? Could be good for another laugh." She reached into her purse and pulled out a pen and some paper.

"Meet you here. If anyone asks, I invited you. No hurry. I'll be there a long time." She winked at me, then sashayed out. When she reached the door, she turned and waved. I looked down at the paper. In round, loopy handwriting she had written a location I was beginning to know well: the Western Rose Hotel.

Janet was not impressed. It took some persuasion, but eventually she picked up her bag and agreed to go.

"If anything looks the slightest bit weird, I mean the slightest, eensiest, tiniest bit off kilter," she insisted as we got into the car, "if there's anyone who could be a pimp, even someone in a leather jacket, I'm out of there. Gone. Disappeared. AWOL."

"You've made yourself pretty clear, Janet." My voice was dry. "I'm glad to hear those Urban Women Warriors are teaching you to hold your own."

She sighed loudly in response to my joke, then settled slowly into the back seat.

"It's not as though I want to be there if there's any trouble," I said. "Of course we'll leave if this party looks strange. Just nod your head toward the door and we'll be out of there before you can say 'paranoid women.'"

"Very funny."

"Think of the Urban Women Warriors," I reminded her. "You can tell your next meeting about your evening on the town. It will be sure to get their ire up."

"Shut up," Dede said from behind the steering wheel. "You have to admit, you're a little nervous, too."

"Of course I am," I agreed. Angie was rapidly becoming my favorite murder suspect. I had been warned to stay away from anything to do with the murders. Kate Whyte knew something about the murders, and she was missing. Why wouldn't I be nervous? When wasn't I nervous these days, after all?

Angie's note had specified the basement. She'd even pointed out that the stairs were beside the front desk. After we entered the main door, the three of us stood in the lobby, looking apprehensively at the descending stairwell.

"This is it." I tried to sound brave, if only for the sake of Janet, who seemed to be cowering in a corner.

"Maybe we should have told someone else where we were going," she piped up. "Something could happen to us and nobody would have a clue where we were."

"There are three of us, Janet. Just think of the safety in numbers. Dede will protect you. You'll be safe." I wasn't used to being the brave one. Janet's fear reminded me enough of myself to be really annoying.

I was proud of my brave words, but I didn't exactly bust the door down when we reached the bottom of the stairs. Instead, I stood and stared at the fading red paint on the door for several seconds. With a deep breath, I raised a fist and tapped. A couple of seconds later, the door creaked open and a ghostlike face looked out. Beside the red door, the face was unnaturally pale, with flesh like rice paper cut by thick black brows. I would not have been able to place a bet on the gender. The features were delicate, evenly shaped, and without makeup. The head, completely hairless, motioned us in. By the time the three of us were inside, the door-person was only a black shadow flitting down the hall.

"Weird," Janet whispered. I looked at Dede, wondering what to do next. She responded with a shrug, then turned down the hall.

"Hey." A soft voice greeted us as we entered a small kitchen. "Glad you could make it." I smiled at Angie, who was sitting on the kitchen counter, wearing a black silk dressing gown. She looked as though she had just stepped out of the shower. Seated at a round oak table were the androgen and two long-haired males, both leaning back in their chairs and smoking.

"This is the party?" Dee asked.

"Most of the action is in the other room," Angie said. "We're just taking a bit of a break."

"Pretty quiet?" I said, my voice rising in a question.

"Must be a slow period." She looked at the two men and smirked. "You guys know what's going on right now?"

They both looked at her and shrugged. For a few minutes the kitchen was quiet as everyone examined each other with questioning eyes.

The awkward silence was broken by a piercing scream. Beside me, Dede and Janet jumped several feet, then looked around nervously. I was wondering how to get them to relax, to look less like they'd just walked in from the backwoods, when a series of screams exploded from somewhere in the house. As they rose in timbre, it quickly became obvious that the screamer was not in pain. In fact, the shrieks were nearing an ecstatic, orgasmic crescendo. Between the passionate outbursts, we could hear panting, moaning, and a low male voice whispering commands.

I froze. I shouldn't have been surprised, of course. I suspected Angie was involved in the porn industry, and from the start her invitation was attached to an ulterior motive. I looked over at her. She was leaning forward on the kitchen counter and staring at me.

"Why are we here?" I asked her. "You know I'm a reporter. The three of us don't look like potential porn stars. What are you thinking?"

She smiled without showing her teeth. Her eyes remained locked with mine. "I thought Vancouver should know what goes on behind closed doors."

"You don't want me to write a story about this?" I remembered Ed Nelson's warning. Angie obviously had another motive, other than titillating me with a glimpse at the adult film scene.

"There's a story here," she said.

"There's nothing unusual about making pornographic movies. They've gone pretty mainstream in the city."

"That depends what's in the movie. Or who's in the movie." She had a strange smile as she spoke, almost sad, slightly disturbed.

"I have to say," I looked around the tiny kitchen, "I had heard there was big money in the business. I would have thought your studios would have been in a more upscale neighborhood."

"Nobody bugs you over here," she answered. "Any cop who walks this street isn't going to care what we're doing when there's so much more going on outside."

"If there really is anything strange, how do you know we won't call the cops?"

"What would you say? You haven't seen anything yet, have you? Some woman having loud sex in the next room is hardly a criminal offense. Making movies isn't illegal, either, last time I checked."

"Why am I here?" I just wanted a straight answer. "I know you want me to write about something, but what?"

"You're the right reporter. I thought Steve could do it, but he's too hung up on sex. You can see other sides to the story."

"Angie," I began. "Nobody reads the *News*."

"I know. I've got a plan that will let you kiss the *News* good-bye. Trust me, there's a story here that will make your career. I know you're anxious for better things. Most reporters would kill to be on the brink of this." She looked at Dede and Janet with undisguised disdain.

"But why the *News*? Why not a bigger paper? Steve isn't the only other reporter in town."

"Quit questioning, Cait. Think of this as your big break."

"Like you gave Steve his big break?" What was she trying to pull on me?

"Just ask yourself the right questions," she told me.

I shook my head.

She laughed. "It's not even the right questions, so much as the right math."

"I have to go to the bathroom," I told her, wondering if she'd let me leave so I could look around a bit.

"Down the hall," she pointed with her chin, a small smile on her lips. "Don't get lost."

The bathroom was just a few steps down the gold-carpeted hall. I paused outside the open door, looking at the other three closed doors in the hall. All I had to do was open one of those doors and I would see exactly what was going on. I took a careful step toward the closest one, my arm extended toward the doorknob. Just silently open it, I told myself, don't let them hear you coming.

"Bathroom's over here."

I jumped about ten feet in the air, turning to look at the corpse-like presence that had let us in. Judging from the high, soft voice, it was, in fact, a woman.

"Oh! Thanks!" I feigned gratitude, then ducked in.

I sat on the toilet with my chin in my hands. I couldn't hear anything happening across the hall. Reaching behind me, I flushed the toilet, in case the riddle in the hall was listening. I stood up, adjusted my skirt, and grabbed some toilet paper to blow my nose. Taking a deep breath, I tossed the used tissue in the wicker garbage basket beside the toilet, then hesitated. Under a pile of wadded white tissue, I could see the corner of a receipt. I made a mental note to remember to wash my hands before I left the bathroom, then plunged my right hand through the used tissue. My hand surfaced with a wadded piece of bright pink paper.

"Hot Pink Video," read the text imprinted on the top. "Meeting all your adult video needs." The store was one of many dodgy-looking establishments lining the south end of Granville. No doubt they had dealings with this suite. I stuck the paper in my jacket pocket, rinsed off my hands, and slowly opened the door.

When I came out, the same unearthly face was staring at me from across the hall. Under that watchful gaze, I dutifully returned to the kitchen. Dede and Janet were hunched over the *Vancouver Sun*, reading the comics as if they were going to be tested on them in thirty seconds.

"Find it okay?" Angie asked with a taunting voice. I looked toward her, my eyes narrowed in what I hoped was a menacing look. We stared at each other, locked in a strange battle of wills. There were heavy footsteps coming down the stairs. Before I could blink, Angie's eyes flickered with fear.

"You have to go," she whispered. "They weren't supposed to show up. Get out—quickly."

We looked around, but there was no way out of the basement suite except by going back up the stairs. The front door of the suite slammed.

"What's up?" A deep male voice called out. The voice sounded familiar. I looked at Dede and Janet, but they both had their heads buried in the comics, sneaking occasional nervous glances around the room.

"Angie?" A man stepped into the room.

I inhaled with shock. It was the man with the ripped jacket, the man who had pulled out a knife on me and Steve only the day before. He turned quickly to me, then to Angie.

"What's she doing her? I told you to keep her away. This isn't what we talked about." He stepped towards her and reached out for her arm.

"Rick, I know what I'm doing," she whispered.

"Oh right. I'm sure you do. I feel so much better." The sarcasm that cut through his voice was eclipsed only by the anger. He gripped her wrist tightly and twisted her arm behind her back. "What the hell were you thinking? You know what her story is."

"I just wanted to show her some of Vancouver's darker side, Rick. Mellow out. She hasn't seen anything."

"I haven't seen a thing," I agreed. Suddenly I was so frightened for Angie that I forgot about myself. "I don't really think there's a story here, though. I mean, everyone can get into the porn business now, thanks to the Internet. I could go home and make a movie myself. That is, if I had a date." Nerves were forcing me to make lame jokes. "I don't know why I was invited here."

"Shut up," Rick spat at me.

"We've just been sitting in the kitchen," Dede piped up. Her voice was surprisingly firm. "None of us have a clue why Angie invited us. Janet and I are opposed to pornography on principle, but all we've done is read the paper."

Rick dropped Angie's arm.

"Now what are we going to do?" He put both hands on her shoulders and started to shake. "They're here and we can't let them go."

I had to give Angie credit. She remained calm through Rick's verbal assault and didn't seem to be bothered by the shaking. She just kept looking directly into his eyes with the same small smile on her face.

"Don't be ridiculous, Rick. Let the poor things go. There's nothing going on here that we have to hide. Nothing wrong with filming a little video, last I heard."

Rick's hands fell to his sides and he nodded at me curtly.

"Get the hell out of here. You and your friends. You can write about the porn industry in Vancouver if you want, but without an interview or any eyewitness account, you've got a pretty dull story. And if you ask me, you media types have written enough about the industry. It's old hat."

"Don't forget, she writes for the *News*. If they find a story, it would be on what kind of food you have catered—is it local?" Dede said as she stood up. "Hey," she laughed when I glared at her, "just trying to lighten the mood."

The braver half of me wanted to stay and find out more but the weaker half won. I shuffled to the door with Dede and Janet.

"We'll talk," Angie whispered, then practically pushed me out down the hallway.

Once we were safely returned to Dede's car, the three of us sat in silence for several minutes. Then Dede exploded.

"What the hell?" she demanded. "That was the weirdest thing that ever happened to me. Who are those people? They're screwed, man. Pardon the pun. Seriously, Cait, you have to go to the police. Not about whatever those fruit loops are doing in that hotel. I guess that's their own business, but because I think they may actually want to hurt you."

"Hurt me? They have no reason to hurt me. I'm just a reporter with some rag no one reads." But maybe they did have a reason to hurt me. The picture Kate Whyte had shown me was burned on my memory. Shelly Bennett made porn movies. She was killed. Kate Whyte knew about the movies. She was missing. Claudia may have also been involved in pornography somehow. She was killed.

I understood Steve's fascination with the red-headed woman. She was teasing us with information, but she hadn't given us nearly enough. She wanted me to figure something out, but I couldn't guess what it was. I kicked the front seat in frustration. I should have asked more questions. What sort of reporter was I? This story was turning into an obsession, but when I was face to face with a key source, I didn't ask any questions.

"Do you think they killed those girls?" Dede was following the same line of thought.

"I don't know. Probably not. I don't think Angie would talk to us if she had. She couldn't be that daring. I'm pretty sure she knows who did, though."

"And she wants you to find out. I think she's setting you up to find the killer."

"Or she wants you as her third victim," Janet blurted out, her voice shrill from tension. "For God's sake, Cait, go to the police."

"No—wait," I interrupted Janet. "She said it wasn't so much a matter of asking the right questions as doing the right math."

"Made about as much sense as everything she said," Janet said.

"Maybe she means doing the math to figure out their ages—the people in the movies, I mean."

Kate Whyte had told me about Shelly recruiting teenage girls at the bus station. It was obvious that something in their movies wasn't entirely legit. And how else could math be linked to pornographic movies? I could see counting being a factor in certain plots, but not math.

"Let's just go home," I told Dede. "I need to think."

"Are you nuts? You're not going home alone. You're staying at my place."

"Dede, you're overreacting. A strange woman invited me to a home video taping. There's nothing dangerous about that, is there?"

"If there's nothing dangerous, why was that creep so mad at her? Obviously, she was taking a risk, and you were about to find out something when he appeared. You've had a rough day, hon. Stay with me. I know you, you'll never sleep otherwise."

She had me there. Two things I knew for sure: I wouldn't be able to sleep and Dede was determined to mother me. Sure enough, twenty minutes later, I was curled up on her couch, afghan around my knees, cat on my lap, herbal tea warming my belly. Dede had gone to bed, after many assurances that I would be fine alone. I was trying to organize a possible chronology of everything I knew about Claudia and Shelly. Somehow, things had gotten too complicated since I had decided to investigate Pete Lloyd as a suspect on my own. It had seemed so cut and dried when I was poking around the Lloyds' house, looking for something obvious, like a bloody knife. If I'd known about the pornography, the threats, and who knows what else, I would have written the kind of story May wanted and returned to covering the first daffodils appearing in Stanley Park.

I picked up Dede's phone.

"Steve? Sorry to wake you. I had to talk."

"Whyte? It's the middle of the damn night. What's up? Is it a story?" The grogginess left his voice when he realized I may have something for him.

"Sort of," I said. "But not for you. You're going to be my sounding board."

"You woke me up to bounce story ideas off of my sleeping brain? Good luck!"

"I spent some time with Angie tonight."

"Angie? You've talked to Angie? What's up?"

I told him about my evening, trying not to let personal panic cloud my objectivity. When I finished, he exhaled loudly.

"Heavy stuff, Cait. I've got to tell you, that's the same way I got in with her."

"She told you she knew something, dangled a story under your nose, gave thinly veiled bribery hints?"

"She invited me to a party, not at a hotel, but a house in New Westminster. I could tell there was some strange stuff going on there, but I couldn't find out more. I told the police about it after this whole thing came down, but when they went out there, there was nothing strange at all. In fact, the house was empty."

"But why does she invite us?" I asked. "What's in it for her?"

"I assumed it was my sexual magnetism, but you . . . well, maybe she swings both ways."

"Steve, this is serious." I should have known better than to expect help from him. "I think they're making movies with underaged girls. I think we need to call the police. I think that's the story she wants us to write. I think she's trying to tell us there's a story there. But why not go to the police? And why target me, of all people, reporter for the city's least-read newspaper?"

"Maybe our stories were the best," Steve suggested.

"Steve, do you think I'm in danger? I mean, I don't want to sound melodramatic or anything, but those women were murdered. Kate Whyte is missing."

I certainly felt melodramatic, confessing my fears, even though I was exposing only the tiny tip of my iceberg of worries.

There was silence on the other end of the phone.

"I'm serious, Steve."

"Sorry, Cait." His voice was gentle. "Hey, do you want me to come over? You don't sound too great."

"I'm at Dede's place." I had to sniff back tears—always a charming sound on the other end of the phone line.

"I'll come over anyway, as long as you can guarantee Dede won't chase me away. We should talk in person."

After he hung up, I sat stroking Dede's cat in her silent apartment. I felt oddly numb, as though my brain had been prepared for surgery.

Steve tapped quietly on the door when he arrived, but he must have woken Dede anyway. She entered the living room just as he sat down. For once she didn't spice him, just flashed a sleepy-eyed but friendly smile.

"How ya doing, pumpkin?" She started to pat my head, but I ducked.

"I'm not dead yet, you guys. Wipe those serious looks off your faces."

"We're just concerned. We don't like to see you as a possible target." Dede flashed a look at Steve.

"I'm fine. I'm just confused," I said.

"It must be a bit frightening, being threatened and all. I'd be nervous and I've been around the block," Dede said.

"I can handle it. I've been around some blocks of my own." I took a big breath. My hands were shaking and I couldn't breathe properly. I tried to say something else, but my voice caught. I was going to tell them. I was prepared to break the code of silence. I tried to speak again, but choked when I opened my mouth. I closed my eyes, then the words appeared.

"I was raped."

That's all I managed to say. I was afraid if I continued, my heart would burst from beating so fast and I wouldn't be able to breathe and I would faint or I would babble like an idiot. My declarative sentence just sat in the middle of the floor, like the cat. It must have sounded strange, out of context, unexplained, as we sat there contemplating the day's events in murder and pornography.

Dede acted first. In the blink of a tear, she crossed the room and hugged my shoulders tight.

"Sweetie, it's okay to cry," she whispered. "Are you going to be okay? Let's get you to a hospital."

"No, silly, it didn't happen tonight." I had to smile. "It happened when I was fourteen. I don't know why I'm telling you this now."

"You're under stress." Steve had crossed the room to sit beside me. "All this talk about murder and danger probably gives you flashbacks."

"I just don't want you guys to think I can't handle what's going on now. I've been through a lot for a small-town girl."

Steve grimaced. "Sorry, Cait. You know I was just giving you a hard time."

"Do you want to talk about it?" Dede asked.

How could I ever make them see what happened? Steve and Dede were leaning out of their seats, foreheads creased with concern. They both loved me, I knew, in their way, and would try to understand. It had been a hard night. I leaned back in my chair and shook my head.

"I don't think I can talk about it right now. But another time. I appreciate what you guys are doing for me. No one else ever listened to me. Of course, that could be because I didn't bother to tell them."

Dede grinned. "Silly girl. You have to be more like me. I've never been shy about expressing myself, letting mounds of garbage and shit and emotions just dump on out of me."

I smiled, then looked at Steve. "Steve, thanks for coming over. I hope all this talk about Angie hasn't upset you. I'm sure she really did like you."

"She's one mixed-up woman," Dede interjected. "Steve, you can do a lot better."

I stood up. Someone had to make the first move to split this up before it turned into a group hug.

"I should go to sleep. I'll be fine in my own place, Dee. I feel better, and I'll get a better sleep in my own bed. But if you hear any mysterious noises, come running to my rescue." I was only half joking.

Dede stood up and hugged me. "Take care," she whispered in my ear.

Steve followed me out the door. He grabbed my elbow as soon as Dede's door clicked shut.

"You sure you're okay alone?"

I nodded.

"I can stay with you if you're not comfortable."

I shook my head.

He kissed me lightly, then left.

Was that a pass? was the last thing to cross my mind before I fell asleep.

Chapter
Eighteen

SATURDAY MORNING, I WOKE with a pounding headache. Instinctively, I began berating myself for drinking too much the night before, but then I remembered my evening. No wonder I felt like a dirty sock. In a mere twenty-four hours, I had been grossed out in the ravine, spent time at a pornography studio, and talked with all my heart for the first time. Really, I deserved to be served waffles and whipped cream in bed, at the very least. Ideally, the morning would begin with waffles, strawberries, whipped cream, a sensitive man, and a story with my byline about the killer's arrest, maybe picked up by the *Globe and Mail*. Thinking about work reminded me I had to call Derek and run my child pornography theory past him. In the meantime, though, the weekend was mine, and there was no reason, after everything that had happened last night, that I couldn't make it a crime-free zone.

I stretched and glanced out the window. The curtain that

I had erected around my bed to give my studio apartment the appearance of a one-bedroom created a cozy sunlit cocoon. I couldn't think of any reason to leave.

Half an hour later, I was woken from semi-slumber by a knock on my door. I checked the clock—too early for Dede—then rolled out of bed and pulled on my housecoat.

"Cait Whyte?" a deep voice on the other side inquired. "Does Cait Whyte live here?"

Too much had happened yesterday for a glib answer and quick door-opening. I considered not answering at all, but I had to draw the line between caution and paranoia before I was unable to leave the house at all.

"Who is it?" I asked.

"Flower delivery," the deep voice replied.

My mother sends flowers every Valentine's day, but that's about the only time my one crystal vase sees any action. Curiosity definitely got the better of caution and I opened the door.

A bouquet of pale pink roses hit my face, almost blinding me with surprise and thorns. I stepped back to get a complete picture: at least a dozen roses, pink like babies, hid a short delivery boy.

"Ma'am, could you grab these?" a voice from behind the pink and green asked with strained politeness.

Could I? I reached across and whisked them away, closing the door behind me. Were they from Pete, in response to our dancing kiss the other night? From Derek, recognizing the stress I was under and looking forward to future coffee dates? Or from Paolo, determined to prove he knew how to woo a woman, despite his behavior yesterday? Placing the roses on my table, I opened the card.

"Sorry about yesterday. I guess my emotions got the better of my good judgment. Is a man allowed to be inappropriate in grief?" Inappropriate in grief—the phrase hinted that there was a touch of the poet about poor Paolo. My concern about his behavior yesterday was fading to a pale shade of pink. It was almost more than I could bear early in the morning. I sighed and thrust my face into the sweet garden on my table.

I knew I would hear from Dede as soon as she woke up. At exactly eleven o'clock, a knock on my door confirmed my prediction. Excited that I could share something other than horror stories from my past and our new acquaintance with the underground film industry, I jumped to the door to let her in. For a split second, we stared at each other. Her eyes still held the concern I had seen the night before when I exhaled the first tentative, painful words of my story. I looked at the floor for a moment. She was still in shock, I told myself. She had thought she knew everything about me and I surprised her by revealing something she'd never expected me to say, considering all her jokes about my allegedly protected upbringing. Soon, she'll remember that I'm the same person I've always been and everything will be back to normal.

"How ya doing?" she asked with forced nonchalance. "You haven't heard from our red-headed friend, have you? Haven't made any plans to explore Vancouver's sordid underbelly?"

I shook my head, then nodded at my table, where the roses were posing prettily in my newly dusted vase. "I've actually been looking at nicer things," I smiled. "From nicer people."

"Which of your many suitors sent those?" She ran over and picked up the card. With the lack of concern for privacy that can only exist between best friends, she read it quickly.

"So, Cait, I hope this doesn't get him off the hook. You see what he's trying to do? Charm you into forgetting his creepy behavior. I think you should cross out his name and write Derek or Pete instead. That way you could enjoy them without remembering that whole scene."

"Dede, don't be so cynical," I protested. "He made a mistake. I'm cool with it. I can only imagine the stress he's under. Like you said—sex and death go together. And haven't you ever done something that made you want to kick yourself afterwards?"

"Ooh, yeah! But I kicked myself. I didn't buy the offended party some flowers and write a schmaltzy note."

"I didn't think it was schmaltzy."

"You wouldn't. Next time I annoy you, I'll remember to call the florist."

"Dee, you're just jealous. How is Janet, by the way? She doesn't seem like the flowers type to me." I regretted the nasty words the minute they left my mouth, but it was too late. Dede wrinkled her nose and stared at me silently.

"I mean," I backtracked, "she seems very intelligent and interesting, but I wasn't exactly impressed with the urban warrior courage last night."

"It's not her scene, Cait. I like her. A lot. You know what? I have to go." With that, she was out of my apartment. I wanted to say something as she walked through the door, something almost apologetic and almost reconciliatory. Just because Janet didn't seem like the sort of woman to buy flowers for her lover was no reason to flaunt my own bouquet to Dede. Maybe I was a little defensive. I made a mental note to talk to her and make amends.

In the meantime, I had some reading to do. All the stress of the last few days had me craving a little R&R on my couch with a good book, maybe some music in the background, and a mug of mint tea by my side. I was going to call Paolo, but I decided to make him wait. I didn't want to look too grateful for the flowers. I wanted him to know that I hadn't completely forgotten what happened in the ravine. Maybe my silence was the sort of game that thin, pink paperbacks advise women to play, but I never said I was above a little feminine strategizing. In the meantime, I was ready to stretch out on the couch. I assumed the prone position and picked up my book. This was what life was all about, not hanging out in porn studios, obsessing over murder victims, fighting with editors, and carrying shaming secrets. Life should be filled with pleasure, I decided, as I got up to fill a bowl with ice cream. I needed more pleasures, both of the flesh and the mind, and lying in the sun reading and eating ice cream with the scent of roses beside me was the perfect way to indulge myself. And, for once, I had some possible volunteers to share other pleasures with.

I had just finished my ice cream when the phone rang. I didn't want to interrupt my celebration of the decadent, but it could have been Paolo, speaking of sharing pleasure. Or Derek or Pete. Just because Paolo had given me flowers didn't mean I had forgotten about them. Or the phone could have been Dede, apologizing and inviting me out for an early glass of wine.

"Hello?" I answered, softly just in case it was Paolo.

"Cait Whyte?" The voice was so low, I could barely hear my name.

"Yes?" I sat as still as possible, waiting for the next words.

"Cait, I think you'd better stay away from the Western Rose," the voice on the other end whispered. "You won't go snooping around if you really like that little girl you've been spending time with."

"I was invited," I said. It felt strange to argue with an anonymous call, but I wanted to make my case. "Angie invited me."

"Well, if you come back, both you and her will be in trouble. And if you go to the cops, you'll have that little girl to worry about, won't you?"

"What do you mean? I'm not going to write anything about last night. And who told you about a little girl?" I was careful not to say Ally's name.

"Sometimes you think you're alone, but you're not. And sometimes you think someone is your friend, and they're not." There was a firm click at the other end.

I sat back on the couch that only moments ago had been a peaceful refuge. How could they know about Ally? The thought of anyone watching her made me sick to my stomach. I looked up at my door to check the deadbolt.

Although the voice didn't sound familiar, I would place a

substantial bet that it was Rick, or at least someone being prompted by him. I went over my visit with Angie, but I didn't see how I had set myself up for trouble. We hadn't been in the hotel very long, no pictures had been taken, and we'd barely talked to anyone other than Angie herself. I wondered briefly if I should call Derek at home. There was one thing I had to do before anything else, though.

Pete sounded surprised to hear my voice. "Cait, we were just talking about you. Ally said you're her favorite sitter."

"I'm honored," I answered. "How is she?"

"Actually, she's sick. I have a couple of weeks of sick time booked, though, so I'm staying at home with the Muffin. Tell the truth, it's kind of fun to spend an entire day with her."

"Is it serious?"

"She'll need another few days at home, at least."

That was exactly what I wanted to hear. Ally was home under Pete's care for a few days. Thank God. That gave me a little leeway to find out if there really was a threat to her safety.

"So." Pete paused. I realized he had no idea why his babysitter had called out of the blue.

"I just wanted to see if you wanted to see a movie or something one day," I said. Ordinarily, I would never ask a man out, not because of any outdated notion of gender roles, but because I was far too shy. Compared to telling Pete the real reason I had called, however, asking him for a date was easy.

"I'd love to." He sounded excited. "But you're my babysitter—what about old Ally?"

"I was thinking of a children's movie," I answered, although I usually don't like kids' movies.

"I really appreciate the time you spent with us, Cait. And I'm glad you didn't get upset by my clumsy behavior the other night. I wouldn't have blamed you if you'd hauled off and decked me."

"I thought it was nice." I was getting downright brazen with men.

"Well, you're certainly my favorite sitter, as well. But are you sure you want to do this? I have to admit, I'm a bit of a train wreck these days. You seem too together to hang out with a down-and-out single dad like me."

"Any friend of Ally's is a friend of mine." I laughed. "I have to check my work schedule, though. I'll call in a couple of days, okay?"

"You know what, Cait? I'm going to work on finding another sitter. That way we can see a movie with real people, not cartoon characters. I'll bring someone in over the next couple of days to break them in."

"Don't worry," I said quickly. I didn't want to be replaced as the babysitter of choice. "I really don't mind a kids' movie."

I hung up with satisfaction. I had confirmed Ally's temporary safety, and I had made a date. The roses looked a bit affronted, but I hadn't made any firm commitments to Paolo, had I?

Still, an hour later I called Paolo and left a message on his machine, gushing shamelessly about the flowers, as if I'd forgotten every magazine article I'd read advising me to play it cool. I was glad he wasn't home, though. After all I had been through the day before, I wasn't too keen to leave the building.

Chapter Nineteen

SOMEONE WAS IN MY ROOM. I gasped and fought at the covers, my heart pounding. Someone was breathing, panting, screaming at me. I sat bolt upright, arms extended straight in front of me. Daylight surprised me. Had I somehow slept through the night? I glanced at the clock. 9:10. It was Monday already. I was late for work. I picked up the phone and dialed May's number.

"May Lee," she barked at the other end.

"May, it's Cait. I'm feeling pretty sick. I think I'd better stay home."

"Home?" she repeated, voice thick with disapproval. "Sick? You've been sick a few times recently."

"I think I have the flu. I just can't shake it," I clarified, then I hesitated. Her disappointment was palpable. "Well, maybe I'll take an aspirin and come in, anyways. If I don't feel better, I'll go home."

"You're sure, now?" May sounded relieved.

"I'll be about half an hour."

I didn't want to spend the day alone, going over the weekend in my weary brain and conjuring up all sorts of intrigue in my overtaxed imagination. I could only begin to imagine what I could brew up. Sex slaves. Snuff films. Lying in the ravine while a camera whirred in front of me, recording my last painful moments. Instead of fixating on these possibilities, I could spend the day with bureaucratic phone calls, dull articles, and a nagging May. As part of my affirmative action plan, I was going to call Derek and explain my theory about underage porn participants in the Western Rose. Excitement about making that call was what finally got my butt moving into the office. Imagine, I thought on the bus, if I gave Derek a few tips and the whole studio was busted right away.

"A notorious black-market porn dealer, Cait," he would congratulate me. "Way outside the bounds of the law. We nailed them, thanks to you. That'll make quite a story."

Real life, of course, was anticlimactic. As soon as I arrived at work, I spent ten minutes looking for my phone book. It wasn't in my bag, where I usually kept it. I had a momentary panic; I felt lost without the tiny, black leather-bound volume filled with numbers of people I'd met since my mom gave it to me on my tenth birthday, but I couldn't waste precious time searching for it. Figuring I must have left it by my phone at home, I dialed the central switchboard of the cop shop and asked to be transferred to Derek's office.

Ron answered the line and told me in his nasal drawl that Derek was out doing an interview. Was there anything he could do?

I hesitated. I wanted to share my discovery with the cops, but I had definitely gone against their orders to stay away from trouble. I remembered the expression on Claudia's face in the picture I'd seen and plunged in.

"Well," I began, "I'm concerned that there may be some underage pornography being made. I was at a ... friend's place yesterday and she implied that some young actresses were taking part."

"I'm not sure I understand," Ron answered, and I didn't blame him. That had to be one of my weakest efforts of late.

"Do you remember Angie, the woman with the tip about the Sabato and Bennett murders that turned out to be a DUI arrest?" I was going to have to be more forthright, even if it got me in trouble. "I was at her place last night. I know—I shouldn't have. Just skip the lecture and hear me out first. I know you know she has some links to the sex trade, but she hinted that she knows about an underage porn ring."

"I'm still not following you, Ms Whyte. How did she hint, exactly?"

"Well, she said I would find a story in the basement of the Western Rose Hotel, if I could do the math." Suddenly, my theory sounded completely implausible. "There's a studio in the basement of the hotel. I'm not sure it's legit."

"I'll see what I can do, but it's all a bit vague, frankly. Steve already sent us on a goose chase in New Westminster, but at this point, we have to check out every tip. I'll get back to you later today. You going to be in the office?"

"Working hard. Thanks a lot, Ron. And can you pass this all to Derek?"

"Anything to further Derek's cause with you."

I was giggling when I hung up the phone. Maybe Ron wasn't so bad, after all. I turned to the pile of memos sitting on my desk, waiting for my attention. I had worked for about an hour when Hannah slipped into my office and left a note on my desk. It was from May.

"Suspect named in Sabato murder. See me immediately." I jumped from my chair. For once, my feet didn't drag into May's office.

"May, I just got your memo. What happened?"

"Apparently they have a suspect. They've brought in someone Claudia babysat for."

"You're kidding?" Events had taken me so far away from

the babysitting theory that I couldn't believe my initial suspicions were being confirmed.

"Guy in Burnaby. No record. Nice guy, or so everyone thought."

I sat back in my chair and let this information register. The news was oddly anticlimactic. I was right all along, despite my recent adventures. Kate, Angie, the men who were following me, porn movies, all had nothing to do with the case. Instead, the story was mundane: a young girl had been working for a predatory older male.

May told me to go to the press conference later that afternoon. I should have been happy that she was allowing me to go, after all we'd been through on this story, but my enthusiasm was dampened. Perhaps I didn't really want to hear the details.

As usual, the phone jolted me out of my thoughts.

"Whyte! Steve here," a more-than-familiar voice barked in my ear.

"Hi, Steve," I replied softly. I felt shy. I had recently revealed my innermost secrets to him, after all.

"Did you hear?" he asked.

"Yeah. How much do you know?"

"Not much. He's just a suspect right now, but they've taken him into custody. I don't know what the evidence is. His kid's at the station. Little girl."

"Poor thing," I shuddered, picturing a tiny child surrounded by burly cops. A little girl, like Ally.

Ally.

"Steve, you don't know this guy's name, do you?" Every muscle in my body tensed in anticipation of his response.

"Let me check.... Lloyd. Peter Edward Lloyd."

I almost dropped the receiver.

"No way. I know him. I've babysat for him. He ... I just can't see it. He's a nice guy."

"That's what they said about Ted Bundy, Cait," Steve paused. "You'll have a good story—babysitting for a killer. I'll bet you'll win an award."

I couldn't miss the jealousy in his voice. Poor Steve. If only he'd had the chance to work for a murderer instead of sleeping with a prostitute.

"Steve, I've got to go. I'm kinda shook up."

"Cait, you call me if you want to talk."

I had to admit the concern in his voice touched me. He hadn't forgotten our talk, even with the excitement of the day's arrest.

"Thanks, Steve. You're a good friend." That was as emotional a talk as the two of us were capable of having.

"Cait!" As soon as I hung up, Hannah burst into my cubicle. "The police are here to see you. They have some questions about the guy they've arrested."

They must have found out I babysat for Pete. Closing my eyes for a split second, I walked out into the lobby. Ron was sprawled out on a chair, pointedly ignoring the No Smoking sign. Beside him, Derek was perched on the end of a chair, looking as if he wanted to take off and fly out of the room. As soon as he saw me, a curtain of scarlet rose up to his ears.

"Cait! I asked to come down here with Ron. You must be a bit shaken up." He caught himself. "If you've heard ...?"

I nodded. "I thought you were out," I said. I was too confused to deal with misinformation.

"Ron was just covering for me. I was busy. Sorry." He looked a bit sheepish for a fraction of a second, then serious again.

"So, you know Pete Lloyd," Ron began, his pen poised above his notebook.

"I babysat for him a couple of times. I find it hard to believe he's a killer." I looked at Derek for some sort of confirmation, but he was looking resolutely at the floor.

"We have something we'd like you to see down at the station. Can you come with us?" Derek was talking to his shoes.

"Sure." I wanted to ask more, but the formal tone that the conversation seemed to have acquired muzzled me. I had no choice but to follow them obediently. All I was missing was handcuffs.

When we arrived at the station, Derek took my arm as I climbed out of the back seat. His hand remained on my elbow and we made our way to an office. Was he just being supportive or did he really think I needed help? I looked closely at him. He didn't give me any clues. For the first time since I'd known him, he wasn't wearing his emotions on his face.

"Have a seat," Ron gestured to a chair under one of Derek's seascapes, then he walked out of the room, leaving Derek and me facing each other in heavy silence. I smiled, then pointed to the painting hanging over me.

"Nice," was all I managed to say. He smiled in return, but didn't take his eyes off the rug until Ron returned.

"I want you to tell me if you've seen this before." Ron placed a small, ziplocked, plastic bag on the desk. I leaned forward. Trapped in the plastic, innocently unaware of its implications, was my missing address book.

I could only nod.

"Does it belong to you?" Ron asked.

I nodded again.

"Where did you last see it?"

"I ... don't remember where I saw it last. I thought I'd lost it. Where did you find it?"

"We can't say," Derek said, speaking for the first time. I knew, though, where it must have come from. I thought back to my trips to the Lloyd house. No matter how minutely I replayed each evening, I couldn't remember taking it out of my purse. I couldn't think of any reason why I would need to look up a phone number. I had called Dede once, but I knew her number better than my own.

"I don't think I would have left it at Pete's," I said.

Ron put another bag on the table. The bag was empty except for a small piece of bright blue paper. I could read it through the bag: *Babysitting. 555-9462.*

"You recognize that piece of paper?" Ron asked.

"I think that's the paper I used to copy down his number. Where did you find that?"

"It was in the book," Derek volunteered.

I shook my head, trying to remember if I'd ever put the number in my phone book. I did have a habit of stuffing addresses, business cards, and other potentially useful scraps of paper between the pages.

"Sorry," I told the two cops, "I'm in a bit of a state of shock. What made you arrest him?"

"An anonymous tip to Crimestoppers. Made on a pay phone," Derek said. "We follow up on all of them. We're releasing the necessary information to the public. It would help us a lot if we could find out who made the call."

"The caller said Lloyd had a new victim lined up," Ron said. "He'd seen your book in Lloyd's house, plus a bunch of your stories. Whoever called figured Lloyd had an eye on you. Of course, he denies it."

"That's not enough to arrest him," I said.

"More incriminating evidence was found in his house," Ron said. "Directly linking him. A knife. A picture of the Sabato girl, topless."

"Just like the one you saw," Derek added, although I already knew.

I closed my eyes, numb, remembering the picture of Claudia, trying to imagine it in Pete's house, a house I mistrusted initially until Pete and Ally's charm convinced me their home didn't contain anything more sinister than dustballs. How was it possible?

"Obviously, we have a lot to learn. Lloyd is denying everything. He says he's never laid eyes on either of them, that the evidence was planted. You're his main babysitter, he says. He had a girl on Sunday morning, but we can't trace her. He didn't have her number, doesn't know her last name." Ron smirked a brief second. "You'd think he'd screen his sitters better. The world's a dangerous place. All he could tell us was that she had red hair."

"Red hair?" I asked with disbelief. "Not a *tall* redhead, by any chance?"

Derek thumbed through his notebook. "Yeah," he said slowly. "What made you ask?"

"The woman who Steve slept with, the one you'd questioned, she's a tall redhead."

"I don't think she's done any babysitting recently," Ron said.

"I've been babysitting, remember? It's not just teenaged girls any more. Maybe she wanted to babysit so she could frame him. Show Pete her picture, see if she's the one." I was overcome with guilt: Pete had been trying to find a new sitter so we could go to a movie. But how did he find Angie? Or did she find him?

Derek made a note in his book, but I could tell he was skeptical. "We'll bring her back in, ask a few questions, see if she has an alibi. Ron sent someone down to the Western Rose as soon as you called with that possible porn tip this morning, but she wasn't anywhere to be seen."

"There was nothing even resembling a porn studio, either," Ron added. "We'll have to file your tip away at this point. Didn't really lead anywhere."

"Kate Whyte did resurface, however," Derek said. "We looked all over the city, without luck, but we kept an eye on the pub where she works. One day, she just showed up. She told us she needed a break, but wouldn't say anything else about where she'd been or what she'd done. Swore up and down she's never heard of this guy, though, of course, she can't guarantee that he isn't Shelly's mystery boyfriend. She's one of the most closed-mouth witnesses we've ever seen. Wasn't very helpful when we tried to get to the bottom of that photo, either."

Kate was out of danger. That was the one piece of good news for the day. I had a hundred questions to ask her, as soon as I escaped the clutches of the police. Of course, she knew that I betrayed her trust and probably would never talk to me again, but the important thing was that she was still alive.

"We're asking this Lloyd character about a possible porn

connection, but since we have no physical evidence, the info we have from you and Steve is just hearsay," Ron said.

"I know there's a studio," I said, although I was starting to question it myself. I hadn't seen a thing, after all. "Where's Ally?" I asked.

"Lloyd's sister is up here to help with her. She lives in Calgary. She's a busy woman, or so she keeps telling us. Defends her brother like some sort of lioness, but she seems more than a tad resentful of the inconvenience of her niece."

I felt a small twinge for Ally.

"Could I take her?" I blurted out. "I'll look after her."

"Cait," Derek said gently. "Don't be ridiculous. I hate to say this, but you're one of our key witnesses against Lloyd. You can hardly babysit his kid."

"But I don't know anything." It was true. I certainly didn't know anything that would link her father to the murders. I may have suspected him at first, but that was only because he was looking for a sitter. I still didn't think anyone that gentle with his daughter could be a killer, no matter how damning the evidence.

"What about Shelly?" I asked. "Is he a suspect for her murder, as well?"

"We're looking into that," Derek said. "He's not saying anything, of course."

"We'll be talking," Ron said. "In the meantime, I assume you know that we have to talk to your editor again."

I nodded numbly. May will love this, I thought. I'm a witness in a story she somehow knew I would be too involved in. How would I explain the babysitting? Should I remind her I was underpaid at the *News*?

"We'll talk soon, Cait," Derek said with a smile. Despite myself I smiled back. We were still friends, after all. The day before, he had dropped in my standings after I had received the flowers from Paolo and made a date with Pete. Now, unknown to him, half his competition had been virtually eliminated with Pete's arrest.

He handed me the phone. "Can you call your editor and ask her to come to the lobby?"

I wondered why he couldn't make the call himself, but I couldn't argue with him. Slowly, I dialed her personal line.

"May, there are a couple of cops who want to talk to you," I said.

She sighed. I could picture her looking up from her screen. "Unpaid parking tickets?" she asked.

"Work related," I said, then left it at that. "And you know, I'm not feeling so well after all. Is it okay if I go back home?"

I handed the phone to Derek. He was staring at me, but I kept my eyes on the floor. I walked out of the lobby and over to the elevator. I could hear Derek introducing himself to my boss over the phone. Her slim back would straighten as she listened, her lips becoming more and more pursed as she discovered my acquaintance with Pete Lloyd. She wouldn't be such a coward, I thought. She would come clean right away. She would stick around and face the music afterwards, unlike me. Shaking my head at my own cowardice, I walked out of the station and into the glare of a tauntingly sunny day. I hesitated at the bus stop, not sure where to go. I'll get on whatever bus comes first, I decided. I'll leave it to chance.

Chapter Twenty

ALMOST EVERY BUS ENDS UP DOWNTOWN. I stood at the corner of Granville and Robson, fingering my keys and watching a parade of groaning buses creep past me. I listed the possibilities: I could go to Surrey and cruise around Guilford Mall; or I could go out to the ferry terminal and board the boat to Victoria; Burnaby was another possibility.

Another plan crossed my mind: I could go to their deli and talk to the Sabatos. That's what a real reporter would be doing right now, I told myself, getting the family's reaction to the arrest. I wondered what Paolo was up to, if he'd heard about Pete Lloyd. If I were a real reporter, I would be on the phone with the family that very minute, probing their most private emotions with a mixture of aggression and forced sensitivity.

Maybe I wasn't cut out for journalism, after all.

The bus to the Lougheed Mall pulled up beside me. I pictured myself wandering the mall, trying on sleazy clothes, maybe, or madly buying a new set of dishes, then eating in the food fair. Or drinking in the Bear Pub, just across the street.

I hopped on just as the bus inched away from the curb. Standing like a drunken surfer as the crowded bus jolted its way east, I tried to rehearse a prepared story for Kate. I knew so much more than the last time I'd made the trip, but I still needed information. Should I just ask her: did Pete Lloyd kill Claudia and Shelly? Who is Angie, anyways, and what does she want with me and Steve? If she tried to frame Ed Nelson, was she also capable of framing Pete Lloyd? And you, Kate, I wanted to ask more than anything, how do you feel safe in this world? Did you run away to feel safer? Is it easier when nobody knows where you are?

The bus arrived at the Bear Pub stop before I was ready. I walked into the McDonald's beside the pub and ordered a milkshake. To my surprise the shake acted like a salve on my suddenly starving body. I'd almost forgotten the smooth, slightly salty sweetness. This is what I've been missing, I thought: junk food. I ordered another, drank it quickly, then forced my sugar-laden body off the chair and out on the street.

Inside the bar, I spotted Kate right away. She was sitting at a table, smoking a cigarette with her eyes closed, as if she had to concentrate to master the inhale-exhale motion. She was wearing a faded cotton baby-doll dress, which made her look somehow both younger and older than the last time I'd seen her. Her hair was tied back, but the strands that had escaped to stick out all over her head were frayed, uneven, and the color of overly sweet lemonade. I looked down at my plaid jumper and clogs and touched my newly trendy hair. Our names may be almost the same, but we would certainly never be mistaken for one another. Still, I felt an affinity with her, as if only my loving family and my opportunity to go to college separated our destinies. I was afraid to approach her, since I had betrayed her trust. If the cops had talked to her, they would have asked about the photo. If she refused to talk to me, I wouldn't blame her. In fact, if she chased me out of the pub with a broken beer bottle, I would understand.

She opened her eyes as I sat down at a table at the other end of the bar. Her brows furrowed together as she walked towards me and sat down across the table.

"Hi, Cait. What brings you out here?"

"I heard you were back at work," I answered. "Where were you? Everyone here seemed worried."

"Somebody told me I should lie low for a while. Somebody who knows who to be afraid of. He said I should stay away from certain people and make sure they can't find me, that they might try to frame me for Claudia's and Shelly's murders. So I spent a day or two cowering. I was thinking of quitting and starting over in another city, maybe Halifax. Then I remembered I'm not a quitter, that I'm in control, that I like my job, and some paranoid warning from a total nutcase shouldn't take that away from me."

"Who warned you?" I asked. "Somebody has been warning me to stay away from certain people, too."

"Someone from the movie industry," she said. "A world I thought I was finished with."

"His name wasn't Ed, was it?" I remembered Ed saying he had worked in the movies. "Ed Nelson? I'd like to talk to him some more."

A strange look passed over her face. "I would forget about Ed. He did move, practically disappeared after warning me. Ed has been frightened of his own shadow since this all went down, even though he talks a good game. That's the thing about men in the business—they're cowards. That's one reason they get into it—they're too scared for normal relationships. I guess I just decided I can be stronger than Ed."

"Ed warned me, too," I said, remembering the fear in his eyes when we talked outside the hair salon. "He told me to stay away from anything to do with the murder, including you."

"You know the police had a tip on him, don't you? Somebody tried to frame him. He said these people were trying to pin the murder on someone else. He had no actual evidence that they had done it, though, and he didn't want to work with the police to find some. Ed doesn't exactly get along with the police," Kate said. "I think he figured he should get the hell out since he obviously had enemies somewhere. I wonder if he's heard they've arrested someone."

"You didn't know the guy they've got?" I asked.

She shook her head. "I've been over this with the cops. I never heard the name and I've never seen the face in the photo they showed me. I really don't know anything. Why can't everyone leave me alone?"

"I know him," I told her. "He's a really nice guy. He has a little girl and he's the sweetest dad I've ever seen. He's lonely and struggling after his wife left him, but he's always cheerful and loving with her."

I watched her closely. As I spoke, a deep trench began to form between her brows, and she started chewing on her lower lip. Her eyes didn't meet mine as I continued. I may not have had any police training, but her body language screamed out that she was hiding something and that my words were disturbing to her.

"You don't know anything that could help him, do you? I really don't think that he did it."

Kate leaned across the table and spoke in a low voice. "Cait," she said. "Are you good at keeping secrets?"

"Yes," I said with the steadiest voice I could manage. "I suppose I am."

"I am, too. Too good, maybe, know what I mean?"

I nodded, thinking suddenly of my own confining silence. "There are some things I should have told people a long time ago," I said.

Kate's eyes searched my face. "Me, too, I suppose." She sighed and leaned back in her chair. "I can't believe I'm having this conversation," she said, looking around the sparsely populated bar. "And at work." She shook her head in disbelief, then took a deep breath and spoke again. "No, I don't know who killed Shelly. But I do know some stuff they don't."

"Why not tell them?" I asked. Of course, I thought, I was in no position to be self-righteous. I'd also withheld information from the police, after all. "If Pete didn't do it, he deserves the truth."

"Too, too. . . ." She looked around the bar as if the right word was written on the walls. "Too complicated."

I waited for her to continue.

"I'll get your drink" were her next words. She got up and walked around the bar, taking orders from the few customers, then returned with a very tall gin and tonic. I stirred the lime around vigorously while we sat in silence.

"Shelly was involved in pornography. You know that. Nothing wrong with that. She needed money. I thought it was better than hooking, myself. But some other people were involved. Not very nice people. That boyfriend, whoever he was. He made her do things that were totally out of character. Not like herself. It's possible. . . ." Her voice trailed off.

"What sort of people?" I asked. "People who would have framed my friend Steve? Maybe framed Pete Lloyd?"

"Have you ever . . . been caught on a cycle of something you can't stop?" She looked at me, waiting for an answer. Clearly, this was not a rhetorical question.

"Sure," I nodded.

"Like what? You have no idea what Shelly went through."

"I don't," I admitted. "But I've done some things I'm not proud of."

"Just a sec," Kate interrupted me with a lifted finger, then pushed herself off her chair. "I'm going to tell Ray I'm taking a break."

While she was gone, I stared into my glass and stirred the lime some more, as if its swirling motion contained a message that would tell me what to do next. I needed a sign from some sort of barroom god. If messages could appear in tea leaves, why couldn't some simple instructions write themselves in lime juice across my gin and tonic?

"No problem." Kate took her seat, a tall glass of Coke in her hand. "So, go on. You've screwed up yourself? Made some mistakes?"

"I guess so." I shook my head. "I'm a coward at heart. A wimp. And you know just how much of a wimp?"

She shook her head. I took a deep breath and plunged in. These still felt like uncharted waters, but I had to gain her trust.

"When I was fourteen, I was raped. I was babysitting for him. He told me not to tell anyone and I didn't. But do you know what?"

She shook her head again, a slight smile warming her face. I took the smile as a sympathetic gesture, took a sip of my drink, wished it could anesthetize the turmoil inside me, and continued.

"He did it again. Raped a fifteen-year-old he'd also hired to babysit. I hated myself." I shuddered slightly, then banged my drink down so hard the lime almost jumped out with the spray of crystal-clear gin and tonic.

"I hated myself," I repeated. "She went to court, pressed charges, he went to jail. But cowardly me, I still didn't tell anyone I was also raped. Not for years. Not until just a couple of nights ago."

"That's not your fault." Kate was wiping my sticky splashes of gin and tonic off the table with her napkin. "It was his fault. He was a creep. Most men are."

"I know a lot who aren't. One's even a cop."

"Yeah, right," Kate scoffed. "Shelly could have told you a couple of things about cops."

"She knew a lot of cops?" I asked.

"Honey, we all do. Nothing lowers your respect for those guys like working in the sex industry."

"You know, Kate," I began, "I've lost many nights of sleep

lying awake, staring at my ceiling, wishing I'd gone to the police and told them everything I knew."

"My break is over. It's been nice talking to you." She began walking away.

I exhaled in frustration. I'd tried to win her trust by laying my heart bare, but I could take a hint. And the speed with which she was walking away made it a pretty strong hint.

"Call me if you want to talk," I said to her back. She stopped and turned to face me.

"Cait, it wasn't your fault that girl was raped. And it's not your fault Claudia and Shelly were murdered. Get over it. You can't do anything. You can't change the world and you can't turn back the clock."

I nodded silently, then finished my drink and left. I had told her everything, but I didn't feel any better.

Now May knows about my connection with Pete Lloyd, I thought on the bus back downtown. *She knows and probably wants to talk to me. Now is my chance to prove I can be brave by going back and meeting what was sure to be a one-woman inquisition. I could prove my courage, if only to myself, by facing May.*

Instead, I did something either stronger or weaker. I went to a porn video store.

The Hot Pink Video receipt I found in the washroom in the Western Rose was still in my purse. I was in the neighborhood. After telling Kate how I wished I had taken action all those years ago, I could hardly walk right past it.

The young guy at the counter was engrossed in a magazine. I stood in front of him for almost a minute, staring at the angry pimples exploding on his pale forehead, before he realized I was watching him.

"Yeah?" he asked, folding the magazine cover to hide an unearthly-looking pair of breasts.

"Do you have anything local?" I asked. "You know, made in Vancouver?"

His eyes turned to scan the bright red shelves lining the

room. Wielding the rolled-up magazine like a weapon of self-defence, he left the counter and came back with four or five brightly colored boxes.

"I think these are made here," he said. "You looking for someone you know?"

"Not really." I didn't offer any more information, just turned over a copy of some sort of twisted version of *Leave It to Beaver*. Shelly's name didn't appear in the credits, though I was learning enough about the industry to know she probably didn't use her real name.

"I know the guy who produced these." His chest puffed slightly. "Comes in here all the time."

"Are they good?" I asked, although I had no idea what sort of esthetic criteria informed a blue movie.

He looked pensive for a split second. "Run of the mill, really. Nothing special." He leaned forward and dropped his voice to a whisper. "I can get their other stuff. Too hard core to sell here, but we do give it to people sort of under the counter, if you know what I mean. It's way cooler."

Half of me didn't want any more information. I didn't need to know what this pimply-faced boy's idea of "cooler" sexuality was. I felt grungy enough. But I had already spoken some difficult sentences that day and I was in too deep to be squeamish.

"What about snuff films?" I asked, feeling a warm blush creep up my neck.

His recoil was instantaneous. In the blink of an eye, he was three feet further away from me, magazine clutched to his chest.

"*That's* sick," he exclaimed. "We don't got none of that."

I clutched my tapes awkwardly to my chest, my face flaming, my mouth sputtering weak words. "I don't. . . . I didn't. . . . You don't. . . . "

"Are you a cop?" His voice hardened. I shook my head. A stupid grin inexplicably appeared on my face.

"You don't seem like one," he said. "But you don't seem like someone who would ask for that stuff, either."

"I'm not into that stuff." I flung the tapes on the counter for emphasis. "I was just wondering if it exists in Vancouver."

He lowered his voice again, although I was the only customer in the store.

"There's a rumor about some guys making some sick stuff. I don't know if it's true. Someone offered to sell us some once. Too twisted for me."

I nodded. "You don't remember who, do you? Or what they looked like? Was it underaged stuff?"

He eyed me again. "You sure you're not a cop? Not that we do anything illegal here."

"I'm concerned about a friend." I smiled in what I hoped was a friendly manner, then asked another question. "Who makes those kind of films?"

He shrugged his slim shoulders. "Creeps. Obviously."

"Is there underaged porn made here, from what you've heard?" I was careful not to imply that he either sold it or watched it.

"I'm sure it's everywhere," he answered. "There are weirdos in every city."

"Well, thanks for your help." I started to walk towards the door.

"Don't you want the tapes?" he yelled after me.

I turned around and stared at the pile waiting for me on the dusty counter. Hours of screening pornographic videos didn't exactly appeal to me, but there was a chance, I supposed, I could see something that would help me out. Perhaps one of them contained a picture of Claudia, a picture that would somehow link the high school student to the pornographic world and explain the picture I had seen. It was a long shot, but I didn't plan to go back to work for the rest of the day, anyway.

"Sure," I said as I handed over some identifying information and a twenty-dollar bill.

"Don't you have a bag?" I asked sheepishly.

He smiled, then popped them into a brown paper bag.

"Good luck with whatever," he said as I left the second time.

Chapter
Twenty-One

TWO HOURS LATER, I HAD SEEN ALL the naked bodies I could stomach. They were all very attractive, but flesh loses its appeal after the tenth naked bum, no matter how firm and well-shaped.

Whatever local entrepreneur had made the videos was operating on a low budget. The lighting was too bright, the camera bobbed up and down, and the sound was fuzzy, not that the dialogue required close attention. I hadn't seen either Claudia or Shelly among the pale, vacant-eyed actors. Frustrated, I turned the television to *Jeopardy*.

I had just settled in when the phone rang. It was Derek.

"I'm just checking up on you," he said with his usual cheeriness.

"Thanks. I'm doing fine. How was your day?"

"Annoying. We spent it with Mr. Lloyd. Uncooperative doesn't even begin to describe him. He insists he was framed.

He's adamant someone planted all the evidence in his house. We're looking for the babysitter he had the other night, but, frankly, we're not sure where to begin. He only got her first name, Brenda. We haven't been able to track down this Angie woman at all. We've got some people on it, though. I can't believe that people leave their kids with total strangers. Speaking of babysitters, we may need you in tomorrow to ask you some more questions."

"What sort?"

"Well, for starters, did you ever leave anything in his house? Beside your address book, I mean."

"To be perfectly honest," I said, "I really don't remember leaving it there."

"Well, either way, you're probably going to be called in tomorrow. Sorry, but you are a key witness."

"Of course I'll cooperate." I've kept enough secrets from the cops, I thought. First my own rape, and now a whole narrative of intrigue. It was hard to believe that I had had the nerve to tell Kate that she should confess everything she knew to the police.

"Have you told the Sabatos?" I asked Derek.

"Yeah," he answered. "And it's a good thing the brother can't get near our man, I'll tell you. He's talking about doing some damage. Not that I blame him, I suppose. If you really had been his next victim, I'd want to do the same. We're still looking for the porn connection to all this, though. Lloyd claims he can't stand pornography, wouldn't go near it, but after you told us about that picture of the Sabato girl, we have to pursue that angle with him. Too bad your Western Rose tip didn't pan out. Anyways, when this is all over, let's go to a movie. A regular movie, PG at worst."

He said it so naturally that I agreed without thinking. Only after I'd hung up and returned to *Jeopardy* did I realize I may have moved Derek to the top of the suitor sweepstakes. Should I have told him that I was seeing someone else? It seemed disloyal to make a date with Derek when Paolo had just sent me flowers.

I awoke the next morning in the hug of my sheets. Stretching out and clutching my pillow, I considered staying in bed for another hour. I could phone the office and tell them I was working on a story. Then I remembered I had to face May.

She was in a meeting when I arrived at work. Hannah handed me some messages as I walked through the door. She treated me exactly as she did every other morning, so I began to relax. No point in getting upset until the boss shows up, I reasoned, then settled down to return some calls.

I was doodling on the back of my dictionary, trying to decide if I should call Paolo, when May walked in to my cubicle. Quickly, I slapped my hand on top of the heart I had drawn with his name in it. She already knew that I had babysat for the killer, but she didn't need to know I was nurturing a crush on the brother of one of the victims.

"May!" I exclaimed in an overly high voice. "You surprised me."

"I'll bet." She raised her eyebrows. "Let's go for coffee. You know we need to talk."

Staring at my clunky feet, I followed my boss's spiked heels out of the building, across the street, and into a tiny coffee shop. We were both silent the entire way. I didn't know what she was thinking, but my mind produced a dozen possible scripts, each ending with me being fired.

As I'd anticipated, May spoke as soon as we sat down.

"Cait, why didn't you tell me you were sitting for Pete Lloyd? A murder suspect? You realize that I'm tempted to suspend you. Working on dangerous stories without my approval is against our policy. Not to mention downright stupid."

"He wasn't a suspect when I babysat for him," I said. "He wasn't until someone phoned in a tip to Crimestoppers. And I wasn't babysitting because I wanted to write a story about it. I just saw an ad and thought I'd respond. It was all a coincidence."

"Do you have any idea who phoned in the tip?" May was looking at me carefully.

"It wasn't me!" I was so surprised by her silent suggestion that I sprang back in my chair as if she'd struck me. "They said it was a man."

"Did you suspect him?" May said.

"Not after I met him," I said.

"You don't find it too much of a coincidence that you ended up at the suspect's house by answering a random ad? You, a reporter who had written about the story?"

I paused. "I pretty much figured there was no way he could have killed anyone. He's a really nice guy, great with his daughter, a musician, funny...." I realized as I listed off his virtues that I hadn't entirely given up on Pete.

"Strange." May seemed to be searching for words. "I trust your instincts about people, Cait. You're usually correct. But your error in judgment—so unlike you—almost cost you your life."

"He wouldn't have killed me," I said. I knew I was right.

"But he'd marked your address book. He'd drawn maps of your daily routine. Obviously he was following you."

I looked up at May.

"Following me...." My voice trailed off as I reviewed the events of the last couple of weeks. I *had* been followed. I had been followed on my way home from Pete's, in fact, by Rick. He knew about Ally, so clearly he wasn't just frequenting the same bus routes. He had seen us in the park. I leaned forward until my face was inches away from May's. Although we were the only people in the cafe, I dropped my voice to a whisper.

"I think I *have* been followed." Quickly I told her how nervous I'd been every time. "I thought I was just being paranoid. You know, I'm a naturally suspicious person. But now I know."

"You've got to trust your instincts," May said. "If you were nervous, there probably was a threat. But you never felt anything around this Lloyd guy?"

"I wondered, sure. You know me. I thought about it a lot. And decided he was safe. Guess my woman's intuition was taking a holiday."

May shook her head. "Something's weird. Go over your steps. Did you tell him very much about yourself? Where did you last see your address book?"

"I don't remember." I tried to think. I have a pretty good memory for phone numbers, so I don't consult it very often. I also use it for e-mail addresses and pager numbers. Pager numbers. Of course—I'd taken it out at the Flying Goat as soon as I spotted Angie, when I was trying to decide if I should page Steve.

"Wait." I sat up straight and grabbed May's arm. "I had it the other night. At a coffee house. And I haven't been to Pete's since."

"You're sure?" she asked, excitement raising her voice, as well. It felt as though we were brainstorming a story idea together, using each other's ideas as fuel for our own as we powered towards the culmination of an article.

"Positive. I took it out to call Steve, but then. . . ." I stopped myself from telling her about my visit with Angie, but my mind continued to race. I'd stuffed it in the top of my purse, then left to go to Angie's "party." I had taken it out at the Flying Goat, so she may have seen it. When I was at the hotel, I had left my purse in the kitchen when I went to the bathroom. Why didn't I think of this before?

I stood up, slapping some coins on the table. "I'm going to call the cops. I think I know what's happened."

"Cait." May stood up and followed me outside. For once, she was the one having trouble keeping up. "Cait, you're still in hot water with me. We have to talk about the fact that you didn't consult with me, that you went against company policy. I'm still tempted to suspend you."

Her voice continued behind me, but I was deaf to her complaints. I was right, I repeated to myself. He's not a killer. He must have been set up. I couldn't wait to talk to Derek, to tell him they were questioning the wrong man, that it was a woman who held the key.

Of course, Ron answered Derek's number. I tried to swallow my disappointment when he said Derek was out of the office again. Sharing a revelation with a self-important, sexist cop just wouldn't be the same. Still, I was on a mission. Picturing Ally, puzzled and scared with her indifferent aunt, I launched into my story.

"Ron, I just thought of something, something important." I took a breath to slow myself down. "I couldn't have left my address book at the Lloyds'. I remembered where I saw it last."

"Slow down there, Cait," Ron interrupted. "You're sure about this? You are a key witness, remember?"

He'd told me I was a key witness about twelve times. Didn't he trust me?

"I know. I have a good memory, Ron." I tried not to sound too impatient.

"We're about to have a meeting on the case. I'll bring this up. We'll give you a call back, arrange a time for you to come in, probably this afternoon." With that, he hung up, leaving me staring at my phone, oddly unfulfilled. Ron wasn't as excited by my announcement as I'd anticipated. I resolved to try again soon, in case Derek returned. At least he'd have the good manners to feign enthusiasm.

I looked around my cubicle. A stack of notes littered my desk. I had e-mail to answer and interviews to set up. It would, I realized, take all the self-discipline I possessed to get even a fraction of my jobs done. I wanted to call Dede and share my thoughts about the address book with her. I had to ask her if she'd noticed Angie snooping around my purse. It seemed obvious that she had lifted it while I was in the bathroom, but how had she done it without arousing Dede's suspicions? I also wanted to call Paolo, but the awkwardness of our last meeting kept me from picking up the phone.

He beat me to it. After an hour of sludging through routine stories, I checked my answering machine at home, hoping that Derek had left a message there instead of phoning me at work. To my delight, I was greeted by Paolo's darkly sexy voice.

"Cait," he began. "Paolo here. Guess you've heard the news. They finally caught the bastard. When I heard, I thought of you immediately. I was wondering if you wanted to go out and celebrate with a drink tomorrow night. At the Four Seasons. I promise I won't try anything inappropriate again. But I'm in the mood to celebrate and want to share it with you."

My heart melted into a puddle on the floor. He wanted to share it with *me*. He'd thought of *me*. He wanted to go to the Four Seasons with the woman who'd helped him through what had to be the worst period of his life: me. All the uncertainty and doubts that had sprouted during our last meeting disappeared in a cloudburst of happy lust. With a warm heart, I listened to my next message.

"Cait, it's Mom." My mom never calls during the day. My ears went on instant alert. "Your father's had some chest pains this week. It's nothing serious, don't worry, he didn't have a heart attack." I breathed a sigh of relief as my own heart slowed down from the jumpstart of her first words.

"But," she continued, "the doctors wanted to do some tests. Just to make sure he's in good shape. We have an appointment with a cardiologist in Vancouver the day after tomorrow. We were wondering if we could stay with you tomorrow night. Just one night. We'll try not to be any trouble. You just do your own thing, pretend we're not there. We love you, sweetie. Don't worry about your father."

Just what I needed—a visit from my parents. I had to convince the police Pete Lloyd was innocent, I was in trouble at work, I had a date with a man I was seriously lusting after, and I had to decide if he was the one I really wanted. And now I would have to fit in some quality time with my parents. They would feign understanding, of course, if I just breezed through my apartment every so often, blowing them kisses and tossing out affectionate words. My parents hated to trouble me. But they had given me life, so I couldn't really ignore them in good conscience. With a surreptitious look at May's office door, I dialed Paolo's number. I got his machine. He'd changed his message since the first time I'd tentatively dialed him, hoping for a quote about his sister.

"I'm not in" was all his answering machine message said, the words followed by several musical-sounding beeps. Judging by the number of beeps, there were a lot of other messages on his machine. Perhaps he'd called me from somewhere else.

"Paolo," I said. "It's Cait. I'd love to go out. But it would be better if we could do it another time. My parents are coming into town tomorrow. Hope you're well."

I hung up, wishing I could rewind my banal message. "I'd love to go out," indeed. What about playing hard to get? Not too subtle, I told myself. I wondered if my unplanned enthusiasm on the phone was a sign that I had decided to focus my interest on Paolo.

I settled back and looked at the blank screen of my computer terminal. Its grayness mocked me and drove home my slow productivity. I flicked on the monitor and typed a couple of words. I should try to call the police again, I thought, and force them to listen to my theory about the address book, but I wanted to ask Dede if she noticed anything suspicious while I was in the bathroom. Also, I had to admit that it was strange to be trying to set Pete free when I had just made a date with Paolo to celebrate his arrest. It was hard work, liking three different men connected to the same case.

"Date, tonight?" I entered into my computer, then added a row of question marks. The words looked bold on the screen. "To celebrate?" I added. "Celebrate what?" I tacked on. Paolo had made no secret of the fact that he wanted to celebrate Pete Lloyd's arrest. But I wanted to spend the rest of the afternoon proving Pete's innocence. I hadn't considered how I would explain this to Paolo. I couldn't lie to him, but could I tell him I might have information that could effectively lead his family back to square one in catching Claudia's killer?

"How's that garbage disposal story coming?" It was May again. I started out of my chair and quickly paged down.

"Fine," I squeaked, convinced that guilt was written all over my face.

"Cait," she said, "some good work on your regular stories could help redeem you and maybe save your job."

I returned to the garbage disposal story for a couple of hours, made the requisite phone calls, and fit all my information into a nice, neat pyramid. It was a classic article, just the sort of thing I'd learned in journalism school, although any high school graduate with a cellular phone could pull it off.

I bounced out of the office into almost opaque sheets of rain. Leaning into the wind, I boarded the bus for home. Although the weather had turned quickly, it didn't bother me at all. Perhaps, I thought, there will be a message from Paolo. He'll want to come over. He'll be damp and cold from the rain, so I'll fix him a cup of tea. No, I'll pour him a whiskey. Afraid to venture out into the storm again, we'll order pizza and curl up on my couch to watch some television.

I cut the fantasy off at this point. Don't go any further, I warned myself, until you have a message from the man, outlining a definite plan. Maybe he wants to spend the day celebrating with his family, instead of with some reporter he's only met a few times. I concentrated on the unrelenting sameness of the gray buildings against the gray sky as the bus sped down Broadway. The monotony was meditative.

By the time the bus pulled up at Commercial, I was almost asleep.

The wind was funneling right through an open window in my apartment. A shower of raindrops blew in, spraying a pile of magazines on my couch. I picked up a damp copy of *Harper's* and shook it. I should have known better than to leave a window open in February. I walked into the kitchen to get a rag. On the way, I pressed the Play button on my answering machine, not even allowing myself to check for the blinking red light.

"Cait, it's Dede," the machine began, the exuberance of my neighbor's voice diluted through the tinny speaker. "Janet and I are going to a rally tonight. It's an anti-pornography demonstration. You know that adult video store, Hot Pink Video? It was broken into. The Warriors didn't do it. Honest! But we're picketing outside to lend our support to whoever did and get some attention while the store's in the news. Call me."

I didn't quite follow the logic, but I had to admit, I didn't really understand anything about the Urban Women Warriors. The machine beeped its agreement, and switched voices.

"Cait, it's Paolo. I just got your message. How about tonight instead? Does eight o'clock sound good? The Four Seasons? I'll pick you up."

I did a little jig in my kitchen, waving my kitchen rag over my head.

"What do you know?" I said to the blinking machine. "I have a date."

"Cait," the next message began. "Derek here. I have to ask you some questions about the address book."

I rewound the tape and picked up the phone. I was going to call Dede first, but as soon as I began dialing, I decided I'd rather see her in person.

I might have thought twice about my in-person visit if I'd known Janet was in Dede's apartment. Dede's "political" friend was seated at the kitchen table when I let myself in. She was reading a thick pile of papers, studiously making notes in the margins. She barely looked up as I entered.

"Cait," she said, eyes on the pile of papers. "Why don't you come with us tonight? You might learn something about violence against women."

Oh thanks, I thought. I know absolutely nothing about that.

"I have a date." I couldn't keep the enthusiasm out of my voice.

"What's this?" Dede walked into the kitchen from the bathroom, the smile on her face a mile wide. "Who's the lucky winner?"

"Paolo," I said. "Wanting to celebrate the arrest of Pete Lloyd."

"You're into that?" Dede asked. "Celebrating with that pervert? After what happened in the ravine?"

"I don't know. I guess it's a bit embarrassing, but I still kind of, you know, like him. . . ." I smiled as I finished, hoping to add a bit of charm to what had to be a lame excuse.

"Cait, he's a creep. Remember, he got turned on in the ravine where his sister's body was found. Talk about issues. And what about this Pete Lloyd thing? Do you think he did it? I thought you liked him. Can you really celebrate his arrest with the victim's brother? Great taste in men, Cait, by the way. One gets excited where his sister was found and it looks as if the other killed her."

I flinched under the questioning.

"I don't know. . . ." I began again. "I guess . . . I really don't know why, but I want to see Paolo tonight."

"Lust," Janet said from the table without looking up. "You find him so attractive, you're willing to overlook all his flaws. Women do that all the time around men. That's why men get away with so much."

"Like you've never done that with a woman, you hypocrite." Dede bopped her playfully on the head. "You know you're not immune to a little sex appeal, either. You're dating me, aren't you?"

Janet continued to read, ignoring Dede.

"But you know where my real doubts are," I continued as if Janet wasn't in the room. "I really don't think Pete Lloyd did it. It's not just that I kind of liked him." I outlined my brainstorming session with May. Dede listened carefully, then furrowed her brow.

"I don't remember Angie going through your purse," she said. "But I was watching the hall the whole time. I wanted to make sure you weren't going to do anything stupid, like decide to investigate what we were being forced to listen to."

"Plus, we were reading the paper. Remember?" Janet spoke up without moving her eyes from the pile of papers. "We were scared senseless, so we huddled over it. But I do think I saw her move Cait's purse."

"When?" I asked, wanting to force her to look at me.

"When you were in the bathroom," she continued. "You'd left it on the kitchen table. As you were walking away, she picked it up and moved it to the counter. I didn't see her open it, though."

"But she could have," Dede interrupted. "She moved your purse to a spot where we couldn't watch it."

"I'm sure she took it," I said. "Somehow, she must have planted the address book in Pete Lloyd's house."

"But why him?" Janet said, apparently intent on never actually meeting my eye. "Do they know each other?"

"I doubt it," I said. "He's pretty lonely, for one. And he doesn't really seem the type."

"You never know with men," Janet warned, as Dede shot her a look of impatience.

"He does have an ex-wife. There may be some conflict with her."

"Maybe Angie is Ally's mother." Dede jumped off her chair, raising her fists in the air triumphantly. "We've got it!"

"No way." Even my imagination didn't buy it. "Too much

of a coincidence. Someone that sounds like her babysat for him Saturday night, though. I think it's pretty obvious that she planted the address book—she stole it, after all."

"Don't knock coincidence," Dede said. "That's where my money goes."

"I'm talking to the police tomorrow," I said. "I'll bounce your theory off them. I have to admit I'm skeptical."

"Why don't you come with us tonight, Cait?" Janet asked for the second time. "It's going to be an interesting rally."

"What exactly is going on tonight?" I directed the question to Dede, not the ironically challenged Janet.

"That disgusting video store downtown was broken into. Someone smashed the windows and made off with a stack of videos. No cash."

"Probably some pervert," Janet piped up. "Not willing to pay for his yayas."

"Why are you picketing? Shouldn't you be celebrating?"

"Just to make a point," Janet said. "While the store is in the news. Hopefully, we can drag it out of business."

I still didn't really understand. It seemed like a show of support for the thief, a person the group had already decided was just a creep, sitting at home, wanking off to his own private collection. But I didn't understand their thoughts on pornography in the first place.

"I just rented a couple of tapes from there," I said. I said it just to bug Janet, but, in fact, I hadn't got around to returning them yet. They were sitting, forgotten, near my door. I wasn't too eager to continue watching, based on what I'd already seen. I made a mental note to return them as soon as Janet's friends ceased picketing.

"No!" Dede laughed. "You actually have videos? Bring them up. We can watch them for inspiration."

Janet finally looked up from her reading to shoot her friend a withering look. "We are *not* viewing any videos. They make me sick," she announced in a firm voice, then she returned to the stack of papers.

"Well, maybe I'll look at some to get me in the mood for my date. I have a good half hour to kill." I smirked at Dede. It wasn't the sort of humor I usually buy into, but Janet was bringing out the worst in me.

"Have fun," Janet said in a perfectly deadpan voice.

"You too," I said. "I hope the rally goes well." I grinned at Dede as I left. She smiled weakly back, then rolled her eyes.

"I'll call you tomorrow," she said. "Have a fun date."

I picked up the tapes as I walked through my door. I turned each one over to read the titles, then decided on one I hadn't seen before, called *Teacher's Pet*, and popped it into my machine. Annoying or not, Janet had given me something to think about. I didn't have a well-defined stance on pornography. As a journalist, I was a supporter of freedom of speech and everyone's right to express themselves. I could even, on a good day, understand some of the attraction, but what Kate had said about Shelly recruiting young girls at the bus station made me wonder about the ethics of the industry. While there were, I knew, plenty of production companies that made legitimate pornography with ready and willing participants, all signs pointed to suspicious practices involving young women by the group that Shelly had worked for. Although all I had seen so far was a lot of anatomy, I still hoped there might be a clue somewhere in the videos: the appearance of Claudia, perhaps, or a sign from Shelly.

I pressed the Play button on my remote, then fast-forwarded past a tedious set-up sequence involving private school girls, school uniforms, and lecherous teachers. Why these things pretended having a plot was beyond me.

Soon, though, all pretense of plot vanished in a series of naked couplings, then triplings. I was fast-forwarding through a gym shower scene when I caught a glimpse of something that made me stop. With the VCR on freeze-frame, I stared at the screen in disbelief.

It was Angie. No doubt about it. Her red hair and pointed nose filled up my television screen. She was walking into the shower, fully clothed, but clearly intending to remove her uniform.

I squirmed a bit in my seat. I felt slightly uncomfortable watching her, like some kind of unwitting voyeur. I knew enough, I decided. I reached for the remote again and stopped the tape. Paolo was due to pick me up in fifteen minutes. While I would be willing to re-enact certain pornographic tapes with him, I had to draw the line at watching school girls. Not only was his own young sister recently murdered, but I certainly did not want to clear the path to any comparisons between myself and the nubile young things on the screen. I switched to the Discovery Channel.

An hour later, the tapes were starting to look more appealing. Paolo hadn't appeared and, worse, hadn't phoned. I pulled my hair into a wild ponytail and walked into my closet, looking for something more fitting for a stood-up woman, like a coffee-stained robe. I was reluctantly taking off my low-cut shirt when the phone rang. Although I had been trying to convince myself that I didn't really care, that he must have more important things going on, anyways, I pounced on the phone.

"Hello!" I tried to sound disinterested, bored, slightly impatient.

"Cait?" It was him. I started to do up the shirt again.

"Hi. Hey, sorry I'm running late. I've been comforting my mother, convincing my father not to go down to the jail and beat up that Lloyd character, you know, the usual stuff everyone does after the man who murdered their sister is arrested. Man, my life is surreal."

There was a brief pause while I searched for something sympathetic to say.

"Can I just meet you downtown?" Paolo continued. "The

Four Seasons? I've made a reservation for a late dinner, too. Hope that's okay with you. We'll have a cocktail first in the lounge."

"Sure," I told him. I began to undo the buttons again. Dinner at the Four Seasons definitely required a more elegant costume.

Chapter
Twenty-Two

I SPLURGED ON A CAB. Before I left, I applied a little perfume behind my ears for the first time since my journalism school graduation. I double-checked my apartment for cleanliness, stashed the box for *Teacher's Pet* under the couch, and left a soft light on, just in case—in the remote chance, for the one-in-a-million event—that we would end up back here.

I was glad I'd switched into a dress when I walked into the lounge. Everything, from the coasters to the model-beautiful bartender, smacked of sophistication. I definitely wasn't on Commercial Drive anymore. I didn't see Paolo, so I chose a deep, lush chair in a quiet corner.

I tried to look as though I belonged when the tall, tanned waiter approached my table. I wanted him to think that I came here all the time, and there was no need to ask me for identification. It still happened, most often in places like this where they were so used to clients over fifty that they had forgotten that a lack of gray roots didn't mean I was sixteen. I looked the waiter in the eye—that was the key—and ordered a glass of red wine. The Four Seasons, I figured, was more of a wine than a whiskey spot. I went for the mid-priced wine. Although it was the same price as a pitcher of beer at WaaZuBee's, ordering the cheapest would have been a sure sign that I didn't come here often.

My wine had just arrived when Paolo strode in. In contrast to me, he looked confident and at ease, as if he moved easily through the Four Seasons of the world and had a right to demand the best service.

"Hey, you look so innocent sitting there." He leaned over and pecked me lightly on the cheek. Just slightly, but my cheek grew warm. I caught a whiff of alcohol on his breath before he sat down. Fair enough, I figured. If I were in his spot, I would have done the same thing. He had enough reason to celebrate, no matter how mixed any sense of triumph would be. In my world, celebrations always included a little libation.

"Sorry about the delay," he continued. "It's been a crazy day. You can't imagine what it's like to see someone arrested after they've destroyed your family. It's a roller coaster—you're happy one minute that they've caught someone, then it hits you that nothing will change. No matter how much that cretin suffers, no matter what sort of well-deserved abuse he takes in jail, no matter how much of his life wastes away in physical pain, nothing will bring Claudia back." His voice caught slightly as he sat back in his chair and shook his head. "Nothing can change the fact that she's gone. Where's the waitress?"

Before my reeling brain had switched gears away from the image of Pete being tortured, Paolo had ordered a double whiskey. I wasn't sure he needed another drink, but he seemed eager.

"Yeah, I've waited for this day forever, Cait. It hasn't really been too long in actual time, but, let me tell you, I've aged fifty years."

I nodded appreciatively. I was starting to feel out of my depth, increasingly aware that I didn't really know what to say to someone celebrating an arrest for a horrible crime. I wanted to talk about my acquaintance with Pete, just to make sure it was all out in the open, but he hadn't left me any spots in the conversation.

"You wait and wait, you lie awake at night," he continued. "You pray, even though you haven't really believed in any sort of God for years. You—"

"Cait!" A strong voice rang out from across the lobby. I turned while Paolo continued speaking. It was Derek, in uniform, moving towards me with a big smile. "Hey, Cait," he continued, "I'm here interviewing...." He stopped when he realized I was not alone. Quickly, his head swivelled from me to Paolo and back again. I could see the wheels turning in his brain and knew how bad this had to look. Not only was I sitting in a posh lounge with another man, but it was Paolo Sabato, the angry brother who complained about the police, who was sitting with me. Derek would either assume it was a date, or think that I was grilling him for information on the police's alleged incompetence.

I couldn't tell which theory Derek was leaning towards. He looked confused, as if he was trying to decide what to say next. Paolo broke the silence for him.

"We're just having a nice conversation over some wine. That's the only good thing to come out of all this: it introduced me to Cait."

There was no mistaking what Derek was thinking this time. His face flushed and he looked at me as if I had stolen the badge off his uniform.

"Glad you're having fun, Cait," he said. I wouldn't have believed Derek's voice could sound so bitter if I hadn't heard it myself.

"What brings you downtown?" I asked, to change the subject.

"Interview" was all he said. He and Paolo were looking at

each other like two dogs squaring off over a roast beef. It was starting to annoy me.

"Cait!" This time the voice was higher pitched. All three of us turned around. It was Ally, running towards me, followed by an icy-looking woman in a fur coat. "Cait," Ally screamed, "I'm staying in the hotel with Aunt Denise." Aunt Denise caught up to her niece and grabbed her by the collar.

She smiled at me with thin lips. "I always stay here," she told me, "but I didn't know how different it would be with a child, especially one with a cold." She extended a perfectly manicured hand. "I'm Denise Robison, Pete's sister," she said, then turned to Derek. "I see you haven't made it too far since we talked."

I looked around at the circle of faces. This was the kind of etiquette situation Emily Post never wrote about. I didn't want Paolo to know that Denise and Ally were related to the man in jail for killing his sister. Although seconds ago his tightly wired mood and slightly drunken energy had seemed exciting, I knew he would not react well if he knew he was staring at Pete's daughter. If that wasn't enough to worry about, my juggling act seemed to have caught up with me. Derek and Paolo were at odds; Pete's daughter and stern sister were staring at me expectantly. I wished I had ordered the whiskey after all.

"Cait is Dad's girlfriend," Ally told her aunt. Leave it to a child to break the tension.

"Really?" Paolo said.

"You have been busy," Derek added.

"You must be very upset," Denise murmured. Her eyes were narrow and she was looking at me as if I had a scarlet A on my forehead. "You know," she continued, "Pete hasn't had much luck with women recently. I think he deserves a little loyalty right now."

We all stared at each other while Ally, nose running, described her hotel suite and I hoped the chandelier above me would fall on my head. Surely death by a thousand glass shards wouldn't be as bad as this, I thought, glancing up hopefully. Just when I was starting to feel that I had to say something, Paolo put his hand on my elbow.

"Come on, Cait," he said, "let's just forget dinner and go back to your place."

I knew what he was doing: marking his territory. I knew that all eyes were on me: Derek looked hurt, Denise looked furious, Ally looked puzzled. If I left with Paolo, I would be choosing him. I tried to meet Derek's eyes, but he wouldn't let me. When I looked down at Ally, her lower lip was sticking out, a thin trickle of mucus under her nose, while Denise patted her on the head.

Just when I was ready to throw my hands up and run screaming from the room, Paolo leaned towards me. "Let's go outside and get a cab, bella." His voice was as smooth as a Four Seasons martini. It was the accent that did it—the gentle lilt with the last syllable of the word "bella." I turned to him and smiled.

"I'll get my coat."

"Have a nice night," Derek said. His voice didn't quite match his good wishes. With a final glance at Paolo, he turned and left.

"Well, it didn't take you long to recover," sniffed Denise, and I couldn't entirely blame her.

"I hope you babysit soon, Cait," Ally said as Denise pulled her away.

As soon as we were securely fastened into our cab, Paolo drew a bottle from his jacket pocket—a slim, silver flask.

"Want some?" He pointed the flask towards me. "It was getting pretty weird in there. I thought we should get out. I don't want to see that stupid cop tonight. He really annoyed me during the investigation, and I don't need to be reminded of that right now. Who was the kid? Or rather, who's this father who is also your boyfriend?"

I shrugged, willing him to stop asking. Fortunately, he

seemed intent on the flask. After another swig, he passed it back to me again.

I've never been one to turn down a drink, but I was nervous about what the driver would say. I was also fighting doubts about Paolo coming to my place. Was I doing the right thing? I wondered what I would say the next time I talked to Derek, and if Denise would tell Ally and Pete what a terrible person I was. I didn't want alcohol to loosen my tongue or wash me with regret.

"Sure." I never had much willpower. I took a relatively ladylike sip from the flask and handed it back. Paolo followed with more enthusiasm.

"Cait, I'm glad we're going to be alone instead of staying in that place. I'm so full of energy right now, I want to celebrate every way I know how. And that includes some festive things I'd like to do with you."

I nodded silently, but my brain was full of doubt. After an afternoon of viewing porn videos, maybe it wasn't surprising that I was gripped with feelings of sexual inadequacy. Could I really handle being alone with Paolo right now?

Paolo stumbled slightly when we left the cab and made no motion to pay the driver. While I took care of it, he swayed toward the steps.

When we reached the door, he grabbed my chin and pulled me closer for a kiss. This was a real kiss, not the polite pecks of our earlier meetings. As my body melted, I knew I had made the right choice.

"I'm so happy we're doing this, Cait," he whispered as I unlocked the door. "I've always thought you were the cutest reporter I'd ever seen. I didn't think it was appropriate before tonight, though. But now I feel we're doing the right thing."

Everything would have been perfect, except for the stink of whiskey. Whiskey is the best smell in the world when it's coming from your own glass, but when a man is kissing you with alcohol emanating from every pore, it loses its luster.

To my disappointment, the first thing Paolo did when he

entered my apartment was take out the flask again. I'd dated drunk men back in journalism school. The evening was always fun at the beginning, particularly if I'd been drinking, too. Sooner or later, though, most men had to cross the line between basking in the magical whiskey glow that made us the most fun couple in the world, and slipping into slurring self-indulgence, a game that only one could play. Paolo, I was beginning to realize with a sinking heart, was crossing that line. Why couldn't more men drink like Dede and I?

He collapsed on my couch and pulled me down to sit beside him. "You're so nice, Cait." He kissed me again, this time hard enough to make me forget about the whiskey. "Why don't we go lie down?" he asked softly.

I didn't know if I had the leg power to make it to my bed. My whole body was weak, my heart was pounding, and I was suddenly worried that I hadn't put on enough deodorant that morning or shaved my legs adequately. This was it, it was really happening: after many fantasies, Paolo Sabato was about to slip into my bed. My dreams never came true. I had no idea how to act, what to do. I was sure he was used to more sophisticated women; I knew I wouldn't measure up.

"Let me go to the bathroom," I whispered back. "I'll meet you there."

He kissed me again, then stood up and stumbled to the curtain that hid my bed. There was a brief scuffle as he tried to maneuver around the curtain, then a muffled crash as he hit the bed. In the bathroom, I sat on the toilet and tried to collect myself. What was the point, I wondered, of an active fantasy life if I ran screaming when the real thing appeared? I had chosen Paolo when I left the Four Seasons with him. Now he was here, in my bed. I checked myself in the mirror, brushed my teeth, applied more deodorant, and left to meet my fate.

As I neared the curtain, I could hear his breathing growing louder and louder. He had the raspy, uneven breaths of a much older man. I pulled the curtain aside. He was sprawled out on my bed, fully clothed and fast asleep.

Thank God. I was so nervous at the prospect of actually slipping into the bed that seeing him asleep felt like a get-out-of-jail-free card. I went back to the couch and listened to the rain pelting on the window. Dede said that when the rain was this heavy, it sounded like stampeding elephants, but I always thought of cows. I wanted to call Dede and tell her about my disastrous date, but I knew she was on a date of her own, if you could call a protest a date. Whatever was happening at the video store, it had to be better than my evening so far.

I picked up a book but couldn't concentrate with the snoring rising from my bed. I turned on the TV and wished I had chosen a more comprehensive cable package. With Paolo's arrhythmic gasps and snorts behind me, I stared at the television blankly. I noticed that although I had carefully stashed the video box, I had left the tape in the machine. Suddenly, the idea of watching a porn movie didn't seem sordid. If I couldn't explore the physical world with Paolo, maybe I could watch with a different perspective. When he did wake up and invite me into the bed, I could probably use a few tips. It had to be more entertaining than listening to Paolo snore. I pressed Play. It didn't take long to remember what was passing for the plot: private school girls, having just finished a rousing game of field hockey, were in the shower. Angie was sudsing down with the other definitely-not-schoolgirls. When she was naked, it was easier to overlook her nose.

A man had entered the shower. A tall, slightly muscular, certainly naked man with a very attractive backside. Something about the back of his head was familiar—far too familiar. The camera zoomed in on his head as he turned to face me. Blue eyes stared right at me from my TV screen as I shrank back to escape what I saw.

Paolo.

I wouldn't have been more surprised if my own mother had appeared. I paused the tape, staring into the mocking blue eyes. The expression was different, but it was him: the object of my lust, the grieving brother, the man whose snores were filling my apartment. The man lying just feet away from me.

Despite all the scenarios I had created involving Paolo and nakedness, this particular possibility had never entered my mind. I was blind. Of course he knew Angie. How else had she known to find me at the Flying Goat coffee house? I had told Paolo exactly where I was headed. How had she tracked down Pete Lloyd to plant my address book in his house? I had told Paolo about Pete, even given him the address. Paolo knew when I was babysitting; if he knew Angie, he must know Rick. It wouldn't have taken a great effort for Rick to follow me out to Burnaby and see Ally, after all. I had thought I was surrounded by coincidences, as if the murders and my obsession with knowing more had opened a door to a synchronicity that existed only in the surreal world of murdered teenage girls, but all along there was an explanation. A handsome, clever—presently snoring—explanation. I didn't even want to think about the way Paolo always mentioned my youth and alleged innocence in light of what I was starting to find out about underaged girls in movies.

If Angie had used my address book to bait Pete Lloyd, she must have been trying to protect someone—the real killer. If she and Paolo worked together in the adult film industry, odds were good that he was at least acquainted with the murderer. But why had he kept his acquaintances hidden? Here was irrefutable proof that he knew Angie, knew her even in the biblical sense, but he had never revealed his link to what was becoming a stronger and stronger connection between the world of x-rated films and Claudia's death. I considered the implications of my discovery.

I crept over to my bed and peeked through the curtain. Paolo was still lying across the bed, sleeping like a man whose conscience was as clear as rain. One arm dangled near the heater, his fingers lightly scraping the floor, while the other was flung across his face.

I inched away, picked up my phone, and dialed, praying the demonstration had ended.

"Dede," I whispered.

"Why are you whispering?" she bellowed back.

"Paolo's here," I replied softly.

"Cait! You got lucky and you called me right away! I'm touched. And congratulations."

"No, no, no. Can you come over? I have something to show you. But don't knock. I'll unlock the door. Be as quiet as possible. It's very, very important. I don't want to wake him up."

I put the phone down quickly and breathed deeply. I didn't want my imagination to get carried away. I knew what my fantasies were capable of, and in a matter of seconds I was going see myself as a hostage, held unwittingly by a madman.

Seconds later, Dede's face appeared in the door. Cautiously, she eased herself into my apartment and raised her eyebrows in a question. I pointed to the curtain that hid my bed, then to the television set. With some reluctance, I pressed Play again, then made a silencing motion to Dede when her gasps filled the room, threatening to wake my guest.

"That's him," I whispered. "That's Paolo in the movie."

"What the ...?" she whispered. "I don't. ..."

I raised my finger to my lips again, then shrugged my shoulders. Think of something, I tried to communicate with the shrug, think of something to get this man out of my apartment before I become his co-star.

"Police?" she mouthed.

"We don't know enough. Just being in a video is not a crime," I whispered back.

Dede's face twisted with thought. I knew that look: the same eyebrow-joining, fine-line-producing expression she had when she sized up a photo shoot. She paced a bit, softly, then slipped out the door.

"Back in a second," she mouthed.

I stood like a statue and listened to pelting rain, Paolo's snores, and my own pounding heart. The light seemed harsher than usual, its yellow glare coloring my skin and bringing the entire apartment into bright relief. Now was my chance, the opportunity I'd looked for these last ten years to prove I could be brave, to show I could take control over the fate of my body. I had an opportunity to vindicate my past, and I couldn't even move my feet. I could barely breathe. I could faint at any minute. Was I really as strong as I'd been telling myself?

Dede reappeared. To my surprise, the frown of concentration had been replaced by a proud grin. Her hands were clasped behind her back, hiding something. I raised my own eyebrows, willing her to be brave enough for both of us. With a barely suppressed giggle, she whipped her hands around and proudly presented me with a pair of handcuffs.

Chapter
Twenty-Three

WHO ELSE WOULD HAVE THE PERFECT captivity equipment in her apartment, existing peacefully with the blender and VCR? Dede thrust the cold metal rings into my hands. I looked at her for guidance. What did she expect me to do, exactly? It seemed obvious, but she didn't think I could actually handcuff him, did she?

With a touch of impatience, she gestured towards the curtain hiding Paolo. I looked over at it. Unless he had moved, which was unlikely, one arm was dangling rather conveniently beside the coils of my heater. I just had to take a few steps over there, open the cuffs, quickly pick up the arm, and SNAP! he was mine, although certainly not in the sense I had imagined earlier in the evening.

I glanced at Dede again. She nodded with enthusiasm. I looked towards my bed. I tried to remember how I'd imagined Claudia before she died, how I'd tossed in that very bed, wishing I could help her somehow. I'd imagined a less heroic physical form of assistance, at my typewriter, maybe making a few phone calls. Handcuffing her brother to my heater had never been part of the plan, but that didn't mean I couldn't handle it.

I tiptoed across the floor and pushed the curtain back. Sure enough, Paolo hadn't moved. In the bright light, his cheeks were flushed and I thought I saw a spot of drool in the corner of his mouth. He wasn't bad-looking, still, despite it all.

I clicked one ring of the handcuffs onto a narrow heating tube, then leaned over slowly and picked up his dangling hand. He moaned a little and squirmed away. I kept my grip, although my hands felt like jelly. I moved his hand in towards the heater, then circled the other ring of the handcuffs around his wrist, like a shark closing his jaw around a bare thigh. Then I snapped it shut.

Click. The snap of metal filled the room with the sound of finality. I had handcuffed Paolo Sabato and there was no way to turn back. I wasn't even sure if Dede had brought the keys.

"Hey," a muffled voice rose from the bed. Paolo twisted away from me, but was stopped abruptly by the metal around his wrist.

"What the—" He tried to sit up again, but his movement was confined to an arm's distance from the heater. "Hey! Cait! What's up?" He looked at me with his soft blue eyes. I stood over him, suddenly unsure of what to do with my own hands. "I didn't think you'd be into this. I mean, you seemed like such a nice girl." He smiled slightly.

"Paolo," I said. "We have to talk."

He twisted violently, pulling on the heater and flailing his legs. My building is old and in need of repair. I looked at the heater and prayed it would stay attached to the wall.

"Paolo, let's talk about your acting career." I wanted to approach his possible role in his sister's murder gently, before he knew what I had discovered.

"What do you mean?" He stopped moving and pasted his

smile back on, obviously confused but determined to remain charming.

"Had many jobs recently?" I asked.

"Not much. Vancouver's pretty competitive these days."

"What sort of things have you done?" I asked. "Commercials? Guest shots? Movies of the week?"

"Just odd jobs here and there. Nothing you would have seen."

There was my opening. He was avoiding giving me a direct answer, but I knew at least part of the truth.

"I think I may have seen you," I began. My heart accelerated. I heard my voice go up at least an octave, ruining my chance to be a cool reporter who confidently and ruthlessly got to the bottom of any story.

"Really?" he smiled politely. He looked, I had to admit, as innocent as a baby, if newborns ever wore handcuffs. "Where?"

"*Teacher's Pet*." My voice was firmer than my legs as I pronounced the damning title. "I was surprised to see you."

Paolo's entire body jerked across the bed, like a fish floundering on shore. His legs pedaled vainly in the air as his arm tugged on my increasingly fragile-looking heater. He twisted around to allow his other arm to play with the handcuffs, but Dede owned the real thing, not some child's version that he could have twisted off like an elastic band. He wasn't going anywhere.

"Damn," he murmured, no longer wearing the mask of charm. "I thought we got all those tapes when we broke in."

"You broke into the video store?" Dede interjected, speaking for the first time. "It was you I was picketing in support of?"

"Picketing? Who the hell are you?" Paolo looked at Dede as if she still held a sign.

"A concerned friend," she answered. I had to admit she didn't look nervous at all.

"You know, concerned friend, I could start screaming

bloody murder from this bed and the police would be here in minutes. I think you're in over your head."

I wasn't going to argue with this last point, but Dede had a response ready.

"Don't be so sure. I'm Cait's neighbor. You can scream all you want, but I'm not going to do a damn thing to set you free until I know more about what's on that tape. The apartment below Cait is empty, and if you think anyone else can hear you above the rain, you're fooling yourself."

The apartment below me was not empty. A single mother lived there, a woman in fact quite likely to be fast asleep and extremely annoyed by any disturbance.

"Yeah!" I added lamely. "Nobody can hear you."

"Cait." He rolled over so he faced me directly. "What are you doing? You shouldn't be surprised by the video. I don't know why you're angry or what has driven you to take me as some sort of hostage. You're intrigued by the video. Don't deny it. You came up here with me, remember? Don't play naive. You knew what you were in for." His voice changed with his words, from the slightly seductive soundtrack of my fantasies to something low and menacing. "That's why you like me. You know, though you deny it, that I can introduce you to things you've never experienced."

"Paolo." The rain bouncing off the rooftop was so loud that I couldn't concentrate on his words. I heard some things I recognized deep inside but I couldn't stop to think. "Paolo, tell me about the video." Dede had moved beside me. I could feel that she was ready to pounce on him but was restraining herself. I hoped she wasn't stopping herself in deference to me, because I certainly didn't have a comprehensive plan of attack.

"Is that why you became a reporter, Cait? To join the criminal world in your own innocent way? I spotted it when we first met. You practically became Claudia when we talked about her."

His words battered my ears with the rain. I had allowed a

psychotic man into my apartment and into my life. He'd fooled me, despite all my fears and phobias and predictions of disaster. I lived in so much imagined fear, I had somehow overlooked real danger.

"Of course," he continued, "when we first met, I didn't think I was meeting you. I was looking for another Kate, a model who wanted to be a reporter. When I got your message on the machine, I heard the name and assumed it was her. I figured Shelly had told her friend, some chick called Kate Whyte she never would introduce me to. I figured Kate was either lying about being a reporter or had just gotten a job with some rag like she'd always told Shelly she wanted to do, and she wanted to bribe me, to get some money for not going to the cops with what she knew, so I went to meet her at the coffee shop. But you didn't look at all like Shelly had described and I could tell you hadn't led the life she had. You were so innocent. Just like Claudia."

There's nothing I hate worse than being called "innocent," especially after handcuffing a man to a heater. I clenched my teeth and launched a renewed verbal attack. Too many things were starting to add up—the video, the picture of Claudia, Rick's following me.

"Paolo, what are you doing in that tape? Was your sister involved in the filming? Did she know what you did? Why didn't you tell me you were in that kind of movie? Did the police know?"

"Whoa! Too many questions. Didn't they teach you in journalism school that you have to allow the subject to answer? Cait, all I'm guilty of is making a dirty movie to help my career. Everybody does it until they get their big break— Madonna, that beauty pageant winner, and dozens of actors who've managed to keep it a secret. I can understand you being upset, since we're dating and all, but don't you think you're overreacting a bit? My sister was murdered and her killer was arrested today. Do you really think I deserve to be locked to your apartment for having a little fun in my youth?"

His smiling face returned. I smiled back. Beside me, even Dede smiled.

"Paolo, we're not going to let you go until you answer Cait's questions," she said. "They shouldn't be hard to answer if you're as innocent as you claim."

"But what are you going to do? Tell the cops that you saw me in a nasty video? They have better things to do. In case you haven't heard, people are being murdered. Or are you planning to keep me here like some sort of boy toy, feeding me occasionally, putting a bowl of water beside the bed, having me handy for your sexual pleasure? I'm sure I could offer you something new." He leered at Dede. She wrinkled her nose in distaste. I shuddered, remembering that only a few hours ago, the idea of keeping Paolo as a sexual slave was actually appealing.

"We've got a plan." Even Dede sounded unconvincing.

I walked a little closer to him and looked down. I'd watched enough cop shows to know a good interrogation can break down even the most cunning suspect. The trick was to catch him off guard, to get him to open up until he unwittingly revealed the truth.

"So, Paolo," I began. "The video was kind of intriguing. Do you like that line of work?"

"Cait, cut the crap. I know what you're trying to do," he replied. Maybe he'd seen the same episode of *NYPD Blue*.

"Seriously," I began again, "how did you start making movies?"

"Cait, just set me free before I slap the two of you with a confinement charge. Just wait until I'm free, boy. I don't think the *News* will think much of your interview techniques— with a victim's relative, no less."

"Or a murderer," Dede said.

I didn't see his reaction coming. I shot a glance to Dede to warn her to be more subtle, then whipped my head around again to face a commotion on my bed. Paolo flopped up and down forcefully, then, with what looked like a wrenching twist to his handcuffed arm, flipped off the bed onto the floor with hurricane force. On my dusty linoleum, he was even more vulnerable, one arm raised above his head to the heater, the other clutching a corner of my sheets, his mouth twisted with pain.

"Damn, I think I may have broken my arm. Cait, you gotta let me go. I think I need help." His voice was strained and his arm did have an unnatural extra bend just above the elbow, where I could see the beginning of some telltale swelling.

"Let me go, Cait, and I'll forget this happened. I'll give you the interview of your life."

"But not the interview that I want." I squatted down beside him. Tiny beads of sweat were gathering above his brow. "You won't tell me what I want to know about your film career—and how your sister got involved." I reached over and touched his arm gently. He flinched and swore at me. I tried not to jump back against the verbal assault. I had to remain calm. A plan had come into place as neatly as the snap of the handcuffs.

"How old were your co-stars?" I asked.

"Old enough to know what they were doing," he answered.

"But too young to be legal," I finished for him.

He shrugged. "Not my fault the law is unrealistic about teenagers having sex. The law doesn't acknowledge when girls are at their prime."

"Paolo," I continued, "was your sister involved in the pornography industry?"

"Cait." His voice was cracking. "I don't know why you can't drop this. My sister was murdered. I made a couple of movies. They're not related."

"But, Paolo," I continued, modulating my own voice, "I know your sister was somehow in the porn industry. I've seen a picture of her naked. She didn't look as though she was having fun. I know you've met Angie before and I suspect she knows who killed your sister."

"Of course Claudia wasn't having fun!" Paolo snapped.

"She was an innocent girl. A genuine Catholic schoolgirl worried about her soul, salvation, and staying a virgin. That's why Rick wanted her. Damn it, I could have killed Shelly. . . ."

Bingo. I walked over to the kitchen. I was about to do something I didn't think I had the power to pull off. My plan, tentative and risky, involved facing the exact realities I dreaded most. I opened a kitchen drawer, took out my sharpest knife, and looked down at the gleaming blade. My face was reflected in the stainless steel, a distorted, unrealistically thin face, but definitely my own. I walked back and squatted beside Paolo. Dede hovered above me. I could hear her breathing, almost feel her shaking.

"So," I said, raising the knife up beside his face. "You knew Shelly."

He looked into my eyes with shock, then back at the blade. I recognized that look. He was mesmerized by the power of a few inches of well-maintained sharpness. His flesh could feel the sharp edge as if he'd already been stabbed. The anticipation would tense his muscles, as if they could form a protective shield from the unforgiving blade. I had, after all, once been at the wrong end of a knife myself. I knew what he was thinking.

"Shelly? Sure. She was my girlfriend. At least, that's what I told her when I wanted something. She was too old, too used, for me but she worked with me well."

I reached out with my other hand and touched his arm right at the strange bend above his elbow. Already, the surrounding flesh was red and angry-looking. I lowered my hand onto the most tender-looking spot and pressed down, gently at first, then gradually applied more pressure.

"Stop." He twisted away to escape my cruel hands. I wasn't sure any longer that they were really mine. "Shelly was mixed up. Really, really mixed up. Jealous. Horribly jealous. She was jealous of my sister. Can you imagine! A whore like that jealous of an angel like my sister. They couldn't have been more different."

"So, did they meet?" I touched the tip of the knife to his arm. I was either going to succeed with my plan or burst into tears and throw up all over the floor. I wished, more than anything, that I hadn't rented the movie, hadn't found out the truth about the man with the beautiful voice and chivalrous manners.

"By accident, once, when Shelly, Rick, and I were downtown. Claudia wanted us all to go for coffee. The worst hour of my life. Shelly hated her on sight, and Rick thought she would be perfect for what we were starting to get into with the movies. She was, of course, but dammit, she was my sister."

"So, Shelly didn't like Claudia?" In my late-night imaginings, the three of us had been friends.

"Not at all."

I raised my hand just above his arm and pressed down again. His arm was yielding in an unnatural way and felt hot against my hand.

"No, don't, don't. Please. Just stop. Dammit—stop. One day Shelly met Claudia after school and told her exactly what I was doing with my acting degree. Then she invited her to watch filming. Shelly wanted my sister and me to fight, to break up our friendship. God knows why Claudia went. Maybe she was curious, like you, about the dark side of life. Maybe she couldn't believe what Shelly said and wanted proof. She definitely planned to repeat the whole thing at confession, I can tell you that.

"Anyways, she went with Shelly and found out what I was doing for a living. She had been so proud of me, but when I arrived, Claudia was furious. She was completely shaken. She said some things to me I never thought I'd hear from her mouth. Then she said she was going to tell our parents."

He shuddered, then grimaced with pain. I raised the knife an inch closer to his face, close to the white firmness of his eyeball.

"I knew she was going to tell them—she was a girl who kept her word. She was horrified that I was involved in something like that, me, her idol, her brother. And I knew just what my parents would do, good Catholics that they are. I would be out of the picture, out of the will, out of their lives. I was going to inherit the house, the business, everything—I am the oldest son, and they are from the old world. It was all going to be mine. But Claudia was going to ruin it all."

"So, you killed her."

"I didn't kill her. Rick was watching the whole argument with my sister. I knew he thought she would be perfect for a movie. He wanted me to film her having sex with him. I was so furious with her that I agreed. I didn't know he would take it as far as he did. Of course, she resisted when he tried to have sex with her. That's what makes girls like her so perfect—they have to be forced. That's what our customers pay for. But she fought with all her life. And he killed her. I didn't."

"You just handed her over to Rick and watched," Dede said.

"I'm not saying anything else," he answered. "You know that you can never use anything I've said. It's coercion. You should know the law."

I had no idea if he was telling the truth or not. I looked up at Dede, who shrugged. I could swear I saw new respect for me in her eyes.

"Don't tell me you don't like this position, Cait. All your notions about yourself as a do-gooder victim are really just a front, aren't they?"

Victim? I was quite sure that I had never presented myself as a victim to Paolo. On the contrary, I usually tried to assert my competence as a reporter and a woman of the world. Was he just goading me or was it that obvious? Or was he unusually skilled at recognizing past and potential victims?

I lowered the knife until the sharp end of the blade rested lightly on his arm. With my other hand, I pressed down firmly on the spot that seemed to generate the most pain.

"Why don't you just admit what you've done?" I asked.

"Maybe it will be useless to me, but won't it make you feel better? You must feel terrible about what happened to your sister if she was so innocent and wonderful. Some big brother you turned out to be. Just get it off your chest."

"She wasn't so innocent by the time my so-called friend Rick finished with her. She didn't die very innocent. Same with Shelly. She wasn't innocent. I don't know why everyone paints her like some sort of victim. What about me? She shattered my family when she told Claudia. She deserved what she got."

"So . . . you killed Shelly?" I knew Dede had found my mini tape recorder, an essential tool for every reporter and definitely handy in extracting murder confessions. She was recording everything he said.

"You know, Cait, Rick is coming over here any minute. That was the deal—I'd get you here and he'd show up as a sort of surprise. Compared to Rick, I'm a kitten. If I were you, I'd set me free while you still have a hope of not joining my beloved sister."

I glanced up at Dede. It was impossible to believe anything Paolo said, but any vestiges of a plan would vanish if Rick showed up. Dede and I could handle one malevolent man at a time, and only if he was incapacitated by a restraining device.

"Trust me, Cait." Paolo must have picked up on our fear. "Rick could arrive at any minute. He'll be a bit surprised to see your friend over here, but he can adapt."

I looked at Dede. She stared back at me, for once without an idea. We looked at the door. Our only choice was to make a break for it.

No sooner had we made a silent decision when there was a loud knock at the door. I dropped the knife in surprise. Quickly, Paolo's free hand grasped the handle and, in a flash, he jerked the blade up towards my head. I leapt back just in time, knocking over Dede, who was hovering behind me with the tape recorder. We fell in a noisy heap just inches away from Paolo but safely out of reach. Gasping for air, I looked towards him. The blade was pointed at me and he appeared to be taking aim.

Another knock. I looked at Dee.

"Cait, it's the police. Open up!" a voice from behind the door commanded.

I leaned back against Dede. Maybe there was a way out, after all. The voice on the other side of the door sounded like Derek's, but I couldn't take anything for granted.

"Can I see some ID?" I asked.

"Coming under the door, Cait." I knew it was Derek before I picked up the identification card. I opened the door. I was ready to hug him when I saw the three uniformed police officers standing behind him, guns drawn.

"Uhh, there's someone here you should meet," I said, pointing to Paolo's prostrate form. He was pointing the knife at the cops, but somehow, faced with the guns, he wasn't as threatening. The uniforms moved in on him, counseling him to drop the knife. It seemed like a good idea even to Paolo. Lowering his head onto my floor, he put the knife down beside him.

"We know all about Mr. Sabato," Derek said to me. "You'll never guess who called the office while I was at the Four Seasons."

I tried to think. "Rick?" I didn't even know his last name.

"No, Kate Whyte. She credits you with inspiring her to come forward. She called the station and said she wanted to talk to someone about the Sabato and Bennett murders. Of course, we leapt on the chance to actually hear her say something. She said you'd taught her something about not keeping secrets that she'd been thinking about, so she'd decided it was time to tell us everything she knew. She told us some things Shelly Bennett told her before she died, some things Kate had been holding on to until you persuaded her otherwise by warning her about the dangers of keeping secrets. She's not exactly a friend of Mr. Sabato's. In fact, they'll probably be facing each other in court. I knew you were here with him, so we figured it was best to make sure everything was okay."

I remembered my last conversation with Kate and how empty I'd felt after finally sharing my secrets. If I hadn't taken that chance and opened up to Kate, she may not have talked to Derek and I might still be wondering what to do with Paolo.

An official pair of handcuffs was slapped on both Paolo's wrists. His face was flushed and he was talking to the officers in a low, confiding voice.

"I think she might actually be insane," he was explaining, nodding towards me. "Out of nowhere she starts torturing me. Must not have liked the way the date was going."

Without ceremony, he was led out of my apartment. As he passed me, he turned his head and blew me a kiss. I stood still, amazed at the frivolous flirtatiousness of the gesture, then turned around and gave Derek an exhausted hug.

Chapter
Twenty-Four

MAYBE IT WOULD HAVE BEEN LIKE THIS if I'd reported my rape, I thought, pulling a yellow blanket tightly around me and raising my hot chocolate to my lips. Across from me, Derek waited.

"Whenever you're ready to talk, Cait," he said, his voice gentle.

"What did Kate say? What did she know?" Part of me was chagrined that she hadn't been able to open up to me. She may have claimed that I was responsible for her change of heart, but she still went to the police when she decided it was time to speak out.

"Kate was a good liar earlier—despite her insistence that she knew nothing, Shelly had told her what happened with Claudia. Shelly and Kate were best friends. Shelly couldn't live with herself afterwards, so she broke down and told Kate. She made Kate promise that, no matter what happened, she would keep it to herself. Even after Shelly was killed, that was a powerful command for Kate. And Kate is bitter enough about her own history with the police that even after Shelly's murder, she didn't see the point in going to the cops. She had promised Shelly, after all, and she's not the type of person to break a promise she'd made to someone who was killed. It wasn't until the arrest of Pete Lloyd and the realization that you were being drawn into it that she knew she had to say something. She likes you.

"Rick and Paolo had written 'babysitting' in Claudia's notebook just to throw us off the trail. They didn't have a very sophisticated plan at that time, but when you told Paolo about babysitting for Pete, that opened up a whole new possibility for them. That's why Rick was following you: to determine the best way to do it, to get to know your routine, to try to get something he could use against Pete. The whole address book thing was pretty clever, I'll give them that. Almost led to a lifetime of trouble for poor Pete Lloyd."

"I feel pretty stupid." I leaned back again. I had not only failed to recognize one of the murderers, I had lusted after him. Then I had practically told him who he could frame for the murder. Then, just to put the final nail in the coffin of stupidity, I had invited him over to my apartment. A dozen different outcomes to the evening threatened to overcome the actual course of events, but I needed to hold onto safe reality for a while.

An hour later, both Derek and I were exhausted. With three other cops and a tape recorder, we'd gone over the events of the last couple of weeks, finishing in my apartment with Paolo handcuffed to my heater. I was approaching tears when a gray-haired cop walked in.

"A lot of twists here," he said. "Pretty complicated business. Paolo turned pretty quickly on his friend Rick as soon as he was in the car—told us exactly where to find him and what he did. He was pretty anxious to clarify that he did not kill Claudia. We've got Rick and Angie both in custody right now, where they'll be answering questions until their throats are hoarse. According to what Paolo told you, Rick raped Claudia, then killed her. Paolo told us where to find the pictures he took, so we have someone on that. We don't know which of them killed Shelly yet, although apparently Rick is pointing the finger at Sabato. Now that we can arrest Paolo as an accomplice in Claudia's murder, we should be able to get to the bottom of his girlfriend's death."

"What's Angie doing?" I asked.

"She's telling us practically everything. She wasn't there when Claudia was killed, but Rick told her that Ed Nelson, who had worked on movies with them before, had done it alone. Apparently, Rick didn't want her to even suspect he'd had a hand in it, since there was already tension between them. He said he'd kill her if she went to the cops, but her conscience got to her. Unfortunately for her, Rick hadn't researched Ed's activities enough and she was afraid to come completely clean so she just gave us the one vague tip about Claudia having babysat for Ed. When her tip to us was discredited, she began her own investigation and it looks as if she wanted you to help her. I think half of her believed Rick wouldn't do something like that, but obviously, she had some doubts somewhere in her mind.

"Turns out you were right, when she gave that hint about doing math, she was trying to point you to teen porn. She has a daughter of her own who lives with her mother. As her daughter has grown, she's started to hate the fact that they use such young actresses. That's why Rick and Paolo had started their own line of work, so to speak. They were working without her a lot."

"I suspected underaged actresses," I said. I may have missed the murderer right under my nose, but at least I had figured out the activities at the Western Rose.

"Pretty impressive, Cait. She practically showed Steve the birth certificates of the girls involved, but he missed it. The night she had you over to the hotel, Rick figured out what she was up to. Since he and Paolo were also using you to frame Lloyd, he thought she was way out of line, that she was leading you way too close. She says he would have killed her if she hadn't redeemed herself by stealing your address book."

"But why did she steal it? And how did she become involved in framing Pete?"

"Rick told her to meet up with you and steal something they could plant. She had a dual motive with the address book, though. She wanted to check out your sources, find out who you'd talked to, maybe even talk to some people. She really rivaled you with the investigative ambitions. When Rick found out she had an address book, he hatched the plan. It wasn't hard to get her involved. He'd been following her daughter's activities as well, so he was able to frighten her into participation by threatening her daughter's life. By this point, she figured out that he meant business. She called up Pete, said she'd found his ad, and offered to babysit. He said he needed someone. That's how she planted the evidence."

Derek stood up. "Cait, I think you should go home for now. We've got enough information for one night. You must be tired. I'll give you a ride."

I followed him numbly down the sterile halls of the police station. Paolo was somewhere in the building. The man I'd tortured purposefully just over an hour ago was somewhere near me. No doubt, he was having an even rougher time at the station.

The rain had eased up. We walked through the parking lot in a light mist, Derek's hand lightly resting on my elbow.

"Do you feel all right going home? You can stay at my place," he said. I knew it was a genuine offer, made with the same politeness that led him to hold my door open as I got in the undercover police car.

"No, I'll be fine," I told him. "I called Dede from the station. She's waiting for me. She'll be crushed if I don't sleep at her place. She's been fretting like a mother hen."

"You guys did the right thing, incapacitating Sabato. I'd

hate to think of what he would have been capable of with both arms free."

We were both silent.

"You might want to consider counseling," Derek said. "Something like this can hit you pretty hard."

"I know," I told him. I took a deep breath and went on. "I know a bit about what's in store for me."

"Just remember, there are resources available," he said. "You're pretty strong, but don't be afraid to ask for help."

Pretty strong. I looked out the window as the car pulled out of the station and thought about his words. I wasn't feeling very strong. I'd been fooled by a murderer, after all. I'd nursed a crush on a psychopath, a man crazy enough to be involved in the murder of his sister and girlfriend. I'd obsessed over the story, but I'd missed the most obvious part of it.

"I can't believe I didn't figure it out," I said, more to myself.

"Don't beat yourself up," Derek said beside me. "You did a great job. You led us to him, kept him in one spot, held your ground, and stayed alive. Sounds like you've got a prizewinning story to me."

He pulled up in front of my place.

"Thanks for being there," I said. "And not just tonight. I'm sure I would have cracked if I'd had to tell the whole story to Ron."

He smiled. "Ron's not so bad," he said. "He did listen to your suspicion about the Western Rose basement. He grilled the front desk hard—got a lot of info out of them. You've got to admit, Ron is a pretty good cop."

Except for his disdain for women, I thought.

"See you soon?" I asked Derek.

"I don't think we should go out for a while, Cait," he said. "I think you need a little time to think. But don't hesitate to call me if you want to talk." He extended a hand. "Friends?"

I shook his hand. Derek had just blown me off as a potential girlfriend, but I was glad for his friendship. I didn't blame him a bit, and it would be a relief, actually, not to have to worry about my trio of men. Having Derek as a friend would be a good trade-off for trying to juggle the three of them.

Dede and Janet met me at Dede's door with hugs. Behind them, I could see Steve hovering nervously.

"Whyte," he nodded. "Glad you're okay."

Dede kept her arm around me. "She's better than okay. She caught a killer."

"I did not," I corrected her with a laugh. "I went on a date with one. You deserve just as much credit. Maybe more—you didn't nurse a crush the size of Georgia Strait on a murderer."

"Good thing I was home," Dede said. She gave me a big grin. "I should have been at the demonstration, but we got in a big fight about non-violent resistance."

Janet smiled. "I guess I can take myself a bit too seriously sometimes. I promised Dee that from now on, none of our dates would involve protests."

I smiled back and sat on Dede's couch. Blood was pumping through my veins and my cheeks were flushed with the cold air. I was starving.

"I feel great," I settled back in the couch. "I've never felt so happy about being in Dede's apartment."

Steve stepped forward for the first time. "Can I get you something?" he asked. "Something to eat? Glass of whiskey?"

"Let's order pizza," I said. The three of them all pounced on a phone book.

"I can do it," I laughed. "I'm fine, you know. I wasn't hurt at all."

"So, Angie stole your address book that night," Janet said. "Why was she giving you so many hints if she was involved? What's her story?"

"Derek said she has a daughter of her own," I said. "There was tension between them before Claudia was killed, because she didn't like the whole underaged scene they were getting involved in. Rick lied to her about who killed Claudia to stop her from suspecting him. He said he would kill her if she went to the police, even if she only had false info. She did anyways, but with little information, all of it easily discredited. She invited us to the studio, hoping we would find something to lead her in the right direction and put a stop to their little kiddie film industry. She did tell us, indirectly, that the studio had fishy things going on."

"When they interviewed me, the cops said Paolo and Rick were trying to make it look as if Pete Lloyd wanted to kill you next," Dede said. "Did they let him go?"

I nodded. Tomorrow, I would go over to Pete's, explain what led me to his house in the first place. I'd offer hours of babysitting as compensation. After everything I'd seen, I could think of worse ways to spend a Saturday afternoon than swinging with Ally at the park. Maybe Pete would even join us. I figured it would be an uphill battle to keep Pete's friendship after he heard what I had to say, but I was willing to do the work.

"Wow," Steve shook his head. "And they followed you around? Did you notice?"

I nodded. "Rick was hard to miss. I've always been paranoid, though," I said. "Ever since...." I let my voice trail off. They would know what I was talking about. "Because I'm always worrying, I assumed I was just overreacting."

"When did you first get freaked out?" Dede asked.

I thought back to the first time I'd heard about Claudia's murder on the news. The flasher earlier in the evening had frightened me. Had it been a warning from the goddess of the inner city? Always looking for disaster had kept my mind too busy to sense real danger.

"Let's take a self-defence course," I told Dede. "With my luck, I think I need it. Of course, you're better in a crisis than me. Instead of getting the handcuffs, I probably would have tried to hide under the couch."

"Don't be so hard on yourself," Janet said. "You were great."

"I was raped when I was younger," I began. I had to talk about it that night or it would fester under the evening's narrative and poison the happiness I felt. "I was babysitting for a friend of a friend of my parents. He offered to drive me home, but he took a wrong turn. He drove up a mountain, then pulled out a knife, and raped me. He said he would kill me if I went to the police. I didn't tell anyone, not even my parents. Then he raped someone else, a young girl. She was braver than me. She reported it and he went to jail. Still, if I had.... She wouldn't...." I couldn't finish.

Dede shot onto the couch and wrapped her arms around me. We sat on the couch in silence. Nothing she could say would change what had happened in the past. In the future, though, I knew things would be different. I stood up.

"I'm going to call my folks," I said. "I'll wake them up and they're coming out tomorrow, but I can't wait. I've kept too many secrets from them for too long."

My own apartment greeted me like a favorite quilt. I looked around with contentment. I felt cozy here, cozy, content, and, above all, safe. I picked up the phone.

"Mom," I said as soon as her familiar, sleepy voice answered. "I have a lot to tell you."